Talismans

Talismans

The Wise Ones Book 1

Lisa Lowell

Published 2020 by Next Chapter
Cover art by Paula Litchfield
Cover design by http://www.thecovercollection.com/
Back cover texture by David M. Schrader, used under license from Shutterstock.com

OWAILION'S ORIGINAL MAP

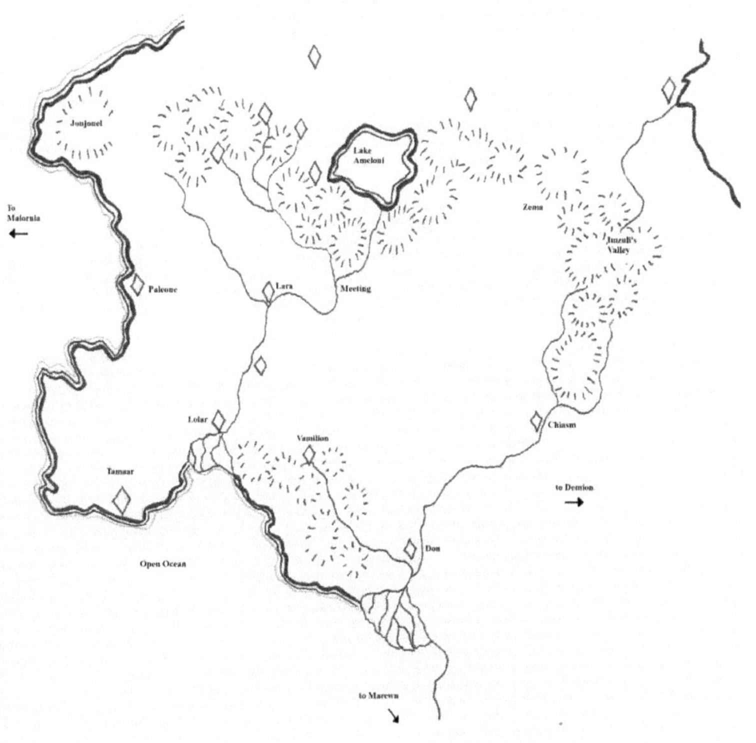

Contents

Chapter 1

Awakened One

A tremendous crash woke him and fine dust fell on his upturned face. He opened his eyes in alarm but saw only profound darkness. Blind? Another explosion just beyond his head drove him to sit up in alarm and he groped across a rough stone floor, feeling his way away from the fearful blasts.

"*You've got to come out now!*" a voice roared, making his head ache with the reverberations.

"How?" he shouted back, groping around for a wall or something to give a frame of reference. "I can't see." A third explosion rocked the chamber and he desperately staggered to his feet. The cavern sounded as if it was crumbling and he could barely remain upright when his reaching hands finally met a wall to help him balance. "What's happening?"

"*You are under attack,*" the deep voice returned. "*You are outside the Seal. You must break through before they find the cavern. Feel your way toward my voice.*"

He staggered against the wall, groping along as the pounding continued, bringing down a rain of rubble onto his head. "I can't break through solid rock. Where are you?" he called again.

"*I am right here. You must wish very hard. Feel for the power. Yes, right there. Now push!*"

The terror of being buried in a collapsing cave, of eruptions, of utter blindness and the alarming awareness that he could not even remember his own name combined to flood him with adrenaline. He wanted out, even if his own death awaited him on the other side of this wall. Out!

Abruptly the rough stone barrier disappeared and he staggered through, almost thrown forward by yet another explosion and landed on his knees on a ridge in bright daylight. With bloody knees, he realized he was naked as a baby and he rose up painfully. At least he could see but the light almost burned. When he finally got his vision to focus he saw something so large he had to step back.

A gold and black iris, flecked with fire and as large as he was tall blinked at him no farther away than his reach. The iris belonged in an eye the height of a house. He tilted his head back to look up and up and found the face of a golden dragon, scales, and spikes flaring about the jaws and sharp ridges over the eye that had come down to his level. An entire dragon lay draped over a black cinder mountainside, gold and glittering like a jeweled necklace on the throat of a lady.

I'm dead, he thought.

"*No, little one,*" the voice rumbled. It took a bit of concentration to understand it, as if this was a foreign language. "*You have just been on a long journey and it will take some time to recover.*"

Journey? He couldn't remember a journey. Indeed, he couldn't remember anything. That observation made him shudder as another detonation rained cinder down the mountainside behind him. Where was he? Who was he? How did this happen to him? Explosions around him, a dragon about to eat him and a vast void where his past must have resided; there was nothing to steady his thoughts.

"*We must deal with the sorcerers now that you have hatched,*" the dragon's voice returned. "*If you will move aside, I will deal with this one.*"

So the thunderous explosions within the cavern had not been this enormous reptile attacking but something else? Without any recourse, the human stepped to the right, as far as he dared on the little shelf that stood out from the mountainside on which he perched. Curiously he watched the dragon's eye close in concentration and then a wave, almost invisible to his eye, pushed out from the dragon's forehead and into the mountain.

The rock wall imploded and avalanches of stone roared above and below. Only this little landing and wherever the gigantic dragon rested remained untouched. The top of the mountain erupted, blowing out the far side in a wave of billowing gasses and washed over, out of sight. The human instinctively crouched down to balance against the earthquakes that threatened to pitch him off the shelf. Then the eruption above eased abruptly and the dragon again rested his head on the ridge again to look at him.

"*There, that's better. I'm sorry that your hatching place was outside the Seal but we didn't know precisely when you would arrive and the mountain just kept growing until it left the protections of the Seal. And of course, that made the outlanders think they could come attack.*" The dragon's golden eye rolled down at the stupefied human. Apparently the dragon's pushing the volcano had done its job for the explosions within the mountain had ceased.

"*We will call you Owailion,*" the voice returned as if nothing had interrupted this singular introduction. "*It is not your true name, which we will keep hidden. Owailion means the awakened one. You are the one we were promised.*"

The human straightened up, stupefied by it all. Owailion....could he accept the name? He couldn't remember his real name. Nothing, not his work, or if he had a family; nothing of his life remained. The looming fear this emptiness created in his soul threatened to swallow him, and he deliberately dropped those thoughts like burning coals.

"Promised what? Who are you?" Owailion murmured, his voice cracked with disuse and the strange language on his tongue.

"*You may call me Mohan. My real name is too long for humans to speak easily,*" the dragon replied. "*And your coming... it is a long story. I will tell you it all when you are able, but for now, we must get away from this volcano before the outlanders return. Also, we do not know how to care for you precisely. You must help us understand what you need."*

Owailion waited for that to make sense and then realized nothing would for a long while until he could remember his life. How would he know what he needed if he didn't remember that? He looked down the slope of the volcano toward the forest below and beyond that in the distance, a chain of mountains capped in snow. None of it was familiar. In his amnesia, he had lost much though he surely knew people did not wake up completely encased in stone. Humans didn't regularly have the ability to burst right through a rock wall and they certainly didn't find a dragon waiting to swallow them on the other side.

In this surreal situation, Owailion reached forward and touched the steely gold scales just below the dragon's eye, and Mohan blinked in pleasure, sending a waft of warm musky air up Owailion's arm. The rumble of a purr echoed up the mountain ridge. That sound alone nudged more pumice and rock to slide down the bare slope.

"*No, Owailion, all this is new to you. We have not met before but you have come a long way to join us. This is the Land... our Land and you are most welcome here, the first and only human to come through our Seal."*

"Mohan? Are you listening to my thoughts?" Owailion asked, just realizing then that the dragon had addressed his concerns and comforted him without the human even saying a thing.

"*How else would I speak with you? You can hear me and I can hear you no matter where we are if you will learn to listen. The language is new to us both but we can understand each other. This is good. Now, you must have needs. You are so newly hatched. What can I do to help you?"*

Hatched? Owailion looked back at the crumbled cliff wall where he had been encased. Did dragons come from eggs? It made sense that Mohan would think he had 'hatched' in that Owailion had somehow broken free just like a chick hatching.

Mohan rumbled like he tried to chuckle. "*What else would I call it? You have broken out of the mountain's shell. Fledglings are weak but you will get stronger with time. What do you need to be stronger?"*

Owailion dropped all his questions and considered Mohan's instead. What did he need? He needed off this cliff. He needed clothes. He needed to understand.

"Clothes?" he asked Mohan in embarrassment. He could not imagine climbing down off this mountainside in his bare feet, let alone the rest of him bare.

"*Clothes?*" Mohan replied curiously.

Had Mohan never seen another human? One wearing something other than their skin? The thought almost made Owailion laugh.

"*We did call you Owailion for a reason. There are other men on this planet, but few that we dragons have seen. The Land is sealed so no men may enter. You are the first human God has promised to send. Perhaps you are hungry. All fledglings are hungry. Do you require food?*"

Owailion thought about that suggestion and then decided it could wait. "No, clothes are more important right now. I don't have scales like you and I'll burn in this sun and unless you intend for me to stay up here, I need clothes to get down off this ledge.

"*I do not understand clothes but if a fledgling needs a clothes you can make this for yourself,*" Mohan rumbled apologetically.

"Make them?" Owailion did laugh this time. He stood naked on a mountainside, conversing nose to nose with a creature he had assumed was a myth. Mohan could swallow him whole and wonder where the rest of the supper was coming from.

"I can't make clothes here," Owailion admitted, motioning to the panoramic but useless view down the mountainside.

"*Why not? You could break free from your shell. A clothes is easier. You imagine a clothes and wish for it and it comes to you.*"

Owailion rocked back on his heels, wondering when the dream would end and he would wake with understanding. "That sounds like magic. What am I saying? Everything I'm experiencing right now – amnesia, breaking through stone, forcing a volcano to erupt, a conversation with a dragon; it's all magic."

"*You are magic, Owailion,*" Mohan confirmed. "*You used magic to break through your shell. The outlanders attacked because you are magic. God sent you to us for magic. A clothes should be easy.*"

"Magic? How?"

"*God gave you magic as you arrived here. It is new to you but I will teach you. Can you imagine a clothes? Wish it into being.*"

Mohan blinked, mesmerizing Owailion into settling his mind. Now, think about clothing and wish them into appearing. Nothing else here made sense so he might as well try. Unwillingly Owailion closed his eyes. He had to tune out his latent fears of large predators, unseen sorcerers, and looming volcanoes and concentrate on something to wear. Then he wished for these things to appear.

Mohan snorted and Owailion opened his eyes in alarm. At his feet, right under Mohan's chin, he saw the clothing he had imagined: pair of leather pants and breeches, a linen tunic and some rugged boots for climbing. Without waiting for the invitation, Owailion sat down on the ledge and began to dress. "That was the most amazing…you say I'm magic? I know a lot about being human, but I didn't know I was magical."

"*Very few humans have magic…unlike dragons.*" Mohan's mental voice held just a tinge of pride in this fact. "*You weren't magical in your life before, but you have come to help us and so now you are magical. You wanted this.*"

"I wanted this?" Owailion prodded as he put on the boots that, to his amazement, fit perfectly. Why would he have wanted to be a magician or to come to this place…the Land Mohan had called it?

"*I thought as a fledgling you would know more of these matters,*" Mohan commented.

Owailion took a deep breath before trying to explain. "I am not a fledgling,…precisely. For a human, I think I am relatively young, but I am full grown. Humans are born, not hatched. I just don't remember magic or anything of my personal past." Then as he stood up in his new clothes he felt much closer to trusting this new world he was encountering. "That's better. Now, can you explain some things while I get down from this ledge?"

"*You will not get bigger?*" This observation seemed to concern Mohan. "*Men are so small. Are all so tiny?*"

Owailion chuckled at the thought. "Women and children are smaller. Does that bother you? It makes me a little worried myself. You might yawn and accidentally inhale me, but this is as big as I get. Why are you...why am I your fledgling?"

"*Well,*" Mohan tried to clarify as he lifted away from the slope allowing Owailion a fuller view of possible paths down the volcano's sides, "*the Land is sealed and there are sorcerers who want to get inside. They think they can take over the magic here. We built your volcano for your arrival but it was too near the Seal that keeps them out. It grew beyond our borders and that is why they attacked, to go through the mountain. They weren't after you exactly, but getting into the Land itself.*"

Owailion scooted off the ledge and began sliding down embankments of cinders as he thought about that. "And you keep saying we. Are there others here?"

As if Owailion's words cast a spell, the sky, the other sides of the slope and even up above the little ridge filled with dragons of various colors and sizes. Over a dozen had all been invisible until he said something. Silver and gold predominated their hides, but with accents of sapphire, ruby, emerald, topaz, and amethyst. No two appeared the same in Owailion's eyes. Some had wings and others, even flying ones, had none. Some had one head and others as many as three heads and an even wider variety of tails. The smallest he could see hovered above Mohan's back and looked to only be triple the size of a large human. Mohan appeared to be the largest, covering easily a thousand feet toward the foot of the mountain. Most disturbing was the fact that every single one of these newly appeared dragons had eyes only for him.

"*We ... my fellow dragons have been waiting for you,*" Mohan admitted, "*but we didn't want to frighten you at first.*"

"Too late," Owailion admitted. "It's the situation that alarms me. You must explain this all. Why do you need me?"

Mohan must have said something privately for the family of dragons disappeared again leaving only Mohan's gold visible although Owailion doubted they had actually left. Then Mohan continued as if this display of power meant nothing.

"*As I explained before, we were promised a man by God and He sent us you. We need your help. You see, we dragons are going to sleep. The Land needs someone else to hold off the sorcerers and stop the demon attacks while we sleep. We need you to take mastery of the magic here.*"

"Attacks like the one that woke me?" Owailion looked over the peaceful countryside beyond Mohan's bulk and saw nothing but forest and summer sky.

Mohan rumbled as he added, "*Yes, sorcerers from the outside and demons within. They grow naturally here in the Land if we do not watch carefully.*"

"And that's why the magic must be mastered?"

"*Yes,*" Mohan stated simply. "*And you will be the masters.*"

"Masters....more than one?" Owailion asked eagerly.

"*God promised that dragons would remain awake long enough to train the first one. Eventually, there will be sixteen humans, the Wise Ones, the ones who will come to control the magic and tame it, so that it will not tempt the evil ones. Power like that normally will seduce man, warp nature and then all will be lost.*"

"Sixteen.... Wise Ones?"

"*Yes, the humans who will not be corrupted by the power. Magic always will ruin a man unless there is something to guide him. You know, I could carry you down the mountain more quickly.*"

Owailion could sense his independent streak resist that idea. While he trusted the dragon to a certain point, Mohan's gaping ignorance about humans left him a little nervous.

"*I wouldn't harm you,*" the dragon promised adamantly. "*You can't be hurt. As a Wise One, you live forever. The magic makes you almost indestructible.*"

Owailion chuckled at that as he sat down on his newly crafted leather pants and made a quick slide down another slope of cinder. "It's the 'almost' that worries me. You don't know how to carry a human and how strong ... or weak we are. And even if I'm magically indestructible it doesn't mean I'm interested in being accidentally punctured or dropped or something. You're awfully pokey and sharp and hard."

"*And you appear to be somewhat...squishy,*" the dragon admitted and pulled farther away from the mountainside, wheeling impatiently above Owailion. Mohan as a dragon sample boasted one set of wings, one head and two tails that twined around him sculpting the air, acting as rudders. Owailion watched him swoop through the sky above and felt distracted by the beauty. Gleaming gold in the high sun, Mohan almost blinded him. The dragon kept a close eye on his human too as Owailion carefully descended.

The dragon groused, "*Do humans always take this long to travel?*"

"Longer," Owailion commented under his breath, as he scrambled as quickly as he could. "There might be a magical way to travel but walking is just about as fast as we can go. With only two legs we aren't as fast as most animals. And you're right, we are squishy. We make up for being rather vulnerable with reasonable brains and good hands."

"*What do humans eat?*"

Owailion was winded and could barely reply. "I'd settle for venison or a nice salmon right now. I love bread and vegetables. Strawberries?"

He should have remained silent, for he abruptly found himself in a torrent of fish slapping down all around him out of the air, and the distant thud of whole dead deer hitting the mountainside. Finally, a hail of strawberries rained down on him until he shouted out in alarm.

"Stop that!" he bellowed, looking up at Mohan in surprise. "Where did that come from? I'm not interested in eating if it comes falling out of the sky at me."

"*Sorry about that,*" Mohan replied. "*The others just want to help. We don't understand your words, bread, and veg... vege... tables. Usually, a fledgling will eat his full weight twice a day for many days before they are sated. You are not hungry?*"

"Hungry, yes, but I don't eat nearly that much and I want to cook it before I eat it and that means on flat ground."

"*Cook?*" Mohan asked curiously.

Owailion sighed in frustration, clamping down on his temper festering within. "Cooking is too complicated to explain. How about I demonstrate when I get down to the bottom and instead you tell about these sorcerers that are trying to get across your borders. Explain about this Seal."

The dragon hovered almost motionless over the forest at the base of the volcano before he answered. "*We dragons magically maintain a barrier around the borders of the Land. No one, dragon or human, may enter unless they are one who has set up the Seal or whose magic supports it,*" Mohan replied proudly.

"You dragons seem to be very good with magic. It seems that you could handle invaders just fine even when you're asleep."

"*Ah, but we don't sleep. Except that is about to end,*" Mohan clarified. "*Four thousand years is a long time to stay awake. Now we wish to rest.*"

Owailion paused in his efforts navigating the slope in order to look back up at his mentor in magic. "Sleep? You dragons don't sleep? Ummm...unless there's something very different about me now, I like sleeping too. There is no way I am going to stay awake that long."

"*No, you misunderstand,*" Mohan replied when Owailion started off again. "*We know that humans are like other creatures; you will sleep for a night and then wake and in the meantime, magic will not run amok. However, it is not necessary for dragons to sleep... until it is; a long sleep, a thousand years at least. Magic cannot go that long unattended. It will break free and start to alter things, warp them into sickly, twisted puzzles of what they originally might have been.*"

Unbidden, an image flooded into Owailion's mind of a panther-like creature. He watched in fascination as the animal began oozing blood, writhed in pain, spitting and snarling. Its hide rippled and the muscles twisted around its stretching bones. The tortured cat climbed into an equally twisted tree. There the beast abruptly sprouted wings and launched itself into the sky. Then the vision faded from Owailion's brain.

"*Demons form with warped, unattended magic. These demons wish to possess others and feed on their pain. Dragons have banished the demons of the Land to another realm, but more come if we are not watchful. There are portals where they sneak in as well. They will surely come if we sleep.*"

Owailion shuddered in horror and almost stumbled as he slid down a bank of cinders. He would be battling demons like that? With magic? Something in him resisted thinking on it. Instead, he changed the subject. "How am I supposed to survive all alone for a thousand years? Usually we humans form nice little packs and help each other in things like this."

"*Packs?*" This insight must have surprised Mohan. "*We did not think of that. I would not worry about needing others. Magic should be adequate for all your needs, surely.*"

Owailion huffed at that. "Magic might supply my physical needs, but humans like to interact with others. Sixteen Wise Ones won't be enough. We like to form families. Pack is probably a bad word. Our families help us raise children and keep us emotionally stable. The families live near each other to make villages and sometimes when there are many of us nearby we would call it a city."

That he had the vocabulary in this apparently new language meant something, Owailion reasoned. He would need other humans or he would go mad, even if there were a few other magicians here. He could not imagine being so isolated here in the Land. If the new language had the words for family, village, and city then they must be necessary.

"*This is not something we considered,*" Mohan replied in a contemplative tone. "*Dragons live apart, left in our eggs until we have fledged. There is a conclave where we gather once a decade, but we rarely see each other in the meantime. Your coming is the first time I have met many of my fellow dragons all at the same time. Is a family necessary if you have no hatchlings?*"

Abruptly Owailion felt light-headed and stopped in his tracks. He sat down with a thump on a convenient outcropping nearby and slowly began realizing all he might have forgotten in this amnesia. Had he left behind a wife and children? Hopefully, he would not have volunteered for this strange change in his circumstances if he were leaving behind someone who depended on him. But no wife or children? No other people at all...except for the eventual arrival of the other Wise Ones? And he was going to be living eternally? It seemed alien to him.

"*Owailion, are you ill?*" Mohan hovered closer and then dropped down onto the mountainside below him. "*You are not well. Did we do something wrong?*"

Owailion did not know why but this final blow to his limited understanding rocked him to the core. Alone for eternity? He could not fathom it and the terror that should have drowned him ever since he had awakened to the first magical blast now descended on him like rain. He curled up around himself and closed down, shutting out everything: the volcano, the sorcerers, demon battling, a massive dragon, his own filthy and tired body, everything. Owailion wanted to sleep away the horror and wake up again sometime later with his memories intact and pick up his life wherever he had dropped out of it.

Without asking, Mohan reached out a claw and delicately scooped Owailion off the mountainside. If he had not been catatonic already the human would have passed out in terror as the dragon launched himself out over the valley and spun down gently into the forest below. Knowing so little about humans did not keep Mohan from acting. Instead, he used what little he did know, finding a creek at the base of the mountain near the trees and wedged his gigantic reptilian body between the trunks and the slope. Then he carefully set Owailion down on the bank of the creek and with a little thought, conjured a pile of twenty fish or so and an equal pile of berries next to Owailion's head.

"*Owailion, are you there?*" Mohan asked in a mental whisper.

The smell of fish rotting in the late afternoon and his hunger eventually overcame Owailion's terror enough and he mumbled something and then sat up. He looked at the fish, the creek and then back toward the mountain but he could only see a bank of gold scales between himself and the mountain. So, with nothing better to do, Owailion began laughing hysterically. It was all too surreal to comprehend.

And his laughter did not help. Mohan reared in anxiety. The dragon probably interpreted his laughter as a sign of distress for the reptile began carefully backing away, which promptly brought trees snapping and crashing in the forest.

"No, I'm fine Mohan. Please, don't move anymore. I'm fine."

"*You don't sound fine. Is that the sound you make when you are in pain? Did I hurt you by picking you up?*"

"No, it's laughter. Dragons don't laugh?

In answer to the question, Mohan demonstrated by sitting back on his two tails, lifting himself up high above the trees and letting out a hacking roar that shook the ground. When he had settled once again the dragon replied. "*That is how dragons laugh. What were you laughing at? I thought I hurt you. You didn't move and your mind stopped speaking to me.*"

"That's probably because my mind stopped speaking to me too for a moment," Owailion replied. "It just hit me very hard that I'm alone and I didn't take that well. I was overcome."

"*You are not alone, Owailion,*" Mohan tried to reassure him. "*All the dragons know you are here in the Land and will protect you. Other Wise Ones will come to help you make your packs. God has promised that. But that does not explain why you were laughing.*"

Letting out a sigh, Owailion admitted, "It was either that or I was going to cry. No, I saw this pile of fish and had to laugh. Humans don't eat that much in a month. Yes, we eat often, but not that much. And now that I'm on level ground I can make a fire. I'll show you how humans cook." Then in a fit of curiosity, he asked another question. "Do dragons blow fire?"

"*Yes, at the sorcerers on the other side of the Seal, but it would probably start a forest fire here, which would not be good for squishy people. If you need a fire to do this cooking, I can teach you how to make one with magic.*"

True to his offer, Mohan walked Owailion carefully through using his power to conjure fire. "*You must draw on the deep of the earth,*" Mohan began. "*Use your mind to see what you want to create. The stuff of the earth will become fire if you ask it to change. Think about its size and the place you want it to grow and the fire will come.*"

Doubtfully Owailion brushed aside a coating of fallen pine needles, clearing a spot for his fire and then concentrated, thinking first of kindling, and then the start of a smallish fire. If this worked he did not want to be the one to deal with a raging forest fire. At his wish, kindling popped out of the ground like dandelions, and Owailion laughed again. Then a poof of smoke showed in the middle of the kindling, and he blew briefly on the smoke. He was rewarded by a simple fire, and then he had to hurriedly add conjured firewood to maintain it. He grew so fascinated with the magic involved that he forgot the purpose of the fire in the first place.

"*Is making fire cooking?*" Mohan asked curiously but sounding not at all impressed.

"No," Owailion admitted. "Now I need a knife and . . . " Owailion used the magic to conjure a knife to gut one of the many fish that had been offered. As he worked with the knife and then conjured a pan to fry it in, he explained the need to cook his food.

"*And you cook your food every time you eat?*" Apparently this amazed the dragon, for he ate a few caribou, his favorite meal, about once a month. "*But look at all you eat. No wonder you eat three times a day. It seems a waste of time to make your food all brown and hot. Well, maybe this is because humans do not have the fire within you so you must roast it on the outside. That makes sense to me.*"

Owailion chuckled at the thought of cooking his food while in his stomach and then went back to questions he had about magic. "So I can conjure anything I want or need just by wishing for it? What is to keep me from conjuring grand things, making myself rich beyond anyone in the world?"

"*You are a Wise One,*" Mohan reminded him. "*You would not be so foolish. Besides, who would care if you made a clothes out of the brightest dragon scales? No one here will see them to be impressed. God selected you because you would not be tempted by that kind of magic. That is where the evil starts among man; using magic out of greed rather than for the service of others. The sorcerers from other lands use their magic for that kind of control and avarice.*"

Owailion looked around at the forest, at the emptiness of the Land and then gathered a fist full of pine needles to feed his fire. "What if there is no one here to serve. Humans are not meant to be alone."

Mohan rumbled audibly at that before he replied. "*Then perhaps God does intend you to be in your pack. He will provide what you need. Never forget, He has chosen you. Have faith in that.*" Then after a pause, he added, "*Owailion, your mind is cloudy. Is there something wrong with you?*"

"Oh, I'm just tired now. You know humans, we sleep every night. If I can sleep, I will be not-cloudy in the morning. Is that enough for you?"

Mohan snorted his agreement. "*What do you require to sleep?*"

Owailion conjured a blanket for himself and lay down without caring about the bed he knew once upon a time he might have enjoyed. "Dark and quiet," he mumbled. And Mohan gave him that.

Chapter 2

Dream of Stones

The dream fell on Owailion like light rain, soft and refreshing. He had not thought, given how overwhelming the day had been to that point, that he would also have a dream so tremendously life-altering as well. It started with him back on the top of the mountain, on the ledge but Mohan was not there. Instead, a great storm cloud loomed overhead and Owailion looked up into it with wonder, expecting an explanation.

"*No,*" a voice announced from the cloud. "*I have a task for you and a blessing. Owailion, you have come to the Land to help and you will be rewarded. You will not be alone for eternity. If you fulfill the instructions I give to you, the door will be opened for immeasurable blessings. First, you must learn all you can from the dragons, for they will sleep soon. You may ask for their help but the work must be yours. I have also prepared other Wise Ones that will walk the Land with you. Have faith that your path will be clear and when it is not, it will be straight.*"

Owailion didn't know what to say to the voice in the cloud, though he assumed this was why he had come to the Land. And he was on the path, even if he could not remember the start of his journey. He said the only thing he could say. "What must I do?"

Another vision imposed itself into Owailion's mind. In it, he held a little bronze bowl as he stood along a luxurious river valley, at the bank of peaceful green water. In his vision, Owailion knelt at the river's edge and filled the vessel. Then he looked inside, hoping to see the future as if it were a crystal ball. The reflection in the water shifted from displaying the sky. Instead, he saw mountains from afar and within the mountain's ring, he saw a deep forest below it. The reflected image swooped as swift as a dragon, plunging down into the trees and until it alighted on the forest floor.

Owailion held the bowl rock-solid in excitement. He was about to witness something magical. The scene passed through the base of the trees, hundreds of them, lined with ferns and then toward a strange clearing. A light dusting of pine needles and ferns lined it but no trees interrupted. Instead, he saw eight standing stones like sentinels within. The reflection was too small for him to study the stones closely but in reality, they could easily be twice the height of a man, all set out in a perfect ring. And most intriguing of all, they boasted writing. He strained to make out the markings in the reflection but they were too small.

In frustration, Owailion was about to dump out the bowl's water when a tremendous wind passed through the forest within the reflection and obscured his view of the stones. When the branches parted again, the runestones had disappeared.

"No!" Owailion shouted, disturbing the image and sloshing water over his hands.

"*The stones have been stolen,*" announced the voice within the cloud. "*This is part of your Seeking. You will build palaces, create Talismans, teach the other Wise Ones. And you will Seek for the thief of the Stones. These are your tasks, Owailion, King of Creating.*"

Owailion woke with a start, frantic, hoping the dream would be forgotten, but it lingered on. He sat up in the forest next to a pile of fish rotting, with the dragon missing and remembered every word. He shook with frustration and wonder, trying not to feel overwhelmed.

Then above him, Mohan appeared instantly swooping over the trees, obviously called because of Owailion's alarm. "*What is it?*"

Owailion looked up through the fir branches above to his mentor and "I just had a very….very clear dream. Do you understand dreams if you do not sleep?"

"*Yes, I have heard of them, but something has alarmed you.*"

Owailion took a calming breath. He needed to understand that this dream, although profound, was not going to be resolved in an instant. He had much to learn first. "I won't be eating fish any time soon. How do I get rid of your…offerings? They smell."

"*I agree, they stink. Just wish them back into the earth and they will return.*"

Owailion chuckled, but also experimented with the wish to make the offending smell go away and they did. He retained the strawberries and ate a handful for breakfast as he thought through things.

"*So, you have spoken with God in this dream,*" Mohan observed, probably hearing Owailion's thoughts about the dream. "*What has He asked you to do?*"

Was that God then? Owailion didn't feel any restriction on sharing his dream with the dragon, and certainly, he needed help with performing these duties he had been given.

"I have several tasks. First, I am to prepare for the others by building homes for each of the Wise Ones and crafting talismans for them; something they can hold that will help them in their own magic. Then I have to find some rune stones."

"*Find them? I do not know what a rune stones is.*"

He looked up at Mohan. "They are the standing stones, set up for a purpose of some kind. I called them rune stones because of the writing."

"*Writing?*"

Owailion sighed with the effort to explain the alien concept to his mentor. He wasn't patient, he realized with surprise and decided to ignore the implied explanation. "The scratches on the stones. They say things."

"*?*" Mohan's mind voice never actually said formal words but his curiosity rippled through the mental link. "*I have not heard them say things.*"

Rather than try and fail to teach a dragon how to read, Owailion tried a different tactic to address the missing stones. "Do you know this place?" he asked and then, with little more than his instincts, Owailion pressed the memory of the rune stones under the trees into the dragon's memory.

"*Yes, it is Zema,*" Mohan replied. "*You call this place rune stones?*"

"Yes, in the dream I had a bowl, a magical bowl. I filled it with water and I saw something in it. I saw those stones I showed you. Zema. And then I saw the stones disappear."

"*Disappear!*" Mohan asked, sounding alarmed. "*Show me.*"

Owailion obediently complied, pressing more of the bowl's vision into the dragon's mind the way he had been shown the demon panther.

"*This is not good,*" Mohan declared as the vision faded. "*I have been to Zema several times and always found the stones there. We must go investigate. The forest is very wet there and the trees grow very thick there but nothing will grow in that clearing except those stones that have been here since before the memories of dragons. We must see if this dream has shown the truth. If they have disappeared...*" The dragon let the worried threat hang in the air.

Owailion came out from under the edge of the trees to look up at Mohan. "How? I know you can fly, but I don't have wings and I need to see this too."

Mohan rumbled in thought for a moment. "*I must take you. You will ride on my back and I will fly... ishulin... to go there. It is a magic transmission. I will teach you. Concentrate on my back, how it would be to stand there; the mountain in the west, looking out over this forest to the east. You will be very high. Think of that and then wish to be there.*"

Owailion swallowed a hot pit of terror at this prospect. What happened if he didn't imagine something correctly? Was this a little like the feeling he must have felt before he came to the Land, agreeing to have his memory erased in order to come here? It must be part of his personality, to take these wild, reckless leaps into the unknown. He felt that pit burn in his stomach and imagined it burned away his fear. It cleared his mind and left him to concentrate. He closed his eyes, imagined the height seven hundred feet above him, with Mohan's spikes running down, as tall as the trees of the forest. Then Owailion leaped.

And stumbled. The gold at his feet was slick as ice, and Owailion sat down before he fell, and reached out to grasp the nearest spine. "I made it!" he shouted in sheer wonder, and he latched on more tightly as Mohan tilted his head, rolling his head, trying to somehow see the tiny human now perched precariously on his forehead.

"*You have good talons,*" the dragon rumbled. "*Do you have a secure seat there?*"

"I will, once I tie myself down." Owailion put words into action and conjured himself a length of rope, threw it around the tree-trunk sized spike he held and then lashed himself to Mohan's forehead. Then he felt safe enough to look around. From that perch, he saw the caved in side of the volcano and when the dragon turned to the north, the vast frozen plains beyond it. At this height, he could not see beyond the volcano, but as Mohan began clambering back up the slope Owailion had come down the day before, Owailion saw the ocean beyond the mountain.

Once he had reached an altitude where his wings would not foul in the trees at the base, Mohan spread his vast golden wings out to the side and without warning, launched himself into the summer sky. His human passenger shouted at the thrill. Mohan wheeled high above the crater at the top of the volcano and then turned east toward a long chain of mountains as if he would fly directly into the morning sun.

"*Ready?*" was all the warning he gave. Then in one downstroke the scene changed. Abruptly the sun was behind them, the forest had changed below and the long chain of mountains had grown close, looming so abruptly that Mohan had to bank hard to the right to avoid the sheer cliffs.

"*That is ishulin, a magic transfer. Once you know where you must go, it is simple. You have to envision it carefully or you will go to a place that does not exist,*" Mohan advised and then turned his head so they could spiral over the thick pine forest below them.

"*This is Zema, short for Imzemalainskalibaz. It means the Place Where Demons Smell. It is a place of suspicion.*"

Without more explanation than that, Mohan began spiraling down toward the trees in his flight path, into the shadows where the twilight fell quickly. Mohan could find nowhere else to land but into the tight forest, using magic to clear a landing for himself. Owailion untied himself and then slid down Mohan's arm. Underneath the canopy of trees, the dark swallowed the sun. Owailion had to conjure himself a torch to walk the few yards to the clearing of stones.

"There are no animals here," Owailion stated the observation, knowing it for a truth, as well as a curiosity. The profound silence gave the place an eerie atmosphere.

"*Yes,*" Mohan replied, still able to see all that Owailion experienced even though he could not follow all the way to the clearing without trampling more trees. "*They don't like the smell any more than we dragons do.*"

"Smell?" but even as he said it, Owailion realized he detected a strange scent, cloying, burning his nostrils. He could not remember smelling anything like it. The odor set his magical instincts on edge. He held his torch high, struggling to see in the semi-dark, with the trees throwing alarming shadows, like walls across his path. Then unexpectedly the trees gave way to bare earth in a ring a hundred yards across.

"*They are gone, just as you saw in the bowl,*" Mohan snarled. "*Something has taken them.*"

"Taken what?" replied Owailion. "Mohan, what were they?"

Rather than explain, the dragon helpfully crafted a memory image that he passed on to the human. Owailion was treated to a much more visible and spectacular display of the standing stones he had observed in the bowl. They were dark granite, unpolished and aligned in a ring. Owailion could see the carefully written lines although the images Mohan provided did not concentrate on the script so he again lost the chance to read it. Dragons would not have thought of the markings as more than scratches an animal might inflict, but Owailion strained to see them. He so wanted to read the words to see if they might be written in his old language from before his coming to the Land.

"What do they say?" Owailion couldn't help but ask.

"*We dragons do not understand these scratchings. I was going to ask you what they say. We never looked closely. We only know that they were here before we came and that the demons leave their stench here.*" Mohan moaned in grief. "*This is not good. Someone or something has come and taken the standing stones without our knowledge. That means they have broken the Seal. We must call a conclave.*"

Disappointed and suddenly fearful that sorcerers lurked all around him, Owailion used *ishulin* to return to Mohan's back where he tied himself back securely to his spot, above the forest tops once again as the dragon tried to reassure him as well as himself.

"*You might as well come also. Perhaps someone has seen this ring of stones more closely than I and can remember the markings… writings for you. We must find this thief.*"

Chapter 3

Conclave

The clear sky overhead teamed with stars wherever it was that Mohan had brought him. The light reflected in the stunning water of a lake so vast Owailion assumed he had returned to the ocean. Instead, Mohan reassured that he had come to an island in the middle of a lake named by the dragons Ameloni or Dragon's Tears. Atop this island was another volcano, obscured in fog and the dark. Its slopes soon would be full of the dragons Mohan had called, but they had not yet arrived.

"*We have our conclave here any time there is important news that must be heard and witnessed by all. It is here we obey the commands of God. It is here we announce the birth of another or the departure of someone we will miss. We have discussed your coming here and the building of Jonjonel, your mountain. We have never had so many of our gatherings so quickly. It is unprecedented. Your arrival has made an avalanche of news. Usually, these conclaves come once a decade at best.*"

"Departure? Do you leave the Land? I thought dragons could not die," Owailion asked curiously.

"*Usually, no, but it has been known to happen that a dragon will tire of magical duty. If we remove our Heart Stone and leave the Land we can depart and go to the stars or other lands and serve there, with less magic,*" Mohan explained.

"Heart Stone? What's that?"

For some reason, this comment seemed to alarm the dragon, who grumbled at his human friend in surprise. "*You do not have a Heart Stone?*" Then Mohan looked up at the volcano above them. "*It is something else we must address then. I will explain after the conclave.*"

"Would you ever leave?" Owailion asked with another drop of fear added to this stressful day. He was not ready for his friend to leave.

Mohan murmured reassuringly. "*I do not see that happening, even with the Sleep coming. I care too much for Tamaar, my mate, and for you and the Land itself. I want to learn what has happened with Zema disappearing. I also hope to awaken someday to a Land with humans protecting it. There is much to anticipate and I would not want to leave.*"

Owailion sighed with relief. "And I would not want you to leave either, my friend. There seems to be so much to learn."

"*It might be wise to do your sleeping now and by dawn, there will be a gathering of dragons here. Then you shall see the dragons in conclave and they shall meet you again.*"

Owailion agreed with that idea and so slid down Mohan's long body and landed on the shore of the island where the conclave was to be held. Instantly he noted the crunch as his feet landed. It sounded like the rattling of dry bones and Owailion shuddered. "What is this?" he asked in private horror. He could not imagine bones were littering the shoreline, but nothing else he could presume would sound like that and feel so loose and disturbingly broken under his feet. He bent and carefully picked up the material from which the shore seemed littered.

"*Dragon Tears,*" Mohan provided. "*We come here only when we share our emotions and these stones come when we come. So we call them dragon tears even though we do not truly drip tears of stone.*"

Tears of stone? Owailion lit a conjured torch again so he could see the pebbles he had gathered and what he saw amazed him. Could these be diamond? The cloudy white stones as large as a hazelnut glowed in the firelight. Without examining it by day he could not be sure, but he yearned to cut the stone and see how it broke, polish it up and discover how these stones had come to cover a volcanic island in the middle of a lake. He could not dredge up much information on diamonds from his former life, for he had probably not been a jeweler but surely the gemstones existed here in the Land.

Without answers, Owailion dropped the gems back into the others on the shore and conjured himself his bedding. He would do as Mohan advised; sleep while the sun remained hidden and prepare for the conclave in the morning.

He had not anticipated having a dream; not like the one where God had told him about the missing stones. This time a woman shrouded in fog walked across the shore of diamonds in the morning mists. The white and blue stones at her feet did not crunch or even stir as she moved. Her long silver gown looked like a wash of water across the pebbles as she floated before him like she consisted of the fog lifting off water. The mist hid her face from him, but her pale hands and the wondrous length of her flowing hair loosely braided down her back told him pointedly that this was again the literal woman of his dreams.

Witlessly, unable to move, Owailion watched her pass in front of him. He wanted to reach out or speak with her, but he seemed frozen. Then, when she almost dissolved into the fog, she reached down and picked up one of the thousands of stones on the shore. Why that one, he could not tell, but then she turned back toward him and brought him the diamond. He watched her hold the little rough pebble in her palm, like an offering and then her other hand passed over it. When he looked again, the stone had become a faceted and polished jewel. Indeed, it showed like diamond in her palm and this enchantress held it out to him.

With trembling hands Owailion could not reach out to take it, and he hesitated when he heard her voice, gentle like water over stone. "Use them to craft the Talismans of our power. Hide them well. We will Seek them."

Owailion stood there, so mesmerized by her finely evocative voice, the sultry tones of it that he could barely comprehend the actual words. Talismans? Seek? He felt incapable of even picking up a stone at his feet, let alone taking the cut jewel from her. He tried again and with shaking hands he reached. He could almost touch her alabaster skin and feel the life there. His own calloused and browned fingers looked so harsh in the mist, but he tried anyway. Before he could touch her, she faded into the morning light and he awoke.

Dawn had come to the lake and Owailion sat up alone in shaken grief. The mist was real, he saw, for the silver fog put everything in a haze. He wanted to go back to sleep and dream of that queen again. And when he looked down, he found that in his hand he held a cut diamond the size of a walnut, but polished and given to him by his dream. Owailion gasped and closed his hand around the precious stone.

Owailion rose and began pacing the beach as he considered the messages of the dream. He had another admonition; to make 'Talismans of our power'. She obviously referred to the other Wise Ones who would follow. Was she one of them? Owailion sincerely hoped so. He wondered at the little bowl that had shown him the theft of Zema. Was it a Talisman for another Wise One then? Was it for the lady in the mists? If so, he felt unworthy to explore the bowl himself. It was a gift for her and each Talisman would be unique to the future owner and possess magical gifts. And this Queen had suggested that the diamonds she had cut would become decorations and reservoirs of power for some of these Talismans?

Suddenly Owailion felt overwhelmed by the duties he had garnered; more than the diamonds at his feet. Find missing rune stones, battle sorcerers, stop demons, build palaces and craft Talismans for the other Wise Ones to find? How was he going to accomplish this all while learning magic before Mohan went into hibernation? He couldn't do it all, Owailion realized. He would be alone soon and the thought terrified him. And when word got out that dragons were asleep, human sorcerers would consider the Land prime property for invasion. How would he do it all?

A sense of panic began to sink in his bones and he sat back down on the crunching diamonds, overwhelmed by the fear and hopelessness. He reached absently for the stones at his side and without thinking about it he grabbed two fists full of the rocks. His frantic mind flared magically and he felt the stones turn to dust. Owailion gasped and opened them again to reveal he had a dozen faceted and perfectly polished stones in each hand.

"So that's how she did it," he breathed out in wonder.

"*It is time,*" Mohan interrupted his ruminations.

Owailion looked around for the dragon in the pervasive fog. "Are you up on top of the mountain? I cannot see you," he asked in an effort to forget the strange dream and its distracting subject. He didn't want to think of new duties or the lovely lady who had demanded them of him. He wanted to concentrate on one thing at a time.

"*Yes, come to the top of the mountain. Join me and you will see Conclave,*" Mohan suggested since obviously Owailion was not going to resolve his confusion any time soon. Owailion scattered the cut gems on the shoreline and drew on the dragon's vision to know how to ishulin himself to the top of the volcano.

His first perception was that he had risen to the clouds and the blazing morning sky greeted him, floating above the earth. On further examination he recognized Mohan's head was simply up above the fog bank that enveloped the lake and the dragon sat atop the dormant volcano beneath the clouds. The mountain on which the dragon stood barely topped the mist.

"*Flames are not just for battling invaders.*" Mohan gave him that as a warning and then rumbling of gasses blasted up within the dragon's body and erupted out in great gouts of gold flames twenty yards out in front of him. The dragon passed his head over the clouds and his inferno burned across the fog bank which disappeared instantly, seared away as if the sun had baked it into nonexistence.

With the fading mist the other dragons were revealed. The glittering of scales and flash of metal blinded Owailion briefly but he now saw the panorama of sixteen dragons sitting on every inch of the island volcano in the center of the massive lake. Owailion could not see the outer shore, as if the island were all the earth remaining and it had become covered in precious metals. All their twisting necks, flared wings and snapping tails created a blur of color. Were they all agitated?

"*We are not happy,*" Mohan began as both a reply to Owailion's unspoken question and an opening to the Conclave. "The standing stones at Zema have been stolen."

A deafening roar of dismay from the dragons momentarily interrupted, making Owailion's ears ring. Then Mohan continued. "*We did not realize the Seal has been breached and someone has taken them for a reason we do not understand. Any who wish to speak, please introduce yourself first so that Owailion may learn your voices.*"

One dragon, green, wingless with two heads growled audibly before he spoke up and helpfully Mohan swiveled his head around to look down at the volcano's base to show Owailion exactly which dragon addressed them. "*Ruseval is how I am called and I warned you Mohan, that the distraction of bringing a human to the Land would be our undoing. You have not watched as you should, and that is why someone was able to come to steal the stones. Or perhaps it is the human who has taken them.*"

That comment got another resounding roar. Owailion could not tell if it were in protest or agreement with that declaration. Another dragon, silver, with three heads in amethyst, emerald and sapphire tones spoke up against that. "*We are Tamaar, and you Ruseval do not know of what you speak. No outlanders have approached our shores to steal the stones or we would have seen them. Mohan is doing his best to prepare this human for when we sleep. If you feared that his coming would distract Mohan then you should have volunteered to teach the human instead.*"

So, the three headed jewel-toned dragon was Tamaar, Mohan's mate. Her triple-voiced words cut straight through Ruseval's accusations. She would be formidable, and a fitting mate for his friend, Owailion decided.

"*You may call me Imzuli,*" added a smaller, white and silver dragon. "*No one was watching where those standing stones were placed, so close to the Great Chain, with so many of us nearby. Even if the human was not a distraction, we might not have noticed when the stones went miss-*

ing. They could have disappeared years ago. They were a curiosity and nothing more."

"No," Owailion found himself interrupting. He didn't know the rules of the conclave but surely a human had never been invited and so they had never decided if he even had a voice. "No, those stones are important. The markings on them, those are writing...a message from one human to another. A message perhaps left for me, to help me protect the Land. Whoever wrote on the stones expected humans to read them, not the dragons. You dragons do not need writings in stone and now I will not be able to know what the message said."

That observation brought an echoing silence. Not even thoughts floated out into the air for a moment. Did they feel Owailion had made a mistake? Maybe the concept of writing had stunned them? Or were they going to punish him for speaking in their conclave at all?

Thankfully, Mohan broke the impasse. "*Do any of you have a memory of the stones that you could share with Owailion that shows the markings clearly?*"

But the uncomfortable silence continued with every dragon shielding his or her thoughts, leaving a void in the morning air. "Then we have a greater problem," Mohan shifted. "How were they stolen? Someone has come and taken that which was placed within the Seal. Presumably someone found a way through that would not alert any of us. Does anyone have a suggestion as to how this has occurred?"

Again, the silence deafened. The other dragons might have been critical of Mohan's involvement but Owailion knew they respected his strength as a magician and would never truly question his ability to keep the Seal solid at all times. They also universally respected Tamaar's assurance that no one had sailed toward the coastline without her thwarting it. But no one would verbalize their true doubts. Owailion squirmed uncomfortably under the unspoken until an inspired idea struck him, emerging from his burgeoning Wise One instincts.

"This is silly. With all the magic at our command, can no one go back in time to see what it was like a few days ago?" he suggested boldly.

Every dragon eye rolled up to look at him atop Mohan's neck. So, it had not occurred to the dragons to try this? Given their tremendous age, perhaps the dragons never realized that there was a past and somehow, they could go back and observe it.

"*You misunderstand, little one,*" Mohan replied for them all, using the nickname he had given to Owailion when he had first hatched. "*We do not know when the stones were taken. They were of little interest to us except when the demons come there. So none of us actively watched them or even checked them in....in probably a hundred years. Do you wish to go back in time and watch them for a century?*"

Owailion felt like he had just been kicked in the gut with disappointment. "Well, at least teach me how to check the Seal to be sure it is intact. Perhaps we can sense how it was broken...if it was actually broken."

"*What do you mean?*" asked a female dragon he could not identify.

"I hate to make this kind of accusation but...but all of you would sense if something broke the Seal, correct? Your magic is maintaining it. Well then, what if the stones have not left the Land by the hand of an outlander? What if a dragon from within the Seal were to take them, hide them or then remove them out of the Land when the interest in them was forgotten? Dragons leave the Land from time to time don't they and the Seal is not broken for them?"

Now the silence rang with the emptiness of thoughts hidden behind powerful shields. None of the dragons wanted to be overheard thinking about his suggestion. It implied that one of those present had broken their oath to protect the Land. They distrusted their human enough to not reply until they knew for sure that the accusation was not true. Owailion sat in the uncomfortable silence and realized that his presence might not be welcome. They did not want to force him to leave, but they also wanted to address his suggestions without human influence.

"If you would let me, I would like to return to the coastline. I wish to study the Seal there. When you wish to have me return, please call me," Owailion announced.

Then without their leave, he used his memory to return to the top of the volcano he had 'hatched' from, Jonjonel. He carefully imagined the dawn had not arrived yet, and steam would still rise from the caldera. Owailion used ishulin and left the dragons to discuss their dilemma in privacy.

Chapter 4

Glass Globes

Owailion emerged on the peak of Jonjonel, looking out to sea. The predawn mist hid the waters below him, and the plain to the north was about to plunge back into winter. The wind off the water tore at his clothing and morning, such as it was, had yet to reach this far west. He conjured himself a jacket and put it on.

Finally, Owailion looked down to where the volcano's skirt met the ocean. The entire coastline seemed to be a cliff as far as he could see. If he were to reach out to touch the Seal, he would have to get down there. He took a careful moment to assess what the scene would be like there at the base of the cliff and then transitioned again.

At the cliff's edge, he looked down and saw the tide was fully in and the surf beat incessantly right against the sheer stone. How would anyone sail a ship anywhere here and expect to climb up the face of the Land? No safe port or dock could be conjured to make that attempt anywhere along the coast. The roar and crash of water, even now in the mildest time of year would leave any ship battered and broken against the rocks. But was the Seal still unbroken?

Experimentally Owailion reached his arm out over the edge, seeking some resistance. Where did the Seal start? Would it resist him leaving it? Could he get back inside if he left? Many questions remained and he had few answers. He wanted to find the rune stones, but human fear and instinctive limitations kept pushing back against magic exploration.

Greatly daring, Owailion imagined himself on a crystal bridge that he could walk out over the ocean, feeling his way forward. He would not fall, plunging down into the water and sharp rocks below, he promised himself. Then, with his arm still outstretched, Owailion took a step out, beyond the cliff. His magic worked and he did not fall, but it took all of his concentration to not look down. He took another step, and then a third and his hand met resistance: the Seal.

Invisible, even to magical eyes, the Seal felt smooth like glass but firmer and substantial as stone. He reached as high as he could up against it, wondering if it formed a dome overhead, high enough to rise over the mountains so that outlander dragons could not simply fly in. Could he breakthrough and leave the Land? Probably he could if he had some idea of where to go, which he didn't. Was he originally from someplace on the other side of the Seal? Or was he from one of the stars above him, just now fading from sight in the dawning light? Would he ever know the answers?

"*No,*" Mohan's voice replied, and then his body appeared behind Owailion on the cliff. Almost startled into falling, forgetting that he floated five feet out away from the edge, the human turned and caught himself and then deliberately walked back to solid ground.

"No, what?" Owailion asked over the roaring of his startled heart.

"*No, you will never have all the answers,*" Mohan replied frankly. "*As for 'can you leave the Land', perhaps. I have left occasionally to fight out at sea and others have gone to other lands and then returned without breaking the Seal, but the dragons who left also used their magic to set up or maintain the Seal. Your magic is not part of the Seal so I do not know, and neither do you. Is it not enough to do; fight demons, battle sorcerers, build your palaces, find the rune stones and even make Talismans for the other Wise Ones?*"

Owailion dropped his head in shame. "I'm sorry. It is a failing of humans, I suppose. We are always curious and wanting to do and see more, even when we already have too much than we could ever possibly accomplish. I just wanted to find out the message on those stones."

"*And touch the Seal,*" Mohan added. "*There are a few dragons, you might have noticed, who do not trust you as a human. I left the conclave when they began to accuse you of destroying the standing stones. You will not be able to assure them if you leave the Land to go exploring. Tamaar trusts you because she trusts me, but she and I are the only ones who spoke up for you and there are many others who have not decided.*"

"It sounds as if you put me on trial," Owailion almost protested, feeling his temper rise like the volcano. Yet he held it in check, unwilling to take his ire out on the dragon who had helped him, defended him despite the innate distrust they all held for the humans as a race.

"*After a fashion, they did put you on trial. But the Land is a paradise, not exile. You would do well to remember that,*" Mohan advised.

"It is a paradise, I agree," agreed Owailion. "It's just that whenever limits are set, humans try to overcome them. There is an old adage; a horse will eat from the far side of the fence. It means that some people will never look at what they have that is wonderful in their life, only what is out of reach and unattainable. I guess I am often like that. I'm sorry. I should be content."

Mohan rumbled an agreement. "*Did you discover what you wanted to learn by coming here to the Seal?*"

"Somewhat. How do I *ishulin* to a place that I have never seen? I could only approach the Seal from the volcano since I've only been here and Zema."

That question startled the dragon, who snorted and for the longest time remained silent.

"How did you learn where you wanted to go?" Owailion prompted.

Sheepishly Mohan replied, "*I don't remember. Perhaps I have always known the Land. I remember being hatched here and learning to fly but I do not remember having to learn where I wished to go. It is as if the visions of all places emerged inside me when I hatched. I have just asked the others in the conclave and it appears that all dragons know where they wish to go and just go. Is this not the same for humans?*"

"No," Owailion sighed in irritation. "How are we going to go anywhere but on foot?"

"*It will take a very long time. If you cannot walk that far I could take you. Where do you want to go?*" Mohan asked innocently enough.

Owailion laughed when he thought of all the tasks he had been given. Eventually, he would have to go everywhere. He would be flitting around a vast continent, defending it from invasion. Also, he would be building homes for the other Wise Ones and finding demons forming. He especially needed instant travel after Mohan went to sleep and that meant he must see everything. How could he remember everywhere he needed to be?

"Is there some way to know how a place looks if I have never been there? It seems unsafe to go to a place that I cannot imagine."

While he asked this aloud, Owailion also found himself with an unusual vision. He could not remember ever seeing crystal globes in his past, but he knew they existed; globes with miniaturized replicas of huge buildings, but encased in glass. He imagined holding this exact location, no matter how the weather and ocean might change as time passed, no matter what angle the sun might catch the mountain. Could he freeze 'Jonjonel's coastline' in glass and return here as a memory?

Without meaning to, Owailion held out his hand and rather than imagining the place itself, he encased his memory into a sphere of glass and wished it to always update itself. He would be able to look and see how this place would appear no matter the erosion of time. And in his hand, the crystal ball appeared.

Beneath him, Mohan rumbled with pleasure. "*Clever magic. You are indeed a Wise One. You must make one of your globes of all the locations you wish to see. Then you may return.*"

"Yes," Owailion admitted, "but I need someplace to put these globes. I'm going to have thousands if I make them for all the places I must go."

"*Put it with your Heart Stone,*" Mohan suggested helpfully.

Owailion waited for that to make sense and while he recalled the term, he had no frame of reference.

"*You do not know Heart Stone?*" Mohan queried. "*It is the key to magic. You must have it or you would not be a magician of the Land.*"

Owailion shook his head and added, "I came out of the mountain with nothing but my skin. Where would I get a Heart Stone?"

Mohan unexpectedly squatted down unexpectedly. "*We must go immediately. Climb aboard.*"

Owailion obediently conjured himself a bag, put the globe he had made into it and then transferred to Mohan's forehead where he lashed himself down as the dragon turned and began to scramble up the volcano's side.

As he climbed, the dragon began explaining. "*A Heart Stone is a gift from God. He gives it to all creatures that are capable of good magic. It is part of a dragon's body, like our brain or lungs, next to our heart from the beginning when we hatch. I have looked inside you and it is not within. You must have left it in the mountain when you emerged. We shall look there.*"

"What does a Heart Stone do?" Owailion asked. "I mean besides make me capable of magic."

"*Good magic,*" Mohan qualified. "*A Heart Stone will not let you do magic if it is evil. It is...a judge of you. It connects your magic with the earth so that you can draw deep on the magic below. There are dragons that deliberately ripped it free and they will not be...be...they become like demons. They will not think of others or do what God has commanded. They refuse to feel compelled to do their duty. They are wild, feral, like animals and capable of evil, lying and deception. It is not good to go without your Heart Stone.*"

Owailion didn't know what to say, for his jaws rattled with each jarring step Mohan took clattering up the mountainside. All he knew was that his dragon guide feared a missing Heart Stone.

"*We are here. You must go back into your shell and find it. God would not have sent you to the Land without one. It is very dangerous to be without your stone.*"

Helpfully Mohan had latched himself onto the shelf where Owailion had emerged a few days before. Weak kneed from the precarious trip up the mountain, Owailion slid down the dragon's shoulder and staggered right onto the landing while the dragon placed his considerable snout right at the edge as if he hoped to sniff out the missing item.

"What do they look like?" Owailion asked innocently enough.

The dragon's reply was alarmingly thorough. Mohan pressed an image into Owailion's mind of a great racing heart, blood coursing through arteries and right next to the beating heart, untouched by the blood and tissue, a perfectly formed glass globe, not unlike the one Owailion had crafted for himself as a memory, but this one swirled with a cloud of blue and lit from within, spinning like mist in the wake of a wind. It seemed small compared to the dragon's heart, but then the size was relative. Mohan's heart must have been the size of an ox.

"*You must scan the mountain and find it. I hope it has not been destroyed when I pushed the sorcerer away,*" Mohan admitted worriedly.

Obediently Owailion turned to face the crushed rock face he had passed through the day he hatched and then closed his eyes and walked forward. Was there even a chamber left? With faith, Owailion passed through the stone wall. He wished a torch into his raised fist and then opened his eyes. Boulders and rubble now littered the once bare floor and Owailion realized the cavern wasn't all that big. His fear and blindness had made it an abyss. Now he could barely squeeze between the fallen stones and the roof that he almost reached with his outstretched hand.

Owailion held his light high, seeking the blue glow of a Heart Stone. He knew it had not been there, at least visibly, for any sliver of light in this cavern would have filled the space. Using his emerging instincts for magic Owailion reached out his mind and sought for the Heart Stone with his Wise One senses. His mind's eye looked through the stone as if it had become transparent. And there, six inches under the original surface of the floor, a gentle glow, pulsed like a heart.

Owailion could not reach past all the fallen rubble but he placed his hand on the stones, right above where his magic told him the Heart Stone lay hidden. Then he wished the globe to rise toward him. He watched in fascination as the glowing blue orb floated through solid rock and reached him. Brilliant light filled the cavern, catching the glint of crystals in the rubble. Owailion doused the useless torch now, just admiring the swirling orb. It hypnotized him.

"I have it," he called to Mohan.

"*Do you feel any different?*" the dragon asked curiously. "*It is supposed to make sure that you are always using your magic correctly.*"

Owailion walked back through the stone cavern wall, out onto the ledge so he could show Mohan, although he suspected the dragon could see through the stone for himself. "I guess I must have already been using magic correctly. How will I know if I do it improperly?"

"*You will not be able to act,*" the dragon stated emphatically. "*It will block you. You can only do good magic, but then, you were chosen because you would not wish to do evil. God chose you to come at this time because He knew you.*"

"So am I ready then, to really start looking for the rune stones and fighting demons?" Owailion asked warily.

"*Ready?*" replied Mohan, chuckling. "*No, but I think you shall learn more if you start to work towards that end. What do you want to try first?*"

Owailion looked out over the forest beyond the volcano and saw the vast chain of mountains sighed. "Where is Zema from here? Could you show me on a map?"

"*Map?*"

Chapter 5

Directions

Owailion carefully explained the concept of a map once they were on flat ground. When he conjured a piece of paper to try to sketch out something, it was too small for the dragon's eyes to focus on the small details. Next Owailion created a leather roll the size of a small cabin's floor and then walked right out onto it. He used magic and his finger to burn a shape right into the surface. "See, this would be Jonjonel as seen from above. And here is the coastline, here along the western edge."

"*Is this the writing you were saying was on the stones?*" the dragon asked in curiosity, blocking out the sun as he brought his great head low over the makeshift map. "*I don't hear the marks speaking.*"

Owailion sighed with frustration and drew in the forest he saw between the coast toward the mountain chain in the distance. "What do you call the forest here?" he asked.

The dragon cocked his head in puzzlement. "*Do you name the place you get your food?*"

Owailion smirked at the thought. "Humans name mountains, rivers, forests, our towns, and everything we locate on maps. Then we write their names on a map. See, this is how I would write Jonjonel." He then wrote out the script. "And this says Western Ocean."

"*I still do not hear it,*" the dragon muttered in disappointment. "*This is a very clever drawing you have made. You are indeed what God called you; King of Creating. But isn't it dangerous to put names on the map?*"

Owailion did not understand that comment and simply asked. "How would names be dangerous?"

In explanation, Mohan turned toward the volcano that loomed above them and demonstrated. "*Jonjonel, erupt.*"

Owailion felt the ground beneath his feet heave and then the echoing rumble in the distance as Jonjonel belched out a column of gas and ash. "*Any magician with enough power may command anything in nature as long as they know its true name. We name our mountains and a few rivers, but nothing more. It would be too treacherous.*"

Gulping, Owailion agreed and then looked down at the map. "I won't put real names on here but we need something to show where Zema is."

Mohan turned back toward the map and then concentrated as the volcano ceased its rumbling. "*Well, I can add some things to your map, now that I understand the symbols. This is the Great Chain,*" and accordingly a vast mountain chain, made in the same style as Owailion's original drawing of Jonjonel began to appear. The range moved across the map, west to east and then bent at a certain point, going almost an equal distance south creating an elbow in the middle of the continent.

"*And Zema is in that elbow,*" Mohan added to Owailion's descriptive thoughts. "*The eastern side of the Great Chain acts as a border of the Land.*"

Owailion looked up at the dragon in wonder. "Do you have any idea how long it would take me to map all of that? It would take hundreds of years. You are amazing, Mohan. Thank you for this."

"*It is my duty to help you and if you need a map to do your work, then I will do what I can,*" the dragon replied humbly.

Owailion stood in the middle of the map, between the two major mountain chains, looking at Zema and then judging the distances. "Now, if I were a human sorcerer, what direction would I take to get the rune stones out of the Land as quickly as possible?"

"*A human? Carrying them? Their weight would be too great unless they used magic to float them. Up over the mountains into the land to the East would be least obvious, but what if they did not come from the east?*"

"Is there a river nearby? You dragons would not think of floating them down a river. It would not even require magic and they could take them anywhere once they were at sea," Owailion suggested.

"*There is a river…*" and Mohan began burning a long line out of the Elbow and down to the south. Slowly the two of them began filling in the rivers, borders, forests, and coastlines of the Land. Owailion had to prompt his mentor about land formations and distances, and then Mohan would provide the actual features on the map. Then finally Owailion wrote shortened titles to the long draconic words for each feature. Within an hour they had crafted a relatively accurate map of the Land.

"Now all I have to do is find out how the rune stones left the Land," Owailion declared as he rolled the leather up into a scroll.

"*I still think they would be easiest taken over the mountains over the eastern frontier.*"

"Perhaps, but you've never had to walk over high mountain passes," Owailion admitted. "I want to know how a sorcerer got inside the Seal in the first place."

Mohan had no answers for such a question and rumbled in discontent. "*It seems that perhaps you were correct to think that maybe a dragon of the conclave has moved the stones, but to what purpose; to thwart the coming of humans to the Land? I will admit that not all of them felt favorably about the idea of the Sleep, or of humans taking over the protection of the Land.*"

"You have no reason to trust humans," Owailion declared. "Are all your interactions with humans like the one where sorcerers trying to blast through the Seal?"

Both Mohan and Owailion turned toward the west, looking out to sea. Fresh in their minds echoed the attack against the volcano as sorcerers tried to get past the Seal because Jonjonel had grown beyond its barrier. And it would only get worse once the Sleep began. That thought burned an ache in Owailion's stomach that he feared to name. How would life, even a magical life here in the Land, be worth living alone? The emptiness loomed like a storm threatening. He had enjoyed

Mohan's curiosity and lively conversation, a perfect antidote to the sheer terror of amnesia, but that looming knowledge that the dragons would all be going into a long sleep, and that he would be left on his own in this vast land, with a pending demon problem and looming sorcerers to withstand, it threatened to swallow him whole.

"*Your thoughts have grown foggy again. Are you sleepy already?*" Mohan asked, reacting to Owailion's alarm.

"What if the Seal won't hold when you are asleep?" Owailion felt alarmed at the reminder he would be protecting an entire country from outlander invasions, possibly without the protections the dragons had already established. "I just assumed…"

"*And we dragons had hoped that the humans on the ships would have given up by now. We also assume the Seal will hold after we are gone, but it was built with our magic,*" Mohan warned. "*It is important that you learn how to use the Seal and also how to roast the sorcerers or however humans battle other sorcerers before we sleep.*

"How do the human sorcerers come here?" Owailion asked. "Only on ships?

Mohan rumbled uncomfortably and Owailion could hear his friend's discontent. "*For the most part, and they keep trying. We do not understand why.*"

Owailion asked with trepidation. "Are they all sorcerers? How can you tell they aren't just traders?"

"*If they try to come close, they have a sorcerer with them.*"

"Do they know about the Sleep?" Owailion asked, also wondering as well why anyone would be so foolish to approach shores protected by dragons.

Mohan rumbled again, "*We do not know, and it is a worry for us. Perhaps that is why they keep throwing themselves against us; waiting to see when we sleep. What will the outlanders do when they realize that you are alone here in the Land? Let us follow the coastline and you shall see,*" Mohan suggested.

It did not take long to go aloft and reach the cliffs that plunged into the ocean. As far as he could see the continent fell sharply into the sea with no harbors or sheltered beaches for a ship to approach the Land. "Nowhere to draw up or even drop anchor," Owailion observed.

"*Look, you can see them there,*" Mohan commented, projecting an image to Owailion. "*With the tall things sticking out, they are easy to attack.*" Mohan's words stirred something and he projected a scene toward his human friend.

In his mind's eye, Owailion saw a memory of Tamaar, gilded silver flashing through a reflection of the light on the water, coming out of the glare at a large three-mast ship filled with dark-clad sorcerers wandering among the sailors. She dove down out of the sky, tearing through the sails and then landed thunderously like some massive figurehead on the bowsprit. The shouts of panic from sailors carried over the water as the sorcerers and sailors gathered, hoping to shoo her away before her weight and her fires cracked their vessel in two.

"Tall things? Oh, masts." Then, without Mohan's imposed vision interrupting his sight, Owailion squinted as they moved south along the coast and indeed saw many ships, all running north or south along the horizon. They mostly gave the Land's shoreline a wide berth, perhaps because they knew the Seal would not allow them an opening and they dare not get dashed against it.

"*We know they have a sorcerer when they come nearer. Like that one there. It is moving south very quickly but it is also close to the cliffs. Perhaps it is the same ones who attacked you at Jonjonel? Shall we see?*"

Without waiting for Owailion's input, Mohan abruptly banked to the right and sped out over the ocean.

"*Now,*" Mohan interrupted Owailion's thoughts about leaving the safety of the Land, "*you must learn how to fight men. It might be more difficult than simply hunting an animal. The sorcerers on the boats are . . . are . . .*"

"Like me," Owailion provided. "Do you ever have to fight some of your own kind?"

Mohan sighed audibly. "*Rarely. We send dragons into exile if they choose not to follow the mandates of God and the conclave.*"

"That cannot be easy," Owailion added, expecting a lesson in how to wage a magical battle. "What must I do?"

"*Can you sense the ship?*" Mohan asked as he banked and circled high above the very visible ship. In other words, Owailion was to open himself to his magical senses.

"No," he replied in disappointment. "What am I going to do when you're in hibernation and I don't even know they are coming? Let them get closer? That's not going to be wise."

Mohan chuckled throatily at the panicking crew. "*It is shielded so you would not sense it. Feel the void in the water? That is how you will be able to tell. As for how you will attack, I really don't know how a human can do this. Dragons do as I showed you; land on the ship and remind them to leave us alone or roast them. Humans can't blow that kind of fire.*"

Owailion sighed with worry. He would just have to figure it out. "We'll see. Sometimes these magic instincts come once I need them."

This ship displayed full sails, racing south, skirting the Land and now Owailion could sense something, a shield around the vessel. He tasted the fear of the crew who frantically brought down the sails in a vain effort to preserve the cloth from shredding at the talons of the rapidly descending dragon.

"Are all the men on board sorcerers or are the crewmen non-magical?" Owailion asked as they approached close enough to see individual faces.

Mohan's thoughts held an element of surprise. "*Crew? What is that? We just tell them to go home or attack. Did we do wrong?*"

"The crew…the men who run the ship. I don't think they are magical." Owailion pointed out over Mohan's nose. "Only he is."

This man stood tall and all alone on the prow wearing a flowing black robe with sleeves billowing in the wind. With his arms arrogantly on his hips, he glared up at the dragon above. He had probably commandeered the ship or purchased passage, but he was definitely separate from the crew and its goals.

Owailion began frantically praying that his Wise One instincts would kick in. He recalled the demonstration of Tamaar nearly breaking a ship in two. In that vision, the men had been scrambling and panicked when she landed on their vessel so he could not see which were magical and which were simple sailors.

"We need to talk to them," Owailion advised Mohan. "I cannot fight what I do not know."

"*Then speak to them,*" Mohan advised. "*But we will stay here aloft.*"

Owailion peered down from the height the dragon maintained, glaring at the robed sorcerer. "Who are you?" Owailion asked, projecting his mind voice down in conversational tone. "Why have you come?"

The sorcerer shouted back to him. "Finally a human has come to greet us instead of sending your dragons." His accent was so thick Owailion could hardly understand him. "Many have doubted that there even were humans in the sealed territory after all. We thought it uninhabited."

Owailion snarled at the thought that dragons were just lackeys in this man's perspective. Mohan also roared his disapproval, startling the sailors and making even the sorcerer flinch.

"Uninhabited?" Owailion barked back at the shielded mind. "The dragons live here. They came out every time and sent you back broken. Explain yourselves. Why have you come?"

The ship-bound magician mocked disdainfully at Owailion's ignorance. "To come to your shores, trade with you, learn of your ways and share our own. Why else does one land visit another…but yours has been sealed? Why?"

Mohan rumbled, and Owailion recognized this was getting him nowhere. Up until this particular voyage, the idea of trading with an 'uninhabited' land was all that crossed their twisted minds? Unlikely, Owailion knew.

Then he suddenly felt an inkling of a strategy. Privately he asked Mohan a quick question. "Is there some way to know if someone is speaking the truth? Is there a spell or something?"

"*A truth spell,*" Mohan instructed. "*If you wish to cast it upon just one person, concentrate on that one and wish to see them as they truly are. This man wears a shield so you must pierce it with a talon of your mind first, and then apply the truth spell. If on all of the men on the ship, think of it as rain, descending, wetting them all. Then observe. Evil shows itself.*"

Owailion nodded and then focused on the entire ship. He imagined the wall of shielding around the sorcerer and then gave himself imaginary talons as great as Mohan's. He pictured himself puncturing the shield wall, crushing it as he went and then flooding the inside of the shield with a mist of truth. The sorcerer's appearance changed immediately. The outlander knew that his personal defenses had been breached, for he panicked, racing to get off the deck, scrambling for the hold, but in his wake, he appeared to carry heavy chains that trailed blood. Before he could escape, Owailion instinctively added a spell of time, slowing the man in his tracks before he could disappear below decks. The sorcerer stopped in mid-motion like some strange statue.

"*I see blood, so he has killed before,*" Mohan advised. "*What would the …the things trailing after him mean?*"

"Chains? That he is a slave of someone else or he carries a heavy burden," Owailion interpreted. "He's a liar too. His tongue is split like a snake and his skin is rotting…I would guess he is evil."

"*And what of the other men…the crew?*" Mohan asked.

Owailion quickly scanned over the remaining men who also stood frozen, but in fear, not in a magical spell. He saw a few with rags and many bloody fists. So they might be angry or brawlers. None of them seemed to be rotting or murderous. "They're not evil," Owailion observed. "Just simple men doing their job. We should send them home, but do something with the sorcerer here."

"*Yes,*" Mohan advised, "*but you do not have a fire hot enough. How would a human deal with this evil?*"

As if to emphasize the point, a wave of pure power bolted up from the deck toward them as the sorcerer tried to swat them out of the sky. Owailion sensed this attack but it barely stirred Mohan, brushing over the dragon's shields, scraping and screeching like metal on metal.

The human looked down at the vulnerable vessel, toy-sized at this height and felt his ire rising. All his life, the life he did not remember,

Owailion must have battled his anger. He hated not understanding. He raged at being overwhelmed or at things not working out in his well-thought-out plans. Most of all he grew angry at frustration. The Wise Ones were supposed to be naturally good people but what stain did Owailion show under a truth spell. Were his chains even longer if he only looked at himself under such an enchantment?

Furious at the sorcerer's brazen attack and racist assumptions Owailion reached out his hand toward the outlander who remained frozen. Here was a frustration, a danger come to mar the sanctity of the Land, hoping to invade, manipulate and spread his reeking arrogance over the plains and mountains of his new home. Owailion did not plan it, but that temper within him blasted out of his mind and lifted the sorcerer off the deck, caught him on fire and catapulted him into the sky. Owailion heard the startled consciousness of the villain snuff out about the time he hit the thin clouds.

Mohan's pleased rumbled broke into Owailion's shock. "*You do have the fire, I see.*"

Horrified, Owailion shuddered as he pulled back the magic he had invoked. What had he done? He should not have…

Mohan interrupted the growing wave of self-loathing. "*It had to be done. If you did not, I would have roasted the entire ship.*"

Owailion looked guiltily down at the crewmen still on board. The truth spell still covered these men and Owailion did not remove it, but he needed to learn more and these sailors were his best source. "Can you tell me, did you take him to the volcano up north?"

The frightened sailors looked at one another tentatively and then one of them stepped forward. "Yes," he called loudly. "There were several magicians. We were commissioned to sail them to the volcano, but three of them died when it erupted. That one survived and swam back aboard."

"From what land did you sail?" Owailion asked next, watching the bespelled men for any sign that they were lying.

"Malornia, to the west."

Mohan rumbled a warning at that. "*That is where most of the attacks originate. Why do they keep coming?*"

"I'll ask," Owailion assured him. Then he raised his voice. "Who sent you?"

Nothing changed in the crewmen's appearances as they shifted nervously. "Our king has commissioned many explorations of your land. He believes it holds great power, or it would not be locked closed. We are only one of the many ships that have come."

Owailion's heart sank with worry. "Then, can you tell me if one of the ships carried a set of rune stones as cargo. They would be very large, taller than a man and with writing on them?"

"No, sir," the leader admitted. "We only sailed to the volcano and now we are heading home."

"Home is that way, not south," Owailion pointed. "You would be well to leave the shoreline. I do not care what currents you will fight. I will send a wind that will take you directly. Thank you for your honesty. Please do not bring anyone like that to our shores again. You can return home."

Owailion then brought a conjured wind forward which made the masts of the vessel shudder. Obediently the crew scrambled to put up the sails again. Then without waiting to see that they were truly floating away, Owailion and Mohan came about and turned for the shore.

Chapter 6

The Lady and the Palace

Owailion conjured a cooking fire and a tent while he watched the ships as they faded in the sunset. Beyond him, Mohan draped himself across the plain, watching the human's actions with fascination. Subtlety the human tried blocking out Mohan's obvious ability to read his thoughts, wanting some privacy. Did he have the power to block out his mentor?

"*What is wrong?*" the dragon asked. "*You are not open to me?*"

Owailion started in surprise. "It worked? I can shield you out? I didn't know if it would work. Yes, I suppose I am. Sometimes I just want to think a bit and not be judged by anyone," he admitted.

Mohan almost purred. "*I would never judge you. Humans are too hard to understand. What were you thinking that you would be ashamed to share with me?*"

Owailion shrugged restlessly before he answered. "So much for shields. I was thinking about that king, wanting to get into the Land because it is sealed, and about the rune stones. We've not come any closer to knowing where they've been taken. And I was thinking about being alone."

Mohan's head shot up. "*You are not alone.*"

"Yes, I know but…"

"*No,*" Mohan interrupted. "*We are not alone. Someone is listening in on us.*"

Owailion wheeled around, looking beyond the firelight, searching the horizon across the plains and then out to sea. He could just make out a distant light on a ship out to sea, far beyond the Seal.

"*Not there, down on the coastline,*" Mohan's mental voice whispered. "*Can you hear it? That is a demon start. It is not a demon yet, but something down on the beach is trying to turn. Magic has combined with nature and is trying to become something evil.*"

Owailion crouched down and crawled over to the west. A hundred-foot fall-off plunged below him onto a relatively narrow beach and then out to sea. On his belly Owailion eased his head over the edge, hoping it would not be visible. Mohan did not move but instead advised.

"*Keep your shields up or the creature will know you are there. Instead, follow my thoughts. I will guide you and show you what to do.*" With that Mohan's mind voice took on an echoing quality, like Owailion was hearing him from a distance. The human strained to latch onto the dragon's thoughts. Then Owailion felt pulled along on a tide of magic toward the cliff and over the edge. Owailion could sense a tang like metal struck by lightning. "*That scent is magic going wild. Watch for it and strike before it turns demon,*" Mohan instructed.

A dragon could not crawl like a human but Owailion sensed his mentor tried to do it, peeking his head over to the cliff's edge. "*Now, we might not be able to see, but I smell the nexus of magical power. It is combining with…a crab? There is a crab down there that is going to become a demon if we let it. This is what you must do.*"

Owailion could see no crabs and barely the lighter sheen of the beach above the waves but he sensed that Mohan was aware of it. Something clicking and beady-eyed snapped in his mind. Then a blast of flame shot unexpectedly out of Mohan's gullet and down onto the invisible crab below. Owailion was blinded, startled and gasping but he got himself in check and listened in again to Mohan's thoughts. When the dragon cut off the flame Owailion recognized that the strange tang of electrified metal had disappeared. The demon was gone.

"*No, it was not a demon yet. Remember the smell at Zema? It was different. You cannot kill demons; just make it move on, back to Other. And that is how you stop a demon from forming,*" Mohan announced proudly and pulled back from the cliff to resume watching Owailion.

"I could barely sense it and you knew where it was without even being able to see it," Owailion said in trepidation.

"*That takes time and training,*" Mohan assured him. "*It is something you must practice before the Sleep.*"

Then, for the first time since Owailion had awakened in the Land, he sensed Mohan was also blocking something, building a shield around the dragon's thoughts. The huge creature was thinking privately, hiding his concern behind a great stone wall of magic that left the warmth of the dragon's presence distant and almost cold.

"What is it? You're…you are…blocking me too. Why?"

Mohan sighed, warming the air with his breath, which was welcome, for the night had grown chill. "*I am….worried for you. It is my calling to make you content and to prepare you for when we dragons have gone to Sleep. I cannot leave you lonely. We dragons are content to be solitary, but not humans. How can I ease that for you, especially if I am not here to be your friend?*"

Owailion could not bring himself to even think of the fear that brought to his soul. Mohan might teach him how to defeat sorcerers and to torch demon formation but nothing could make it easy to be alone. Owailion took a breath and then looked down. He could not and would not think about it. Instead, he changed the subject.

"I will deal with that in time," Owailion murmured. "Meanwhile, teach me how to do that wall around your thoughts."

* * *

The next day as they flew south along the beautiful coastline, watching for ships Owailion abruptly asked Mohan to land. "There's something here," he announced, surprised that he had sensed it and the dragon had not.

Owailion slid down Mohan's back before the dragon properly folded his wings down and the human began searching this new patch of ground. "Just back there, I felt ... feel something. It is a strange kind of itch. It is magic, but I don't know enough about it yet to give it a name,"

Mohan seemed to ignore the implied question but then turned back from the sea to speak with Owailion. "*Let us investigate your itch, as you call it.*"

"Can you feel that?"

"*I feel nothing... of myself. I can feel what you are feeling though. You call this an itch?*"

Owailion felt his palms tickling and rubbed them against his thighs but he could not ease the discomfort. "It's exactly an itch. It feels like I'm about to sneeze but it won't come or as if someone is lurking behind me and I cannot see him. I just know I am supposed to do something here."

"*Dragons call it a compulsion. You have not felt this before? It is a signal that there is something here for you to do. Your action is required. You must do magic here or it will 'itch' until you act. That is how we find demons, sorcerers, and even our mates. God guides us to what we need to find.*"

Owailion froze in the act of sliding down Mohan's shoulder. "Wait a minute, God arranges your matings? You don't fall in love?"

"*Love?*" Mohan asked, with the same curiosity he had applied to clothes and maps. Obviously, the concept eluded him.

Owailion slid down to the ground, walked to the edge of the cliff and sat down abruptly with his legs over the lip. He could not explain the concept so instead, he asked, "God gives you this itch?"

Mohan almost managed a human shrug. "*Yes, at least that is how He does with a dragon. I do not know if this itch is how you will find your mate and I presume she will be another Wise One. If you are not meant to be alone she will come and you will help her the way I am helping you.*"

"And how will another come here if the Land is sealed?" For some strange reason, Owailion didn't feel alarmed by the prospect of having a magical itch guiding him to other humans, especially of the female persuasion, but he didn't think he would fall in love with her instantly. He doubted a compulsion could drive him to it.

Mohan must have been listening in on his thoughts, for he commented. "*You think that now, but the compulsion you are feeling now is not a strong one. It is asking you to do something and then it will fade,*" Mohan warned. "*I do not know what you will feel when you meet your future mate, but it is far more powerful than this that has stopped us here.*"

Owailion laughed at the thought, but he knew that for whistling in the dark. He wanted to be rid of the itch he sensed. "So, what am I supposed to do in this particular spot that magic is making such demands of me?" he asked to change the subject.

Mohan tried to shrug, imitating his human's mannerisms. "*I do not know. It must be a human thing, for I do not sense this magic unless I am listening to your soul. If a dragon was meant to do this act, I would feel it instead. Do you see something or imagine something here?*"

Owailion sighed. "No, I feel only the itch. Do you always know what your promptings are asking you to do magically?"

"*Rarely do I know the full purpose of the compulsion. For example, I knew the Land would be hosting a human when I was given the prompting to bring a volcano – Jonjonel – into being, but I had no idea the two were connected. I still do not understand the reasons for the Sleep either. However, I have already learned to obey the prompting even if I do not know its purpose. God will reveal Himself in time.*"

"Are you tired then? Is the urge to fall asleep too strong?" Owailion asked.

"*Do not ask me to wait here long without something to occupy myself,*" warned Mohan. "*It is not a very comfortable or safe place to sleep a thousand years.*"

"Safe? Why would this be unsafe?" Owailion asked in alarm. Then he looked out to sea and remembered the ships full of sorcerers he still could not confront on his own. He could easily envision attacks against the Land after the dragons slept, especially if the Seal weakened under Owailion's watch. Deliberately he shook himself away from the vision and realized he had gained an answer to one question. "I know I need to build here. God wants some kind of protection here on this cliff," he announced.

Mohan rumbled in a pleased fashion. "*The 'where' and 'why' is a place to start. The 'what' and 'how' will come if you meditate on them. This is good.*"

Owailion found himself shaking his head even before the words died in his head. "No, I have to move on. You are growing sleepy, I can tell. I should keep going to find all of…the… the palaces. Palaces? I am supposed to build a home and this itch, it is telling me that this is the spot for one. It will one day have a Wise One here that will watch the western coast for all of us. That is the compulsion I'm feeling."

Owailion could not believe it had come so easily, but the itch eased even as he said the words.

"*That is good. It is a human task then. A dragon would not begin to know what a human Wise One needs in a palace…if we know what a palace even is. It is a duty for you. How long will a human palace require?*"

Owailion almost snorted with surprise. "I have no idea what it looks like? How big? What materials? Why a palace? Humans never really need something that large. A palace…it's a ridiculously grand thing…like wearing diamonds and gold to pull weeds. A simple house is all most humans require."

"*You understand it more than I already,*" Mohan chirped. "*What can I do to help you?*"

Owailion stood and looked up and down the shoreline and cliff edge. His mind spun with the overwhelming sense of all that would be involved, even with magic. How would he move stone, bring water, find materials, design these homes? Was he an architect in his old life?

"*Well, I don't know what a palace is, but I presume it will take a long while to create, even with magic. Do you mind if I go find something to eat while you work on that? If I stay long here I will fall asleep and that won't be good.*"

Horrified that he had inconvenienced his friend, Owailion immediately encouraged Mohan to go and take as long as he needed. The human suspected he would be weeks here and he couldn't imagine having the dragon slowly petrify, or worse, grow ravenously hungry while he waited. He watched as Mohan lifted off to the east, launching himself off over the plains. What did a dragon eat, Owailion wondered idly and was reassured, just as Mohan disappeared from view. "*It has been a long while since I've tried buffalo. That's the big game out here on the open plain.*"

Owailion chuckled as he turned away, grateful he did not have to watch a buffalo being hunted by a massive dragon. In the meantime, he considered what he wanted to eat for himself, and began by conjuring himself a fire and his tent again, just to have the reassurance of normalcy, and as soon as it grew dark, Owailion went to sleep.

Owailion slept soundly with the wind gentle, even here at the edge of the Land and the ocean booming at the base of the cliff. He dreamt that he walked on the beach below, looking up at the white cliff wall above him like a barrier, blocking him in. That thought chilled him and he looked farther up, seeking the top of the cliff. And there he saw her – the woman from his dreams.

She stood at the crest of the cliff, draped in misty veils that flowed like water. And behind her stood a great glistening mansion fortress of faceted stone looked out over the ocean, facing it defiantly. Owailion's dream self-wished himself up atop the cliff beside her and his wish was granted.

He found himself standing beside her, with her graceful gown trailing away, blending in with the stone walkway and over the side of the cliff, spilling like water. Her hair and face remained obscured beneath a waterfall of a veil, held in place by a gold and silver circlet of woven lilies. Owailion yearned to lift the veil and see her face, know her name and ignore the obvious purpose for her coming into his dreams.

"No, Owailion," she whispered in her voice like water. She did not let him divert from the task at hand. Instead, she reached out and drew him toward the palace, and he thrilled at her touch.

Obediently he looked up at the palace he was meant to build here. Strong, thick marble-clad walls with stylized ironwork atop them lined the cliff, both menacing and yet beautiful in a majestic way, challenging any to come. The patterns engraved in the stark white walls in bas relief caught the light of the setting sun. And above the outer protections a spiraling tower, with a blinding gold roof. The iron gates repeated the decorative theme while still appearing fiercely stalwart against all comers. Atop the highest spire, Owailion saw a blue banner rippling like waves in the sky and a golden eagle circled, guarding the whole complex.

The lady then pulled him forward, toward the formidable gates that opened for them, swinging wide as they approached. Together they walked inside on a path made of flint and agate through gardens, fountains and practice yards set under cultivated shade trees. Outbuildings for weaponry and horses hid among the gardens, discretely spread throughout the grounds and complementing the landscaping. With an effort Owailion took note. He knew this dream would show him what to build if not how and he needed a sense of the person who would live here, not be distracted by the wondrous beauty that walked silently with him.

As they approached the doors of the main building, he paused in wonder, looking up at the polished gray wood that stretched two full stories above his head. Into each side of the passageway, a knight in full armor stood carved in bas relief, one holding a sword and the other a spear as if guarding the way. The Queen of Rivers kept moving, slipping from his hands and Owailion moved forward to take her hand again as the polished doors swung open for him.

Inside they had entered a grand foyer, complete with two staircases that wound up into the heights above and a gold chandelier that reflected off the blue and gray polished marble floors. Full suits of armor stood in niches around the oval space, and several doors, inlaid with gold and more of the bas relief soldiers led off the main floor. Owailion drank it in, wondering at the beauty and grandeur, even in a military fortress. This Wise One would be a warrior, he was sure.

He followed the graceful queen as she flowed up the spiral stairs. Her gentleness contrasted with the weapons hung like pieces of art in between grand tapestries depicting scenes of eagles and dragons in flight. Wood, metal, glass, and stone blended richly as building materials and Owailion felt grateful for magic, for no one could have gathered such a variety and quantity of raw materials, let alone built it all in one lifetime. This was a palace for the ages.

Carefully, the dream-queen opened every room for him and some part of Owailion's mind cataloged every feature. They discovered a forge, a library, more weapons stores, and a workroom completely dedicated to sharpening and repairing all the various tools and weapons. Then he found more typical places; a kitchen with several ovens and a huge wooden cooking surface. Beside it stood a large table with simple chairs for eight. Nearby he found a larder with access to a kitchen garden surrounded by a marble wall so no one outside would know it even existed. The queen, with her regalia, fit better in a much grander dining hall that could easily seat twenty with regal blue and gold tapestries lining four fireplaces and glittering with light from candelabras and braziers. Eight private bedrooms, each with a privy and bath filled the upper stories, each with small balconies and stained glass windows with the soldierly motif etched into them.

"Where is there a private place where a Wise One could sit and just relax after a long day of fending off demons or sorcerers…or in this one's case, whole armies?" he asked his queen escort.

"Above," she whispered, sending shivers down his spine.

She then beckoned gracefully for him to follow her up one more flight of marble stairs. There she stopped before a single gray wooden door guarded by the sculpted sentries, this time with an eagle perched on one shoulder each. She opened these doors for him, but then held up her hand to stop him entering.

Inside he discovered the room he had anticipated; comfortable chairs in royal blue, large welcoming hearths and splendid light coming from crystal openings in the arched ceiling as well as a grand chandelier of iron, silver, and gold. The floors of marble continued the military motif but a cerulean carpet with a gold star covered most of the sitting room and a stunning suit of armor, gold, platinum, and silver-lined steel stood at the ready, complete with a blue plumed helmet. Owailion, standing stunned in the doorway, yearned to approach for a closer examination and took one step toward the beautiful room but found his way blocked.

"No, my love," the gentle voice of the Queen of Rivers rippled through his mind. "Look and remember, but here you cannot enter. Not until it is given to another. This is the Chamber of Truth. Each will have one. Here only the truth will be revealed and you will see all as it should be."

Owailion had no reply, but the chilling challenge quelled his regret and he stepped back. He would build this palace just as he had been shown and one day he would see the fruits of his labor. He turned away regretfully from the wondrous room, wanting to speak with the lady, but as the doors closed behind him. Her veiled face turned away and Owailion woke with a start from the dream of the Lady and Palace.

Owailion sensed Mohan's sudden alarm and abruptly the horizon above the plain filled with the alarming sight of the dragon looming like a golden storm above him, wings spread, with a buffalo hanging from his jaws and an extra one clutched in one talon. "*What is wrong?*" the dragon asked frantically, settling down on the ground, spitting his prey out and licking his bloody chops with his black tongue. "*Are you harmed?*"

Owailion tried to calm himself, swallowing his fear at the sight of the predator nibbling on his food in chunks ten times a man's size. "Oh, no," Owailion tried to brush off his thundering heart. "You go on and eat. I just woke up from a dream. You eat and we can talk later."

"*I can talk and eat at the same time. What has this dream done to you?*"

Dawn peaked over the horizon and Owailion regretfully realized he would have to explain. He began packing up his blankets and conjured a fire to cook some breakfast while he tried to think of how to explain.

He deliberately turned his back on the dragon as Mohan picked up his fallen prey and stuffed it back into his maw, hide, horns and all.

"I dreamed about the Queen of Rivers again and she showed me the palace that I need to build here. I think I can build it but… I want to meet her and…and why keep the rest of humanity away if we are the only ones here to enjoy these grand homes? Having only sixteen humans doesn't make any sense to me."

Owailion also allowed Mohan to hear the thoughts he could not put into words. It made sense that the dragons were the only sentient beings in a country sealed against humans. He very much doubted having humans and dragons at the same time would go very well for either species. And yet having a sealed Land, with the dragons sleeping and just a handful of humans, made little sense. Were these sixteen Wise Ones expected to repopulate the entire continent? Well, if so, he had the responsibility to make the newcomers comfortable too.

Owailion sighed, with no answers. "You go finish your meal," he advised Mohan. "I'm just going to sit here and think on how to build a palace with no idea of who will live here in some distant future."

"*This sleeping you do, it seems to teach you much,*" *Mohan commented.* "*I wish dragons could sleep as humans do and gain such insight and guidance. How does sleeping lead to this? You don't seem to be doing anything.*"

"Dreaming is all we do when we sleep. I don't know if dragons will dream but I hope so."

"*Dream, I do not understand this word very well.*"

"Here, let me show you," and Owailion passed a compressed vision of all that had transpired in the night into Mohan's mind. Then he added, "When we sleep we most often see many things that are silly or random. And sometimes, like in this dream, they are a message from God of what I must do."

"*You must create that…that place?*"

"Yes, for one of the Wise Ones who will be a warrior, or so it seems."

"*And what is its purpose? It is a very large…cavern for a small creature like a human.*"

Owailion chuckled at that observation. "It is. Most humans would find one room in that place adequate for their entire family. However, it must mean something more. Each of the Wise Ones is supposed to have one of these palaces for their home. I was shown how it appears and I know I can do it with magic, but I do not know the purpose. Maybe the magicians who attack the Land will fear us more if they see this...this extravagance."

"*That is often the case,*" Mohan commented sagely. "*When the outlander sorcerers see a dragon's magnificence, they often fear and turn back,*" Mohan said this humbly, without a drop of understanding human instincts.

"I very much doubt it is just your magnificence...only." Owailion enlightened his friend. "A dragon your size is going to freeze any human in primal fear. You forget we don't run fast, don't have claws and talons, or blow fire. Your sheer size is most intimidating."

"*I am the largest,*" Mohan observed, again with an innocent embarrassment that he had to point this out. "*How long will it take you to build this place?*"

"I don't know," Owailion considered. "Do I have to even be here to monitor it if I tell magic what to do?" Without expecting an answer he stood up and considered the effort needed to build this dream into reality. His magical instincts began stirring, drumming deeper than he had gone thus far with his shields and conjuring. He could sense deep below where water, long gathered in natural cisterns had pooled and he would tap into them. He felt for the bedrock of the cliff under the thick topsoil and with a flick of his mind began lifting that earth away, making it disappear into the ether. He would found the palace on stone deep below the prairie surface. He gave magic its instructions and then turned away, looking for something to distract himself, testing if he needed to concentrate on the excavation once he had ordered up the magic to do it.

"Are you done eating?" he asked Mohan as if there was not a gaping hole appearing right next to him on the cliff.

Mohan looked a little startled; his gold eyes bugging out at this prestigious use of magic and had to tear himself away from watching the dirt fly away. "*Ummm, I've never eaten so much before and yet, I don't feel that I'm stuffed. Thank you for asking.*"

"It sounds like gorging," Owailion pointed out, "like bears and other carnivores that hibernate. They eat a tremendous amount before they sleep for the winter. Is that what you're doing?"

"*I don't know. No dragon has done this hibernate before. Is gorging normal then? I ate sixteen buffalo and I think I could eat as many again and not feel bad about it.*"

"Remind me not to go wandering off in the mountains alone any time soon if your entire species is out gorging right now," Owailion teased. "Do you feel up to continuing our journey or do you need time to digest? This palace seems to be building itself once I tell magic what to do and if we keep moving you will stay awake longer."

Mohan assured him that he could fly on with no trouble. Owailion ate his own breakfast quickly as he surveyed the progress of the deepening and widening hole his magic drove into the earth, reassured it would work independently of his concentration.

"I need to give it a name, for the map," Owailion commented before they left the site. He pulled out the map and noted the approximate location with a diamond on the western coastline. "How do you say fortress in your language?"

The dragon tilted his head awkwardly, blocking out the sun so Owailion couldn't see well enough to continue his drawing. "*It is another language, I suppose. I would say…Paleone. It is strange, I did not think of it as another language. What you and I speak to each other is not the same as we name things. True names are spells to have power over a thing. When we name it we give it magic. This naming of things…it is human magic I think.*"

"Paleone it is."

Chapter 7

First Talisman

"*I think you should meet with Tamaar,*" Mohan announced.

"Why?" Owailion almost squeaked in sudden alarm at that prospect as they took off again, leaving Paleone as an active dig site on the cliff.

"*First of all, she is an expert in Seals. She has set a double shield around her territory and she can teach you the fundamentals. Also, she guards the southwest coast. That is where most of the ships are met. If anyone has taken the stones as you say, perhaps she has seen them in her forays.*"

This sounded well enough to Owailion, at least in principle. He needed some new way to search for the runestones as well as a goal to get away from Paleone as it was coming together. He had made a memory globe of it so he could easily look in and know its progress, but now he needed a new project. Facing Tamaar, Mohan's mate might sound like a positive step but it also carried a large chunk of intimidation with it.

"Very well," Owailion agreed.

It took no time to arrive at the edge of Tamaar's sealed territory, and they landed on the northern edge of a forested peninsula that jutted out into the ocean. Just as they landed and Owailion slid down, the sky just beyond the cliff, filled with a blinding flash of silver, gold and bronze dragon. Tamaar, three-headed and with shadowy wings filled his view. She couldn't match Mohan for size, but the amethyst, sapphire and emerald eyes mesmerized. She hovered, unwilling to land, displaying an alarming array of teeth, each one the size of his arm. Owailion straightened up in sudden fear as the incredibly long necks and heads snaked above him. Then some instinct drove him to do something strange.

Owailion bowed to the dragon, lowering his head and murmured, "Lady Tamaar, thank you for meeting me." Exposing his neck to a dragon was the most unnatural act he could recall but he clamped a shield of steel over that thought and waited to be acknowledged.

"*Lady?*" Tamaar's mind voice came in three tones, all speaking at slightly different times.

"A term of the highest honor to the most beautiful females," Owailion provided as he lifted his head, wondering if he would have to translate 'human' to Tamaar as well, or if she was just surprised at his manners.

"*We know what a lady is,*" Tamaar's triple voice replied haughtily. "*We are just taken aback by a warrior using it to describe a dragon.*"

"I am no warrior…at least I do not think I am. In my memories and magic, I'm only a few days old and do not remember my former life. That is why I have come to speak to you. I wish to learn more about seals as part of my duties for when the dragons are all in the Sleep."

"*Not a warrior? You will be,*" Tamaar's reply dripped with cynicism. Then she turned one set of glowing emerald eyes toward Mohan, keeping amethyst and sapphire warily on guard on Owailion. "*Has there been more news about the standing stones, Beloved?*"

Mohan's manner seemed to lift with the endearment, and he rose up on his haunches before he answered, spreading wide his wings. "*Owailion believes they have been removed from the Land by ship and was thinking that you might know of a ship that has passed by carrying them.*"

"*By ship?*" This caught Tamaar's curiosity again and her three sets of eyes swiveled back to inspect Owailion all the more. She finally came to land on the cliff right next to the much-dwarfed human, nearly bowling him over with back winging. He felt exposed and naked again on the mountainside facing her intense gaze as if she could see into his soul. "*What makes you think this?*" the triple tone rang in his head. "*Earlier at conclave you thought that it might have been a dragon who took them. A dragon would not use a ship to carry them.*"

For one frightening moment, Owailion could not dredge up a reply. "Yes, but a dragon would also never think they were important. Yet a human would value them highly. He might persuade a dragon to give the stones to him and then take them back to his home."

"*And what would you, with no wings, do if you found the ship that carried them?*" Tamaar asked with an insinuating tone as if she mocked him for his powerlessness.

Owailion felt his heart sink. She was right; in this situation he was powerless. Yet he could not refuse to answer her. He waited breathlessly, thinking behind his shields. Then the Wise One instincts finally kicked in and he did not fight the prompting.

"Lady, I shall defend the Land with all the power at my disposal," Owailion swore, feeling the Heart Stone pulsing in his chest.

And at his oath, the most amazing thing happened. One moment he stood on the bluff in the simple utilitarian clothing he had originally conjured for himself that first day on Jonjonel and the next moment, without any intention, his clothes changed. He suddenly found himself dressed in brushed leather breeches dyed a soft dove gray, with silver stitching on the seams and over that he wore a velvet jerkin that shimmered and shifted through shades of silver, with patterned stitching of gold and silver in it, richly decorative. The sleeves of a cloud white shirt billowed in an unfelt wind. Across his body, a molded steel bandoleer carried a platinum sword encrusted with diamonds. It held down a silver velvet cloak lined with white fur, also embroidered until it stood stiffly, barely stirred by the magical wind. And most alarming, on his head he could feel a crown. He didn't dare reach up to inspect it, for the dragons, both of them reared back in alarm at this transformation. Owailion could understand the reaction.

"*What is this?*" Tamaar's three voices and Mohan's one simultaneously rumbled through Owailion's head.

"I....I....I don't know," he replied honestly. "I didn't do this."

"*Your... coverings... they change?*" Tamaar pointed out the obvious.

"*He calls them clothes,*" provided Mohan helpfully. "*But I have never seen them change before. A dragon does not change his scales.*"

"A human changes clothes so they can be washed but...but this...this is magic. I didn't do it, I swear," Owailion sputtered.

"*I think that is the word. You swear or take an oath and this happens. Have you encountered this before?*" asked Mohan.

"No," Owailion replied honestly, and as he did so, his clothing, without any action on his part, returned back to his original attire. "No, I've never imagined something like that could happen. It's like the palaces I'm supposed to build; too grand for any normal person."

"*Palaces?*" the sapphire mind of Tamaar queried.

Mohan provided the answer helpfully. "*God has commissioned him to build caverns...he calls them houses or palaces, for the other Wise Ones. They are also glittery...like those clothes. But God wants them.*"

Owailion nodded and then realized he had an opening to continue his interview with Tamaar, despite the distraction of the regalia appearing. "That is another reason I have come to speak with you, Lady Tamaar. God has asked me to build palaces throughout the Land...as outposts so the Wise Ones may take up the guard of the Land. One of these palaces may be in your territory and I must be near it to sense where I am to build it. May we have permission to enter and see if there is a Wise One who must stand guard in your lands?"

Tamaar let out a strange sound, half bark, half chirp, in alarm, and reared back, with the amethyst head even hissing. Mohan growled low, a calming purr. "*Tamaar, he comes with God's commission. He cannot harm you, the Land or anyone in your protection. He can do no evil.*"

Owailion wanted to know what caused her distress at his coming to visit, but he held his peace. Mohan had more credibility in his littlest talon than any human would ever garner with her, and if anyone could convince the tri-colored dragon, it would be her mate.

"*He holds a Heart Stone, yes, but he can remove it. What is to keep him from throwing it aside?*" Tamaar reasoned.

"By nature he is good. Humans are like that. They either are slaves to their nature as the ones you have battled, or they are like Owailion; trained to be good by nurture. See him in truth spell and witness for yourself his soul."

Owailion again underwent Tamaar's serious glare and this time watched for what dragon magic might emerge. He waited for some wave of power but instead felt nothing until he found his appearance once again had changed, back into the silver and white regalia. This time he pulled the crown off his head and inspected the silver circlet decorated with a faceted diamond the size of his eye. He could not catalog the changes he had withstood but he knew last week he had been a typical human, ignorant of this world of dragons and magic. He had been called the King of Creating and now he dressed as a king. He had become a sorcerer and immortal… unless this she-dragon ate him, and he would never be able to comprehend it all.

"*I see no falsehood in him,*" Tamaar declared.

That comment made Owailion look away from the crown and up at the dragon again. She had done to him as he had done to the sorcerer on the ship; put him in a truth spell. Was this wondrous costume how he truly was now and his common clothes were the disguise to help him blend in like a normal person? He almost laughed to imagine tramping crossing the Land wearing such finery.

"*You must be what you say you are; a good man, for you appear as this….this…glittery human and that shows you as honest,*" Mohan explained to the flurry of questions that tripped through Owailion's mind. "*You are not bloody, serpent tongued or showing as a demon. It is difficult for a dragon to speak a falsehood but man has the ability. However, as a Wise One, you probably cannot lie either if you appear so…what is the word in human terms?*"

"I appear as….I think the term is a King. Only a king in the world of men would dress this way. And can I lie? I don't know why I cannot…and …."

Owailion experimentally tried to say something, anything false. He could barely think of something; he preferred summer over winter, but the words would not come out of his mouth. Why couldn't he say a simple untruth?

"I can't. I can think of a lie but the words won't come out of my mouth," he gasped after struggling over forming just a few syllables. "That is so strange."

"*That you cannot lie, it is a good thing. Dragons find it very strange, but humans find lying too easy. There is no reason to be false,*" Mohan advised and then turned back to his mate. "*Does he have permission to enter your territory and learn about seals? I will be his escort. He is mostly following the coastline... creating a map.*" And Owailion heard the gold dragon pressing the concept of 'map' into his lady's minds.

"You are welcome to see it when I am finished," Owailion added.

All six of Tamaar's eyes flashed in a glare at him. "*We shall not need that. We will grant you access.*" haughtily Tamaar replied. "*We will also leave you something we have found so you can train him,*" she added for her mate's sake. Her sapphire head reached out and brushed lightly against Mohan's jawline and a gentle cat-like purr. Then she pulled away. Owailion bowed low once again in thanks to the lady-dragon and then mounted up on Mohan's neck while Tamaar dove over the cliff and into the sea.

Two weeks later Mohan and Owailion flew away from the lush jungle forest under Tamaar's influence. They left behind the start of another palace, this one themed for the ocean, with aquariums and mother of pearl in the planning. He had enjoyed yet another dream, escorted by the lovely Queen of Rivers who had remained shrouded and elusive, walking him through this palace as well. While it felt nice to begin – and be able to continue the palace at Paleone simultaneously – building at Tamaar with no further answers disturbed him.

Owailion also had learned how to create a shield, at least in theory. He could defend a wide area, almost as large as the palaces would be, but nowhere big enough to encompass the entire Land. That was still beyond his abilities and might be forever unless he could combine with the other Wise Ones. Tamaar didn't have the patience with him and he did not have the capacity to study more under her tutelage so they gave up. Perhaps the yearning to meet the Queen of Rivers distracted him too much so he and Mohan left Tamaar's territory just as fall was descending.

Now, just outside Tamaar's seal Owailion faced a dilemma; go up the wide river he now encountered or keep following the coastline. Traveling into empty mountains - Mohan's definition of dragon-free– that lined the coast, did not appeal and so Owailion decided to follow the river, filling in the map rather than the perimeter of the Land. If he trusted his instincts – which he did not- something waited for him up this river.

They had flown only a few strokes up the river when Owailion asked Mohan to stop. The glorious river valley, deep and rolling, with the rising sun glancing off the water spoke to him and he felt the now familiar itch of another palace. They landed just where the water spread into the channel and into the northern tip of the delta. There Owailion found an island in the middle of the wide flow, calling to him.

"*How many of these palaces can you do at any one time?*" Mohan asked as Owailion began stripping down to swim over to the island. He wanted to inspect the island where the dragon probably would not fit. The deep river valley with the steep slopes was forested more naturally than Tamaar's magically maintained jungle and tickled at a lost memory from his old life.

"I have no idea," Owailion replied. He had regularly checked in on his two projects so far and noted that Paleone had reached the stage of walls of white marble lifting into the sky and Tamaar's foundation had not been excavated quite yet.

"*What are you doing?*" Mohan asked curiously as Owailion dove in.

Apparently, Owailion felt at home in the water as if he swam all the time in his old life. "Swimming of course. What's the name of this river?" he asked as he climbed ashore.

"*We dragons call it Laranimilirinilolar, but you might call it the Lara,*" Mohan replied.

"Lara, the river and I'll call the palace Lolar," Owailion called to him. "Shall we stay the night here to await inspiration?"

"*I am hungry again,*" Mohan admitted sheepishly. "*At this rate, I'll get fat. Is this normal?*"

Owailion chuckled but didn't speculate as Mohan launched himself into the sky for his customary 'while dreaming' meal. Then, when the valley had fallen into shadow, Owailion lay down in his bedroll to go to sleep, anticipating a dream about what he should build on this island.

To his surprise, the dream did not start here along the river, or on this island. Instead, he was walking on the banks of Lake Ameloni again, where the conclave met. However, snow blanketed the diamonds on the shoreline although he could still hear their crunching. The volcano was lost in the low clouds that added to the ankle-deep snow. Owailion looked down the shoreline and finally saw her, the Queen of Rivers. He reached his hand out toward her, expecting to be shown a new palace to build, but he was wrong.

She wore the thin veil of silver and gold, with an elegant gown embroidered with more of the silver on gray silk and chilly blue. Like the frozen lake beyond them, she did not move. Instead, she simply looked at him and he could almost make out her features through the gauze and patterns of the veil. Her alabaster hands were cool, even through his gloves and the moment he realized this, he looked down to see he too had changed into the glorious regalia he wore in the truth spell.

His dream-self began to speak words he knew he should say. "I, Owailion, before God and this conclave, do take you…"

Then Owailion awoke.

He gasped, sitting up in the dark. No moon and only a few stars filled the night sky in the river valley and he could see nothing in the shadows of the hills. Owailion shivered miserably. He knew nothing of the mansion he must build here and felt empty, useless. Owailion yearned to touch her and see her face. He felt some kind of compulsion but unlike the itch prompting him to build the palaces, he could not scratch this. Loneliness descended on him like a great weight.

"*She is meant to be your mate,*" Mohan's unexpected commentary interrupted Owailion's thoughts.

The human looked up again into the night sky, wondering if the dragon had returned from his feeding early.

"*No, I just heard the alarm in your mind and thought you might like to talk about it. You have never been more….agitated. Remember, God promised you more because humans don't do well on their own. So why would she not be your mate?*"

Owailion put his hands over his eyes, trying to press the distracting after-images of burning light out of his mind. He could not concentrate, not with that alluring shape seared into his thoughts. "I don't know. Usually, we get to select our mates, not have them selected for us. It's just so…I have too much in my head right now. Maybe three palaces are too much…but this one, thinking of her…it's very distracting."

A draconic chuckle filled Owailion's mind. "*You sound like me the first time I met Tamaar. This Queen of Rivers is your mate. Now you just have to find her.*"

"Uggg, I can't think about that right now. I'm supposed to be learning magic, battling sorcerers and building palaces, not thinking about…about a woman. It turns my mind to… I'm confused. Why would God show this to me when I'm supposed to be doing so many other things? I don't need this distraction."

"*Of course you do. No one, even a dragon, can do as much magic as you are doing and not have a distraction,*" Mohan declared.

"I start a palace and walk away," Owailion protested. "I've not found any demons to fight yet."

"*You will. Demons will come and the invaders now know you are here too. I do not want to think about what will happen when they discover you are alone here in the Land and the dragons have fallen asleep. You cannot be the only one protecting our borders. She will come before we go to sleep, I think. Besides, she must be beautiful, for a human. Yes?*"

Owailion let out one quavering breath, trying to regain his bearings again and then admitted that Mohan probably was right. "She was more than beautiful. I've never….well I assume I've never met another of her like."

"*Then let me give you something else to think about,*" Mohan suggested. "*This is a puzzle.*" The dragon then plopped a rock in Owailion's lap, as if he conjured it.

"A puzzle?" Owailion echoed. "Oh, this is what Tamaar gave you to train me." Should he be surprised or worried by the lump of stone about the size of his fist that he now had to heft up and examine as if it were precious? It made him think of what a cat would bring, some dead mouse it had played with for too long and now had dropped it before her master on proud display. See what I've given you?

"Ummm, thank you?" Owailion said aloud, hoping Mohan would not understand the awkward comparison.

"*I do not know what a mouse is,*" Mohan shattered that hope, "*but I have given you a puzzle with which to work some magic. This will keep your mind off the pretty lady. You can work with it and then when you discover how to deal with it, share it with me.*"

"Are you going to grow sleepy if I stay here a while and work on this?" Owailion wondered warily.

"*There are other things I could do while you work at it. You can call me when you are ready.*"

Owailion watched his friend lift off into the air. Barely aloft and free from the close-set trees, the gleaming dragon disappeared in a flash, leaving the early morning sky empty. Heavy with thought, the human returned to his bed, and the puzzling rock that Mohan had left behind.

With no other occupation, Owailion reluctantly applied his mind to the simple rock. With magic, he could sense it contained copper, tin and simple silicates. Bronze, he remembered could be crafted with copper and tin. This must have been something he was trained in, not incidental knowledge. Was he some kind of smith in his prior life? Puzzle indeed.

Gradually the rock shifted in his mind's eye, coming alive, like a pill bug finally unrolling once the fear of being touched had eased. It writhed and unfolded. Owailion resisted the urge to open his eyes and see if the rock truly was shifting. If he looked, the stone would undoubtedly look exactly as it had the first time he had touched it.

Unexpectedly he remembered the demon cat that Mohan had shown him that had sprouted wings and flown away.

Owailion's eyes flashed open, unsure and alarmed now. No, his imagination was getting the better of him. He looked at the simple ore and shuddered. He could not blow fire like a dragon but something in this rock was going demon. The only way he could think of erasing this unease was to make something of it before it came alive; some hard-cased centipede crawling over him in the night. Owailion dropped the puzzle stone onto his bed and couldn't help but rub his hands against his knees to brush away that disturbing thought.

Very well, he would use what he knew. His magic reached out and felt its way through the innards of the stone, separating copper from the tin and other trace elements. When he opened his eyes he saw three different powders in neat little piles on the blanket he sat upon. Owailion reached out and felt the materials, sensing none of the potential life writhing through them. He felt only purpose, with no lingering intent. So what would he do with the minerals?

Again he thought of bronze, and that decided him. He conjured a simple wooden bowl in which to mix the powdered copper and tin. He didn't feel a need to fire up a kiln or melt them down in order to form something. Indeed, the elements followed his magical command to come together and solidify. Powder became solid alloy without forms or heat. They pressed into the same shape as the wood within which they had been placed. Then for beauty's sake, Owailion's mind etched a decoration around the delicate base; reeds and lilies from the bank of the river up the side of the pottery. He then simply tipped the bronze bowl out of the wooden one and he had a charming little dish that rested perfectly in his hand without the fuss of a forge. It glowed in the golden sun, but as he watched, the age of years descended and it grew green with patina.

Somehow he liked it more just for the greening. It fit the river environs and oddly enough made him recall his dream of the lady. She had been silver, gold over river green, fresh and new and all the other things this bowl made him imagine. The river would always pass by and be new, never the same, flowing from a never-ending source. He knew now that this dish he had crafted would be magical too somehow. And it would be hers – her Talisman.

Then he remembered his first dream, where God had given him duties…and had shown him the stolen stones of Zema. He had seen that part of the dream through a little bowl. He had just created that very magical bowl. He would not use fire to stop things warping into demons; he would change them into the Talismans that God had asked of him.

Owailion eagerly carried the vessel to the water's edge and filled it. He wanted to test out this new creation. He then held it high so he could see the reflection of the sky, and waited for something to appear on the surface. When nothing appeared he sensed a moment of doubt. Why have a magical bowl with no power in it? Then his own magical gifts reminded him of something; he needed to wish for something. Owailion closed his eyes in concentration. He knew what he wanted to see, yearned for it in his mind. Show me the coming of the Queen of Rivers.

Obedient to his command, the surface of the still water changed. The sun shifted angle to reflect sunset, and a soft breeze stirred the trees, but little else altered. The river valley visible in the Talisman's reflection remained virtually the same. Then the gentle flow of the reflected passing water stirred as if a fish had breached and left a single ripple ring. The sun off the water blinded him briefly. Then her head rose out of the water.

Owailion gasped, and the reflection shattered as he dropped the bowl. She was coming right here, right now. In a panic, he conjured a simple box and put the bowl inside it burying it right there on the shoreline, down below the sand, deep in the mud so none but a magician could retrieve it. He knew the Queen of Rivers would find it later. Meanwhile, he had to prepare.

Chapter 8

Raimi

"This is the place. This is where she is going to arrive. Can you feel it?" Owailion shouted in excitement as Mohan settled on the far bank, called by his human's announcement.

"*The Queen of Rivers is coming here? I do not sense her. Before your coming the tension was great…and the humming to welcome…*"

"Humming?" But Owailion did not pay attention. Instead, he looked out at the still, deep water and realized he was not going to see her until all was calm; the water, the air, the birds and most of all, his heart. The scene was not set for her yet. With a thump, Owailion sat on the bank, with Mohan on the other side of the trees, but well able to see from his enormous height above.

"No, in the bowl's vision, it was so peaceful."

"*Then that makes this a human experience. I think that my presence will not help this event. She will come if I leave.*"

Owailion didn't want to tell Mohan that his great golden head popping above the trees would probably mar the anticipated arrival, for he knew how much the dragon would be interested in witnessing it, but there was nothing like pure terror at your 'birth'. Also, part of Owailion's mind recognized this needed to be utterly private. He struggled to calm his breathing and center himself, letting go of his anticipation.

"This could take a long time. Besides, I know she comes when you are gone. You were not in the bowl's vision. Do not be hurt, but I do not think this is a thing for dragons."

"*I am not offended. She is your mate. This is her time with you. Call me when you are ready to travel on.*" Mohan then lifted away and disappeared.

Meanwhile, Owailion sat in the sun, anxiously analyzing the sound of water birds wading around the bend, and the gentle wind rustling through the drying branches of late summer. He could hear the swifter water upstream, crashing over cataracts and plunging into the deep, clear flow right in front of him. That remained placid and utterly still.

Then he realized he had been camping for weeks and really should try a little grooming and take his hygiene in hand. After all, he might be meeting his future wife in a few hours and the thought made him cringe. Rather than disturb the peaceful river Owailion conjured a full tub already warm and steaming and washed thoroughly for the first time since his hatching. He shaved and for the first time actually looked at himself in a conjured mirror. Perhaps he had forgotten his appearance along with his real name and his past, but he did not recall having snow-white hair and eyes as dark as coal. It was disturbing to look at a stranger's face.

Awkwardly he made a sad attempt at trimming his hair with a conjured set of scissors. The results did not reassure. In the end, he simply magic-ed his hair cut neatly and although he was sorely tempted to change its color, he left it white. He was a magician after all, and maybe that was a sign of his new talents. Finally, he conjured himself new clothes, of a finer quality and fit than the rugged leather and linen he wore with Mohan, simply because he did indeed feel like he was going to meet the woman of his dreams and he wanted it to go well.

And still the sun crept across the sky and the water never changed. Eventually, he sat on a blanket on the beach and drifted off to sleep in the gentle wind. How long he slept, he could not tell, but something in the air changed and it woke him. The sun came from his right, low and burning. He squinted against the bright light on the water and remembered how he had been hypnotized by the light in the bowl. The sun must be low and the air almost frozen with tension, waiting for a single ring in the water. The smell of the river, rich and musty with life, echoed a forgotten memory.

A single ring rippled out from the center of the deep water.

Exactly how he had seen, her head rose out of the water, coppery and completely in silhouette. Owailion's breathing stopped as he watched her rise, gracefully patient. Somehow he rose to his feet, watching her, but didn't recognize he had done so. Her lithe figure perfectly formed remained below the sinking sunlight, and then began walking toward him. Each footstep crafted a single ring on the surface. Owailion resisted the urge to reach out when her arm lifted. Instead, he conjured a silvery satin robe for her without consciously doing so.

And the moment her foot touched the earth and not water he was able to see her face. Her eyes reflected the sky; a coppery gold outlining brilliant green. She smiled and her sweet mouth melted a hollow in his stomach that he didn't remember being there. She lowered her head, just now noticing how she was not dressed and he slipped the robe over her bare shoulders before she could blush.

"Welcome," he managed to whisper, hoping his voice didn't shatter the spell of her arrival. "I am Owailion." Was it a lie? He had no other name to give himself, and he was not blocked as he might have been with a lie.

Her bashful glance was instantly charming when she whispered, "Raimi."

Owailion almost gasped. Her voice ran like cool water down his back as he felt his mouth pop open. Did she remember? He had not even considered what name to give her, assuming she would come with no memories of her former life as he had, but for some reason, God had sent Raimi to the Land with at least that memory intact. Owailion could not think of how to ask what she did remember. He found it hard to bring his mind around to logical lines with her expectant and bright eyes looking at him that way.

"Where am I?" she asked simply, relieving him of the pressure to generate something to say.

"This is the Land. The Lara River. We have been waiting for you."

Curiously she looked back at the river as if she didn't remember that either. Surprise rippled across her face. "I don't remember...falling in? I don't remember..." Her confusion stabbed at him and he had to release that distress before she grew upset.

"It's a long tale. Here, sit down and I'll try to explain." He almost conjured a set of chairs but thought better of it and he escorted Raimi to the blanket on the sand. She did not need to be more overwhelmed than she probably already felt.

"Tell me what you do remember?" he began, hoping that he could learn how she retained her name before he filled her mind with all the wondrous things he had encountered in the last few months.

Raimi looked around, only now realizing where she found herself. Her bright eye caught the emergence of the evening star and the setting sun. The night sounds along the river began before she found words. "I remember coming out of the river. And my name, but the rest..." Her eyes filled with unshed tears. "It's all gone. What happened to me?"

Owailion struggled to not reach out to gather her into his arms and comfort her in that first realization, but no one had done that for him. He dare not impose his emotions onto hers. Right now one overwhelming emotion was enough. "All is well. The same thing happened to me; amnesia...only I didn't even remember my name. This is the Land. We were brought here without a memory of our former lives because ... because... because God needs us to protect this place. You see, we are magic. I don't remember having any magic from my former life. Other things like speaking, writing, and all the things about being human, those I remember enough to do them, but nothing specific from my past...and not the magic."

Raimi's face finally grew still, placid as the water beyond her, and Owailion could not interpret her gaze. She lowered her head to master her tears and then looked up again before she spoke. "Magic...as in...

poof, things move and fly and such?" Her voice dripped with fear and disbelief.

"Here, let me show you," he provided. Then without needing to use his hand, he reached out, touched the sand at the edge of the blanket and then lifted his hand away as he created a fire that merrily burned on conjured wood, lighting the growing twilight. "This is called conjuring. I just concentrate and wish it into being. If you want, you can conjure something as well. Are you hungry…cold?"

Raimi looked at the fire with wonder in her eyes, and he heard her thoughts as she realized he had offered her a chance to do this for herself. "Warmer clothes?"

Owailion's smile deepened. Her wish reflected his first magic as well. "Very good. Simply imagine what you want to create," he advised, "and then think of how the deep center of the earth will give it to you. Then wish the clothing to appear, right here in front of you."

Raimi nodded as if she understood and then lowered her head in concentration. Her still damp hair clung to her face, and Owailion felt tempted to brush it aside or add a conjured comb but he resisted. Mohan had done none of that for him and suddenly he was grateful for the training the dragon had given him.

"Oh!" she gasped, drawing Owailion back to the here and now. In her lap, she had created a simple shift, a gray/green wool dress and a bodice to go over it. She couldn't resist and reached out to feel the fabric with her gentle hand. "It worked."

"You did very well. Can you try shoes and a comb perhaps?" Owailion suggested.

Her startled smile winded Owailion. Sheer girlish delight at the thought of being able to add to something with so little effort made her almost giggly. Owailion listened to her mind as she recognized that she might be overwhelming herself. She suppressed a stab of fear and Raimi visibly calmed, forcing herself to concentrate and closed her brilliant eyes. Owailion shamelessly watched her mind work out carefully what she wanted and presently a simple bone comb materialized in her lap. Then she furrowed her brow before a sturdy pair of boots landed beside her.

"Boots?" Owailion asked with a quizzical look.

Raimi opened her eyes and then peered meaningfully into the night. "It seems wise. I don't see the lights of any town nearby. We might be walking for miles and …and I think I might be used to this kind of terrain. I've worn boots before."

Owailion chuckled. She had the same instincts he had, latent memories of what would be needed but no true recollection of how she knew. "Why don't you go up into the trees and get dressed," he suggested. "I'll make something for supper. You are right; there are no towns nearby."

Raimi looked up the beach into the dense undergrowth and the dark there. Owailion could read her mind easily, for she had used no shields to protect her thoughts from him. In them, he overheard Raimi's worries about bears and other large predators but also about him. Would he follow her into the trees to molest her? She must have had a past laced with danger and attacks if she worried about those things echoing from her past. No wonder she was shy and so wary. Without meaning to, Owailion reached out to magically ease her fear, erasing it and at the same time hoping he wouldn't make it worse by doing so.

As she took her new clothes and crossed the sand to the nearby underbrush, he asked, "What would you like for supper?" He deliberately pitching his voice to carry so Raimi would know he wasn't following her as she picked her way deeper into the bushes.

She must have gone far into the trees, for he could barely hear her reply. "Whatever you have is fine. You cook?"

He did not answer. Instead, when she came back into the firelight he had conjured a table, complete with fine white china, a tablecloth, and candlelight. He pulled a chair out for her but she stood stunned, on the verge of the beach, dressed in her new clothing, hesitating to come closer. With her mouth open in awe at the obvious display of magic, Raimi held out the robe to him.

Owailion smiled welcomingly as if she had not frozen in shock. He didn't want to embarrass her, but instead, let her master her feelings.

So he continued, "No, I don't cook really. I conjure whatever I feel inclined to eat. If you need some time, dinner isn't going to get cold. Are you well?"

Raimi took one tentative step onto the sand. "What did you say your name was?" She looked abashed, sorry to have forgotten something as simple as his name.

"I'm Owailion...and it's easy to forget things when there's so much that is new."

She held the robe out to him again, taking another step toward the table. Owailion shook his head. "No, you can also un-conjure something. Can you make it disappear back to the earth I made it from?"

Raimi stopped and stared doubtfully at the satin in her hands and then tried not to gasp when it disappeared.

"See, you're good at this," he noted proudly. "Are you willing to try something more complex?" and he again motioned to the chair.

"You're better at the magic," commented Raimi but she took another step and sat down at the table. "This is beautiful," she added with her eyes drinking in the fine table settings. "Where did you think of this?"

Owailion shrugged and sat down in the other chair. "I must have seen a fancy supper like this in my old life. I don't remember it either. I have only been here in the Land since mid-summer and it's just coming on to fall now."

Raimi's lively eyes flashed back to the trees, across the river and into the sky, as if verifying his estimation of the season. "And was your first memory walking on water?" she asked.

"No, I woke up inside a mountain, completely sealed in it, like an egg. I had to break my way out. Mohan knew I was there and encouraged me, but I had to use magic to get out and when I did, I came face to face with Mohan. He's an enormous dragon."

To prepare her for eventually meeting Mohan, he pressed the memory of that first encounter into her mind, so she would get an idea of his sheer size. The vision of the dragon did not seem to frighten Raimi any more than she already seemed as if she had been familiar with the creatures in her former life, not like it had surprised Owailion.

More frightening for her was the unknown situation. "Will you please explain to me what is going on? You said I can use magic? But I don't remember being magical…though I seem to know other things, like how to dress or speak…is this my language?"

"I thought the same thing too when I came…awoke here in the Land," Owailion assured her. "It seems like certain words are foreign and others are not. I often have to explain certain terms to Mohan because he doesn't have the concept, being a dragon. For example, writing. It was alien to him and when I say that word, it's like from my original language, not the one I woke up speaking."

"Strange," Raimi agreed. "And is conjuring all you…I can do?"

"Oh, no," and Owailion almost laughed, "But it is the most basic. If you'll do the conjuring for something to eat, I will tell you. There is so much to share."

Raimi looked at the empty plates and then closed her eyes. She carefully concentrated on a small hunk of crusty brown bread, and then added a pad of butter. Owailion was just hoping for something of meat when she added a haunch of roasted rabbit and then for good measure, a vegetable Owailion had never before seen. When she opened her eyes and saw her plate, her eyes grew huge, as if she had never seen such a grand meal.

"That's perfect," he complimented her, though he realized she must have had a simple upbringing if this rustic fare were the best she could imagine. Had she experienced a rough, hardscrabble life? He wanted to know, but she could not provide that information. She seemed so elegant and regal in his eyes; gentle and soft-spoken in her mannerisms. He found it hard to imagine her tromping about in boots and eating peasant food. "What do you call this vegetable?" he asked to refocus himself.

"It's *kol*," she replied in surprise. "You don't know it?"

Owailion shook his head. "Well, we've established that you and I do not come from the same place. I've never heard of nor eaten *kol*, but it looks tasty," and he picked up his knife and fork. Then as promised, he began to open up to her about all potential abilities.

The first thing he introduced, mind-reading, immediately alarmed her. "I don't want that, sir," she protested. "It is...what about...I couldn't ...I don't want to know what others are thinking. It would be too..."

He was beginning to understand a little of Raimi's distress when she finally conceptualized it in her mind though she did not speak aloud. Instead, he overheard it all. *How can I endure all the other thoughts? I can barely stand my own. I don't want to know another's insecurities and doubts and I don't want them to know mine. It's an invasion of privacy. I don't like being near people just for that reason. I will leave so they cannot learn how bad I am. I move on and they won't realize all I've done that went wrong. I'm like the river; no one notices and I'm content.*

Owailion let her mind go on until she acknowledged all her fear but it surprised him. She had been brave enough to accept God's invitation to come here and to explore the Land with him but she could not face others who might be critical of her? She was afraid of what they would think of her, not what she might hear of them? Well, Owailion could at least reassure her a little. Some latent Wise One instinct guided him to reply to her gently, not addressing her fears, but almost ignoring them.

"You need not hear their thoughts if you do not wish to. A magician can shield others out, but you will want to be open to some thoughts if you want to speak with Mohan or any of the other dragons. You can talk aloud and they will understand you, but they only share words mentally. You can even speak with them thousands of miles away."

"Shield?" she asked, and he heard her dropping her fear like a pebble lost at the bottom of a stream. "Can you teach me?"

Owailion nodded reassuringly. "Of course. And also, consider this; you cannot misunderstand me, and I won't misunderstand you if we listen to each other's thoughts."

"But privacy..." It seemed to be something Raimi prized highly.

"I will teach you how to block me from listening in on your thoughts at the same time as I teach you how to hear them. It is a skill that goes hand in hand. What if you want to share a thought with me only and not with Mohan? That will require a little more deliberate use of magic. I've not had to try that yet...seeing as I have only really worked with him."

"You have not used magic around other people?" asked Raimi in surprise.

Owailion recognized, much to his chagrin, that he had resisted telling her that they were indeed the only humans in the Land. Had that been on purpose or was he instinctively avoiding that fact because he knew it would alarm her? Well, he had best reveal it immediately.

"Raimi, there is only us. The Land has been Sealed to humans for over a thousand years. The dragons are the ones who first settled it and sealed it off from mankind. I was the first human allowed past the Seal and now you have come as well. We were brought here and given magic to become the stewards of the Land, the sixteen Wise Ones that God promised to the dragons so they could sleep."

As he spoke, the flurry of questions rippling through Raimi's mind allowed him to keep going, helping her understand before she could even voice her concerns or observations. Oddly enough she felt almost relieved that the Land was empty. Perhaps the crowds of her old, half-recalled life intimidated her. Carefully Owailion avoided the implication that they were meant to be mates and instead concentrated on the fact that there would eventually be others with whom to share her magic. She might have known just on intuition that they would inevitably be drawn together. But when he stopped speaking, allowing her to absorb all Owailion had explained, Raimi's only reply caught him completely off guard.

"Is that why I like you?"

Chapter 9

Going Outland

Mohan had not deliberately misled his friend. He would go hunting, but the dragon had prey he did not intend to eat. Instead, the great gold creature conjured a dozen dead buffalo to himself as he settled for the night in the forest of Zema to watch the lost rune stones. He simply intended to eat and do some deep magic at the same time. Owailion was right; there would only be discord if the human went back in time to see who had taken the writings on stone. And it would never have occurred to the timeless dragons to go back to witness the theft, but Mohan had learned much from his human.

Carefully Mohan used his innate understanding of the Land, knowing how every place looked despite changes, to imagine the clearing with the stones in the winter past. It would be icy and miserably rainy, unfit to fly. He could work his way forward and see the various times and seasons at this place. For good measure, Mohan also cast invisibility over himself so that the dragon or human who did come for the stones would not know of his observation. As he suspected, the stones stood there undisturbed at midwinter, just two seasons before.

Mohan ate juicy buffalo while considering the next passage he could move toward. He had started to build Jonjonel about the beginning of spring and the ash from its growth would have made for spectacular sunsets throughout the Land. He drew on the spring equinox at high spring in the evening and shifted time. This new scene, with the ash high in the air visible in the west and red sunset over the trees, provided the anchor for drawing the dragon forward slightly toward when the thief would arrive. Still, Zema's stones stared back at him.

The next shift would take the dragon to the day at the height of summer when Owailion had hatched. The forest around the dragon swayed gracefully in the warm air, brilliantly green and verdant. The ash in the atmosphere had faded, leaving the horizon golden again, but the sky still slightly hazy with the eruptions from earlier in the year. Mohan would be a fool to not think that the coming of man had not initiated this thievery. With all the dragons excited and watchful for the impending arrival of the promised human on the other side of the continent, someone had taken advantage of the distraction. It had to be then that the thief struck.

And still, the runestones remained undisturbed. Mohan grumbled at his lack of success. These shifts through time took a lot of energy and he couldn't eat enough sitting here waiting to make up for his loss. Better to sit in one place and watch than to shift again. He would wait a few hours and then try a different path.

Eventually, the lure of falling asleep descended on Mohan with a heavy claw. He could not stay here much longer and just watch the stones without turning into one himself. However, just as he was about to give up, a booming noise shook the air and rattled the trees around where the dragon rested. He almost roared with shock.

Then he saw that the stones were gone.

The loud sound and their instant disappearance happened simultaneously. Frantically Mohan stretched out his mind, seeking someone's magic nearby, but all he sensed was a solid and decidedly draconic shield around someone's thoughts. Was the echo that still rippled through the air meant to distract or was it the result of the removal? Mohan had no way to know.

Perplexed, Mohan remained, now fully awake and alert, with his tails flicking in irritation. He could not smell humans nearby. Usually, he recognized that scent from miles away. The scent of dragon, phosphorus, and sulfur, pervaded, but that was because he'd been sitting here for hours. He had lost his chance. Mohan contemplated returning to Owailion, disappointed and thwarted, but still on the hunt.

Instead, Mohan decided to try another investigation possibility. He briefly called Owailion and got the reassurance that his friend would be occupied with the new Queen of Rivers for several days. Mohan determined to use that time to its fullest. This would be the most dangerous and daring of his enormously long life. Only he could perform this service before he went to Sleep.

Mohan was leaving the Land.

Mohan flew swiftly above the cloud cover, with the blue sky above and autumn clouds all across the sea. If Owailion was right, and they left by sea, then they had gone across the Western Sea. Most invasion attempts came from there and carrying the stones overland to the south or east seemed cumbersome.

As he flew Mohan kept his mind shielded and protected tightly. Exiled dragons fled mainly to Malornia in the west and these renegades might hold a grudge. According to legend, the forests and unexplored mountains sheltered demons that went unchecked over this frontier and every moment Mohan remained in Malornia he risked being attacked on every front. At least up high he could see the danger coming.

As he flew over the alien land Mohan mourned for the people, both human and dragonkin who lived in Malornia. He had heard the tales. Magic had warped the landscape. Twisted mountains, malformed trees, toxic deserts, and salt-riddled lakes evolved with uncontrolled use of magic; a paradise for demons. The humans who lived here crowded for protection into cities on the coastline, behind high walls with still more magic to keep demons away from them. The human magicians kept careful control over the population, but it was difficult to say which resulted in a better lifestyle. Dragons in Malornia became weapons of terror, controlled and abused by the powerful human sorcerers, but they willingly submitted to have access to something only a human population could give them; power through fear. Mohan did not understand the attraction.

Although he flew high above the clouds, invisible to those below, Mohan could easily see through his magic eyes how life faired below. The humans struggled to harvest their crops and bring in their stores while sorcerers and their pet dragons kept watch covetously. These enchanters counted the people under their influence like jewels. Farther west the forests and wild places teamed with demons and even a few of those dragons exiled from the Land. Mohan dreaded seeking out someone he might have once known, but he had to know.

Mohan had participated in the Conclave of Exile for only one dragon in his lifetime, but Tilziminik had chosen his lot. The black dragon had been so anxious to spread the borders of the Land, expanding the Seal that he had been willing to attack other lands, driving out the humans in order to expand, no matter the cost to others. This was counter to the Law and Tilzim chose exile rather than submission to the borders God had prescribed for the Land. Now Mohan remembered his former friend with regret. Pride was as much a draconic flaw as it was a human one.

And now he feared to see how Tilzim lived in this twisted land. Malornia, the land of the lost, Mohan thought. But would Tilziminik want to punish humans so much that he would return to the Land to steal the standing stones? Did he even care? Mohan had come to ask his former friend just such a question.

"*Tilzim?*" Mohan called at his strongest, longest range, hoping his call found itself into the correct mind. Mohan felt a flicker of acknowledgment to the northwest but it stifled itself quickly. So the gold dragon turned his flight path toward that direction, sped up and again called. "*My old friend, I need to speak to you.*"

A magically sent snarl, completely devoid of words came through the golden dragon's mind.

"*Have you gone so feral that you have lost your words?*" Mohan replied, hoping to insult the dragon into revealing himself. The ultimate debasement, going feral, would get a reaction if, in fact, it was not true. But if Tilzim had indeed given into his animal tendencies, abandoning all civilized discourse and logical reasoning, then the dragon would feel no offense. Could a refined and well-educated dragon fall so low in only a hundred years?

"*No, but I might go wild on your insulting wings if you come any closer,*" Tilzim replied with an echoing snarl, helping Mohan narrow in on his location. "*You come here at your own risk.*"

Mohan knew better than to bother. He didn't need to be closer to be sure it was his old acquaintance; they had been friends before the Conclave and he knew Tilzim's voice still. The gold dragon hovered in the air above a mountain, tested the presences there and then settled on a warped mountain top like a bird on a branch, ready to take flight again at the least provocation.

"*I have come to speak with you, which I can do without coming into your territory. I just need to ask a few questions and then I will leave you in peace.*"

"*What would the all-knowing Mohan have to say to me since he was part of the Conclave that sent me here?*" Tilzim snapped.

Mohan replied carefully. "*I am not all-knowing. Only a fool would think he knows all, especially when I have learned that there is always more to learn. That is what brings me here. Do you recall the standing stones at Zema, in the forest at the Elbow?*"

Silence greeted that question, but Mohan could tell that Tilzim was listening and he could comprehend the words so the gold dragon continued. "*They have disappeared. They had markings on them that a human can read, so they are of value only to another human. Can you think of any of the men you know here who would want them?*"

The roar of disgust reached Mohan's physical ears as well as his mind, but it echoed off the mountainsides, making it impossible to point to a specific location and the golden dragon dared not try to track it. He had made an implied promise not to come closer and Tilzim was still willing to talk to him...from this distance.

"*I have not fallen so far that I would consort with humans to know their types or desires. Here in Malornia humans enslave other magical beings. Why should I let that happen to me?*"

Mohan sighed in resignation. "*I just hoped that since the message on the stones was written to men, and yet behind the Seal, that perhaps it foretold of when men come and manage to break the Seal... as a message to those about to enter.*"

"*Man will never enter the Land,*" Tilzim stated flatly. "*The dragons see to that and defend the borders.*"

So Tilzim did not know of the promise of the Wise Ones. He knew nothing about Owailion. This did not surprise Mohan because God announced this to the conclave and presumably no one else. Accordingly, Mohan moved on to other topics. "*And have you felt the urge to Sleep?*"

"*Sleep?*" Tilzim's reply dripped with mockery. "*Dragons do not sleep. Why would you think I would stoop to such a human act? You must think I'm a fool.*"

This news did surprise Mohan. He had assumed that all dragons, no matter where on the planet, would have to obey the instinct to sleep. Alarmingly Tilzim did not have the compulsions of the dragons in the Land any longer. So why only dragons in the Land? That seemed strange. Why would God...

Interrupting Mohan's thoughts Tilzim made a final voluntary comment. "*One thing I will tell you; there are plenty of evil men and sorcerers here in Malornia who would pay your weight in gold for possession of those stones. Some have the gold to do it.*"

Now it was Mohan's turn to go silent, keeping his thoughts solidly behind shields. How would Tilzim know this and yet not know about Owailion's coming and the Sleep? This whole situation was confusing beyond belief. How did this help discover the thief who had taken the stones? For that matter, did he trust Tilzim's news?

"*I will keep that in mind, my friend,*" Mohan replied carefully. He did not know what else to say, for he feared to think deeply and become distracted in his thought while he remained unsafe here. "*If I do not speak with you again, be well and free.*" Mohan then launched himself back into the sky, rose into the clouds and then turned east to return to the Land.

Mohan could have used magic to launch himself directly back home, but instead, he elected not to. Owailion did not need him at the moment and while Mohan still felt in danger flying directly over the heart of Malornia, he coveted the time to think. His discussion with Tilziminik had done little to reassure him.

Obviously, dragons in exile, even those that retained their sentience and magic, remained outside some of the factors of those dragons in the Conclave. How could they not be included in the Sleep? God was allowing only the Conclave to sleep because they needed to and the wild or exiled dragons did not? Was it only because of the constant burden of protecting the Land? Did vigilance come with such a cost? Somehow Mohan doubted that. There must be something more. Back when Tilzim had been evicted from the Land no one had known or even suspected the Sleep was coming. Prophesies of men coming to the Land had been introduced at the same time as the Sleep so the two events were linked. Why had God withheld that need from other dragons? Why was that fact withheld from the Conclave?

As he flew Mohan considered why God would have kept them uninformed of this. Mohan held talon-tight to his utter faith in God's motives and purposes but not knowing had a way of niggling at one's mind, driving you to doubt other things that before you need not question.

"*You have not needed to know and do not need to know now,*" a gentle voice in Mohan's mind admonished.

Mohan recognized it; the peace and love the voice bore for him could not be feigned nor forgotten. Suddenly the dragon needed to stop flying, just to concentrate and to be in the right state of mind to listen to what God would share with him. He wheeled down toward the ground and with relief found he had come far enough to be out to sea once again. He alighted on the water, tucked his wings in like a duck and awaited this singular interview.

"*If I do not need to know, then please do not share it if it will not be wise. I am not worthy,*" Mohan replied humbly, hoping he was not being too bold.

"But Mohan, you are curious and you will think about it until you have every question and no answers. No, my son, you need to know if only to keep yourself from speculating. But this which I will share with you must not be revealed; not to the Conclave and not with the humans who will come after you. It must not be shared when you pass on your knowledge of the Land. This is for you alone until I will reveal it to whom I will."

"*Yes, my Lord,*" Mohan promised.

"*Very well,*" said God. "*This is the mystery I will share. The Sleep is for the dragons of the Conclave only. It is for a wise purpose that I do this. You must sleep, for you are going on a long journey to a new world that I have prepared for you. Where you go, the other dragons outside the Conclave and mankind cannot go. The Land has been prepared for a purpose, where the gifts of magic are controlled and refined by those only who are worthy. It was done in wisdom with dragons first. In man, it has yet to succeed, for mankind is not as easily led in the paths of virtuous magic. If the Wise Ones that come after you can hold to the values the Heart Stone instills within them, then they too will be trusted with greater, deeper powers. Then they may progress as have the dragons of the Conclave.*"

Mohan sighed with wonder. A long sleep for a long journey, like the one Owailion, had taken to come to the Land? They were not going to just sleep, they were going to travel? All of them in the Conclave? To a new world? Mohan's mind reeled with wonder and excitement. He wanted to ask so many more questions but knew that patience would reward him and he would know eventually all the answers. It would be unseemly to ask more. But…

"*And the runestones that were stolen? Is it for man or dragon to discover their meaning?*" Mohan could not resist asking.

"*There are many purposes in the rune stones. The writings are for the Wise Ones. They contain a prophecy of their coming and their type. The stones also were planted there as a mystery for the Conclave. In them, one in the Conclave will reveal themselves as unwise. Evil will be set in motion…not of dragon creating. A simple, innocent nudge of a pebble can lead to a great avalanche. It is grievous that the stones are lost but more so is the act that has sent them away from the Land. Owailion will find them eventually and the message will be revealed. At this time, before the Sleep, what must be revealed is the one who would sell the prophecies. They were given to evil men who will try to use them to overthrow the Land when you are gone. That is not the Conclave's mission."*

"*Be at peace, Mohanzelechnekhi. You have done well. Your stewardship is almost complete. The agency of others is no longer your concern. Know that Owailion will do well, no matter how long his road. He will fly alone, but he will stay the course and one day he will find joy as you have found.*"

Mohan felt humbled and relieved. He did not have to find the rune stones. Owailion would oversee that task. The dragon lowered his head, almost to the water upon which he floated in grateful honor to God who had revealed this to him. He would not share this with anyone, not until the time he was given permission when all would be revealed.

"*Then I am not to confront the thief?*" Mohan asked, sensing one last, very grim task.

"*They will be revealed and you will know what to do when that time has come. Be at peace and know that all will be well with the Land and her inhabitants. Now go, do your duty and stay the course.*"

And with that, the interview with God was done. Humbled and in a solemn mind, Mohan shook himself, lifted his wings and rose above the waves, seeking the Land.

Chapter 10

King and Queen

Owailion and Raimi talked the night around, focusing on magic as the main topic, but also what they could glean of their pasts, talents, and interests. He shared how he found the skills to build things and became the King of Creating, but resisted telling about the demons and sorcerers. Instead, he showed her the map in hopes that she recognized the writing he had applied to his work. When she looked at it she drew her fingers across the words with wonder.

"These aren't the right symbols…and yet, I can read them," Raimi commented in puzzlement. "How is it that I can read this new language?"

"I wondered that myself. There were some rune stones that Mohan tried to show me but the stones were stolen. We are supposed to find them so we can read them. I was so curious to see if they were written in a language either you or I understand," replied Owailion. "It's a miracle that we came here, let alone that we understand each other, and can speak and read the same language."

"It is a miracle," Raimi agreed, but then asked. "Why not bring magicians already trained? What are we to do here? Why us? What does the Land need with protecting?"

This question at least Owailion felt qualified to explain. "We were chosen because the magic would not corrupt us. We are good people by nature. Other lands beyond the Seal have human sorcerers, and I've already fought one trying to infiltrate. Too often these men and women are corrupted and crave more power. So the dragons distrust humans because of their evil nature. You and I, however, have been brought here with a Heart Stone. Which reminds me; in the morning we have to go looking for yours. It's probably in the middle of the river."

Helpfully, before she could ask Owailion brought out his Heart Stone and showed it to Raimi. "This acts as a conscience that prevents us from doing evil with our magic. You'll find you cannot even lie as a Wise One."

Raimi looked in fascination at the glowing globe he held out to her. The white and blue orb lit her eyes more than the firelight. Before he could become equally bedazzled by her glorious eyes, he put the Heart Stone back near his heart before he continued. "And with it comes other gifts. I've already found insights I know the old me would never stumble upon. Our duties are to use that magic in the protection of the Land from outlander magic and demons."

"Protection from…from demons?" Raimi's fascination bore a note of recklessness. She was not as gentle as she seemed, but fierce in the face of a challenge.

"Yes," and Owailion then shared a vision of the crab going demon and how Mohan had dealt with it. He was about to tell her more of the Talismans he had created from the stone 'going demon' but something blocked him. The bowl he had crafted for her was to remain secret.

Instead, he equivocated. "I don't blast them with fire. I just redirect that magical energy into Talismans that I then hide and the other Wise Ones must discover. The effort of seeking these Talismans will strengthen our magical skills."

Raimi thought over his explanation while Owailion shamelessly listened to her mind and learned more about her with every moment. He began to realize she wasn't afraid of anything, except perhaps of herself.

"It seems," she eventually sighed, "like pioneering is what I've come to do in the Land. I told you that I thought I had worn boots before. Well, I get the sense that some kind of frontier life has been my experience. I think I left my old life behind on purpose. I wanted to go off on my own and explore, cutting my path. Does that sound realistic?"

Owailion smiled at the recognition of the symbolism of her words. "Like the path of a new river," he replied. "It sounds no more unrealistic than my experience. Sometimes I even have dreams that give me instructions on what to build. I knew to wait here on the river for your arrival, even though I have never been here. I just have to be wise enough to listen to the promptings."

Raimi nodded in understanding. "In my case, I think…," she paused thoughtfully and changed tactics. "I'm not very outgoing. I don't want to interact with people or lead them. I want to be left alone to explore."

And in the back of her mind, unsaid Owailion heard something pitiful.

"*I just don't want to hurt others,*" Raimi's mind whispered.

It was enough to make him wonder if she remembered more than she was admitting. How had she hurt others in her past life?

Meanwhile, Raimi continued, unaware of his distraction. "That's why I was a pioneer. No one will make demands of me that I could not fulfill. I want to be alone so I don't have to be… "

Alone? Owailion rocked back in surprise and his shields slammed into place even if Raimi had not yet learned how to listen to them. Did she want to be alone? Well, the Land was empty, but for him and a few dragons. She could be alone if that was what she wanted, but Owailion swallowed a terrible disappointment. Raimi was lovely, sweet and shy. He knew he never had encountered a woman more attractive to him. With time he would get a grasp on her personality but if she was saying that she wanted to be alone, how would that comfort him? Owailion felt the exact opposite; he wanted a companion, a confidant, a support system that would help him build what God had wanted.

Something in Owailion protested. She was being cold. Raimi had the gifts to be his companion and she was just as magical as he. The promptings Owailion himself felt could not be so wrong. Would she reject him and his help just for want of her privacy or a forgotten fear of responsibility? Then, just as he realized he was upset with her, a Wise One impression washed over him and it calmed him instantly. This quelled the foolish reaction the old Owailion probably would have made. Instead, it slowed him and reminded him that he possessed magic.

Listen to her thoughts.

Obediently Owailion plunged deeper into Raimi's unguarded mind. And what he heard stabbed him through the heart.

"*I can't, I can't. It is wrong. If I get involved it will all go awry. Everything I touch will be ruined. He will be so hurt by me. How can I want this... want him? I want magic and it is wrong. How can God change me so much? I am not worthy of this world, of Owailion, of magic. And...*"

Owailion cut off his listening and looked at Raimi's face, so placid, like the river behind her in the dark. To look at her refined and gentle expression in the firelight you would never think she had any fears, pain or such pitiful self-esteem. No wonder she had rejected interaction with anyone and become a pioneer. Her thoughts and fears lead to leaving the world behind because 'everything I touch will be ruined'. Why? Did she remember more than she was sharing? Instinctively Owailion waited for the inspiration to open the door through which he could walk to understand Raimi. He now realized why she had retained her name. She needed to know who she was so that she would acknowledge how much she could change.

"Raimi," he whispered reassuringly, "you will not ruin everything you touch. You cannot harm me; I'm immortal, as are you. If you learn magic, it will only be good magic. You can trust that."

Carefully, slowly he reached out and touched her gentle hands, cool as the water. The touch felt right; not hurried or alarming to her. He said it again, this time only in her mind. "You cannot hurt me."

Raimi's face looked like stone, expressionless but the placid water flowing beyond them in the night began to roil in response to her hidden fear. Deep waters seemed calm, but the undertow could pull him down and the dark murky bottom remained unexplored. Deliberately Owailion sent calming thoughts and slowly the river settled back down, still swift and deep, but her emotions did not express themselves in the water.

"Do you see what you did there? You are the Queen of Rivers. Every one of the Wise Ones will have an affinity. Yours will be to the rivers and any flowing water, deep, but always moving on. You are that pioneer. You will find you feel most at ease on the river. Perhaps it is a little like your old life. You always wanted to move on because that is what rivers do. They are always moving on."

Slowly Raimi smiled again, deeper, with relief. Could she believe that?

"Come," he abruptly announced. "I want to show you someplace." Owailion helped her to her feet and then pulled his bag back into existence. "I found a way to travel magically." He lifted his hand and his collection of globes appeared in the real world, looking like stars brought to earth to hover over the sand. Then, aloud so she could hear how he did it, he summoned the orb that he wanted. "Paleone," he commanded.

The corresponding globe floated toward them and he pulled it out of the air. "Every place I visit, I make a memory orb so that I can return. It constantly updates so that I know where I will be going, even if events change its appearance. I told you about the palaces I have to build? Well, you helped show it to me. I dreamed about this place, Paleone. You showed it to me in my dreams."

Raimi's eyes grew huge with wonder and the light of the memory orb caught the green of her eyes, reflecting it in the night. "You want me to see it?" she whispered in awe tinged with fear. "Where is it on a map?"

Helpfully he pulled out the map. "We are here," and he showed her where the Lara met the sea. Well, there is meant to be a palace here on this island in the middle of the river, but I was not given the inspiration yet on how to build there. I think....I know it is supposed to be where your home will be."

Then Owailion held up the memory orb again so she could see what image had been set into the crystal. "And Paleone is already started, here." He pointed to the diamond on the coastline. "If you take my hand, I can show you in person," he promised, delighting in the excited flutter of anticipation in her thoughts. She might be afraid that she would ruin anything she touched, but she had an adventuring spirit that also drove her as well. This, she could not resist.

Her hands grasped his and he deliberately looked at the orb so he would not be distracted by her excited eyes. He concentrated a bit and then pulled her with him toward the bluff above the ocean, five hundred miles from the sheltered river valley. Her gasp of wonder told him they had arrived, and he opened his eyes again, luxuriating in the majesty of the wind above the ocean. High flying birds sailed in the brightening sky. Just beyond them, the excavation and conjured ring of foundation stones for the palace stood out perfectly.

"Let me show you how it will look," Owailion offered and then pressed into her open mind the dream of Paleone. The dream Raimi escorted him once again through the luxurious grounds, the finished rooms, the exquisite art. Owailion watched her while she attended to the vision, smiling at all he saw in just observing her delight.

"It's…it's heaven," Raimi whispered in reverence. "And you say that you are going to build a palace like that, for me?"

Owailion hoped he had not been too forward in showing her that. Too late now, he thought. "Yes, when I get the inspiration. I will build there on the delta when the dreams tell me what to build. I have started one other, but I…I was told to wait. Maybe it needs your input. Raimi, this will be your home, safe from the world,"

Her green eyes drew back toward him like a lodestone. "I am the Queen of Rivers? And what are you the king of, Owailion?" The way she whispered his name stirred him. He loved the sound of her voice; soft like rushes in a light wind mixed with the distant song of water over rocks.

Owailion reluctantly shook off her voice to break her spell over him. He breathed deeply the scent of the sea in the morning and then spoke. "I have an affinity for creating things. I love to study how things work and make them function to help people. That's why God chose me to be the builder. It is my duty to make the Land a place fit for humans. Your duty will be to seek some things I created for you; Talismans of your powers."

"And why me next?" Raimi asked, looking around at the building "Why bring someone into the Land who just wants to wander?"

Owailion struggled with that question himself. He had to wait a bit for the wisdom he had come to expect from his gifts to enlighten him. And when he knew what to say, he recognized that this would alarm her.

"Raimi, I will be a hundred years in my work, moving around the Land, building and creating. But there was one thing I asked God for when I accepted this task. I asked him for you."

The blank look Raimi gave him stabbed Owailion in the heart. "You asked…"

"…For someone who would be willing to tramp through the Land with me. This country is wild and empty. There are no cities, roads or other people. I am doing all this because there is no one else to do so. If…if you are used to moving on, sleeping in a tent for years, willing to master magic and using it to defend this new country, that is what we are committed to doing. You would not have come here, not have risen out of the water like you did if God did not know that is what you were capable of doing."

Raimi's eyes pierced like a pike, glittering in the morning light, till he lost her in the silhouette again in the sun. She could not say a word. Owailion listened to her thoughts for the longest time as she watched him. Did she have the faith he did, to trust that God's plan in dropping her into this world? Did she dare trust herself with magic? Somehow she recalled her old life enough, the bad decisions and fears. She must have volunteered for this adventure because she needed an escape.

But Owailion's implicit faith in her melted the frosty fear that lined her life, threatening to close her off in a winter of her creation. God and Owailion together had enough faith in her. She only hesitated in fear of some past mistake. She dreaded hurting him and she knew magic could not prevent all pain. Was Owailion strong enough to take her on and meet the demands of her past? Could he keep up with her? She would move on, she knew. Something would go wrong and…

"And we will face it together," he interrupted her string of thoughts. "If you will just share with me whatever the problem might be."

Finally, Raimi's emotions, the thick, dark thoughts, like the trees and hills of some forgotten past fell away, not blocking her path. She could see the possibilities. That fierce independence led her way. She took one step closer, so close that Owailion could feel her cool breath on his skin and he stood in the shadow now, able to see her alabaster face. He almost drowned in those eyes and he again wondered at the magic that could make him love her so profoundly in just that moment. He felt the still, deep waters of her soul and knew somehow that Raimi would dive in and meet him here.

"I will."

Like magnets, they seemed drawn to each other. Owailion loved the freshwater scent of her hair, and could easily drown in the green of her eyes. He didn't feel to ask to kiss her, he just knew he could. He lowered his head. Just then Mohan appeared like a storm above them, massive and back winging enough to bowl them off their feet.

They broke apart, the moment gone.

Raimi's hands clenched in Owailion's at the sudden interruption, but she mastered her instinctive fear and stepped away from his protective arm.

"*Welcome,*" Mohan called cheerfully.

Owailion carefully clamped down on all the muttered thoughts going through his head and made the introductions. "Mohan, this is Raimi, Queen of Rivers. Raimi, this is Mohan, my guide and teacher."

To Owailion's relief, Raimi displayed no fear of the huge dragon, as if she had encountered them in her previous life. She talked with him without reserve and freely shared her experience in the Land thus far, little as it was. When she began to explain coming out of the river Mohan found this fascinating as a complete departure from anything a dragon birth entailed. In her first experimental magic, she even shared a vision with the dragon so he could witness for himself her 'birth'.

Owailion just stood back and watched her delight in the dragon and these magical exploits. She was an adventurer alright. Her self-esteem aside, she would never back away from anything it seemed.

But what were they to do now? Owailion had a few ideas of what he wanted to do for his Seeking, but he did not feel right taking Raimi along with him on a dangerous trip, especially if he must also train her in magic along the way. There was just too much to do.

"Raimi, Mohan, we need to decide what our next step is. We need to find Raimi's Heart Stone and get her training on magical travel, more conjuring, shields, everything. And I need to find who stole the rune stones. I also must investigate that King who is sending all the sorcerers to invade the Land, which will require your help, Mohan. Maybe the king is the one who took the rune stones, but it's not safe for Raimi to go with me until she has a better understanding of magic. And I don't dare stay here long to teach her while you wait because you will grow sleepy, Mohan."

"And I want to explore. That's what I came here to do," Raimi assured him. "But I also want… " She didn't verbally finish the sentence but Owailion could hear her remaining thoughts. She wanted to be with him.

Gratified, Owailion smiled, for he felt the same way. "And yet that won't be all that safe either."

"*Why?*" Mohan asked. Although he had heard the entire conversation, he did not seem to understand the temptation being with each other held for Raimi and Owailion already.

"Because a lady and a man should not be together without a chaperone until they are married," Owailion sighed, locking eyes with Raimi.

Mohan at least had the sense to not ask for further clarification.

"*Would another teacher be helpful?*" Mohan suggested.

"What did you have in mind?" asked Owailion eagerly.

"*There is another dragon who might be persuaded to take Raimi, guide her as I have done for you.*"

"Really?" Raimi and Owailion said in tandem and then smiled at the coincidence.

"*Imzuli, the white dragon who guards the northeast mountains above Zema is more than anxious to meet humans. She will be willing to escort Raimi if you are willing to answer her questions about being human. Imzuli loves everything about humans.*"

"But…" Raimi looked at Owailion with an abrupt flash of panic in her eyes. "I only just…" and she could not finish the thought.

Owailion understood immediately. "Imzuli will need to feed and we as humans still need to sleep. How about every evening we speak with each other about our adventures and share what we have learned?" He too felt something profoundly wrong with leaving Raimi's side when she had only just arrived in the Land. Was this compulsion part of being a Wise One, or was he already able to say he loved her and could not bear to be apart? Yet he also harbored the fear that if he remained with her, he would give in to the temptations he felt when near her. It would be wrong to follow such desires, at least before they were married.

"And how do we marry here?" Raimi asked.

Owailion's stomach did a flip and he felt more frightened than he had when he first awoke with rock raining down on him at Jonjonel. Had she said what he thought he heard? Was she already committing to marry him? Yes, they had been drawn together immediately, physically, emotionally and most of all, magically, but he never thought she would expect that. He had never implied…

But even Mohan could sense it.

"Mohan, can Raimi and I speak privately for a moment?" Owailion said after taking a steadying breath.

"*Of course,*" the dragon complied. "*I need to feed again, and I will speak with Imzuli and see if she is available.*"

As they watched the dragon depart again after just arriving, Owailion felt ashamed at his fear. "I don't know how to speak with you about this with him here. Are you…"

Wordlessly Raimi cut off his words with their interrupted kiss. Her sweet lips washed away his fear and Owailion sank into the lovely light in his heart at her bold freshness. Raimi never questioned her fate here in the Land or that God was arranging their emotions to help them fall in love. Again, she would just jump in and make it work.

When he could breathe again, he pulled away and looked into her gold-rimmed eyes in wonder. "How can you be so brave? You don't know me. You have no idea what kind of world you have fallen into. What if I'm not who I say I am, and this is all an illusion? What if…"

Again she interrupted him, this time with a finger to his lips and then ran her fingers through his thick, alarmingly white hair. "You are like an angel. Don't you feel at peace? Peace and strength. That is all I feel and I've never felt this way before."

"You don't know what you have felt before," Owailion pointed out logically.

Raimi shook her head, "But I know what I have *not* felt before; peace. It will work. I have hope and faith that somehow this will work. I promise you that…"

Raimi stopped as her simple clothes changed into the regalia of a queen. She was looking at him through a veil of silver and white, trimmed with gold and wearing a moiré blue and green damask silk gown that flowed over the grass at their feet like water. The green of her eyes shifted in wonder and Raimi trembled, almost like she might faint.

"Be careful what you promise," Owailion put his arm around her, holding her securely. He was finally able to see her face through the watery veil now that he looked without dream eyes. "Here in the Land, when a Wise One makes an oath, wondrous things like this happen. It also happens when you use high magic." To demonstrate, he surged magically and put himself into his finery as well.

"And…and…this…"

"Every time you make an oath. You promised me that my faith in magic and God's plan for us will work out," he finished for her.

Raimi steadied herself and Owailion reluctantly removed his hand. "Well, I meant what I said. If all this is God's plan, then it's best to jump in with both feet. I will do whatever this Wise One life asks of me."

"Even if it means marrying me?" Owailion asked carefully.

Raimi froze, her face as placid and featureless as a winter pond. Then, in a fit of irritation, she lifted the bothersome veil over her head so she could look at him without its interference. Then she let the emotion fade before she cracked a smile. "Especially that."

And she kissed him again, enthusiastically.

"*What are they doing?*" asked an unfamiliar dragon voice, feminine and an octave higher in tone than Mohan's. Imzuli, no doubt, but Owailion did not let go of Raimi as he was enjoying this luxurious kiss and draconic curiosity could wait.

"*I do not know,*" Mohan's mind voice interrupted again. "*But they wear those strange coverings when they do magic.*"

Owailion could hear the two dragons settle on the cliff edge before he let go of Raimi. Then with a satisfied sigh, he explained. "That is called kissing. It's what humans do when they are going to get married."

Only Raimi gasped when the humans returned to their normal clothing at that comment, but she recovered quickly and smiled at the new arrival. Imzuli was a much smaller dragon, perhaps three times the height of a human and brilliantly white. Her silver and diamond accents flashed in the late summer sun till the humans almost had to squint.

"*May I present Imzuli, of the northeastern mountains and my daughter,*" Mohan introduced.

"*I'm very glad to help one of the Wise Ones,*" Imzuli added sweetly. "*And what is this word, 'married'?*"

"She promised to bind herself to me and we do that with a ceremony called marriage," Owailion supplied, though his eyes kept drifting toward Raimi. "And a kiss shows that promise," he added for good measure. "When is the next conclave so we can get married? The dragons can be our witnesses? We'll find a priest and bring him here if that's possible."

"*Conclave is usually set at midwinter, in about three months,*" Mohan replied.

"We can't…" Raimi began awkwardly, but her thoughts continued openly. Could they grow to understand each other, nurture their relationship with Owailion traveling all over the continent for months? Would they survive, not giving in to the temptations? Perhaps they could come together to share every evening so they would grow to know each other? "We can't continue just …. three months…"

Owailion could sense Raimi's tension building, but its cause still eluded him. Where was this brave, brazen pioneer? What was concerning her? He wanted to send the dragons away again to ask her privately, but they could not keep doing that. Instead, he experimented and built a private shield around Raimi's mind so her thoughts would go only toward him. Then he spoke to her in that private shell.

"They do not understand our attraction for each other. Dragons only mate when there is a need for hatchlings. They want to watch us," Owailion warned her. Then he tried a more teasing tactic to test Raimi's comfort. "We could always demonstrate. Me, I'm probably an exhibitionist."

Raimi stifled a yelp at the suggestion and put her hand over her mouth. She knew it was joking but human intimacy went far beyond any dragon's need to know. Then Raimi stilled her mind, diving back into her cool reserve, and practiced tentatively sharing her thoughts without spoken words. "I don't know if I would be the best prospect for that. Owailion…I'm not sure that…that…"

Owailion pulled her in close so only he could see her full expression. "That you have ever been with a man?" he supplied the awkward words she couldn't even manage to think. "I'm fairly sure I'm not a virgin though I don't remember any wife or children in my former life. I doubt God would have selected us for this calling if we were abandoning obligations and loves in our other lives. It doesn't matter. That is literally in the forgotten past. When the time is right, as you said, we will be perfect together."

Raimi replied intently, her eyes focused on the plains that stretched out beyond the dragons. "How? There are no priests here. I will not just make due. I want it to be right the first time. Magic might throw us together and make our emotions kick in but we are not animals, driven by basic instincts. I want you, Owailion, far too much to just fall into bed with you without that commitment. I will only do it right," she swore and her clothing shifted again, making Imzuli cock her head in curiosity.

"We can't just stay in one place, or the dragons will fall asleep," Owailion pointed out logically and then released his shield to include the dragons. "And that is why we have invited you, Imzuli, to join us. We need your help."

Carefully Owailion outlined his plans. He and Mohan would travel to Malornia to investigate the king and whether he was responsible for the missing stones. Also while there, they would hopefully find a priest who could come to the Land to perform the wedding. Meanwhile, Imzuli would teach Raimi the finer points of conjuring, magical travel, and mind-reading as well as shields. If they encountered anything going demon, hopefully, Raimi's Wise One instincts would emerge to help train about that without the need for dragon fire. Finally, they must locate Raimi's Heart Stone. Every evening they would contact one another and share all that they had learned on that day. Hopefully, these tasks would be enough to make the three months pass more quickly and give them the hope to continue their path.

"I'll teach you how to make the memory orbs so I can go back to where you've been as well. With your help I'll have the Land mapped in no time," Owailion added, making it sound like a privilege. He made the map reappear and handed it over to Raimi. "You're the adventurer. Time to go adventuring."

Chapter 11

River Travels

After the briefest of goodbyes and much to the delight of the dragons, Raimi kissed her new fiancé again. Owailion reluctantly broke away from the embrace and then mounted Mohan's neck. They departed in a flash, leaving her alone with the white dragon. Suddenly terrified, Raimi looked up at Imzuli and sighed. "I've not had any time to plan this. What should we do first?" she said hopelessly.

"*You've had no time? Neither have I,*" Imzuli chirped. "*But I am excited about this opportunity. Let's focus on what we must do first. Are you tired? Hungry? I know humans need to sleep every night and eat several times a day.*"

Raimi looked at her new teacher and smiled. "Not right now. There's so much I want to learn. Like how to ride a dragon. You're smaller than Mohan. I don't think I could ride on your forehead as they do. Shall we experiment? I've never flown."

It took some trial and error before the two ladies established what might work. Raimi could climb to a spot between Imzuli's wings and conjured a bit of lashing to tie, like a necklace around the dragon's neck. "*Like a necklace,*" Imzuli commented. "*I've seen human ladies wear them but they are prettier than just a rope. I shall make mine diamond.*" And the dragon put words into action and added silver and stones to the new accessory.

"And where shall we fly to?" Raimi added. "Owailion's palace here and the delta island are the only two places I have seen here in the Land."

"*You are the Queen of Rivers. Therefore I will take you to the rivers,*" Imzuli announced, and they launched into the air.

The two new friends traveled far and Raimi gloried in flying. She begged to go high enough that she could see the edges of the earth. Flying southeast, over Tamaar's territory they revisited the island on the delta where Raimi's home would eventually be built, and then they passed over the nameless southern mountains. Out of these, a river flowed due east and Imzuli flew low over them until it merged with a larger river that the dragon called Hedanilinidon.

"I'll call it the Don," Raimi insisted. "It is strange that none of us use the language we were born to. We share this language only. What does Hedana...whatever, mean?"

Imzuli spiraled down, toward the spot where the eastern river met with the Don and landed on an island in the center. "*It means 'The water that flows straight into the Sea'. And yes, the language is different. God has given you these words, but not dragon words. In other countries, they speak other languages too.*"

"I suppose God wanted this. Do you realize, Owailion and I do not come from the same place and probably never spoke the same language either?" Raimi then eagerly untied herself from the dragon's neck and climbed down. "If other people ever come to the Land from other countries, they must be able to speak with one another. I wish we could give that gift, to be able to speak the same to all who come to these shores."

"*Really? Are more humans...more than just the Wise Ones going to come to the Land?*" the white dragon asked in wonder. "*Humans breed far more quickly than dragons....but then you also do not require the space that we do. I understand you also die off rather quickly too. Perhaps others will come and it will not grow too crowded.*"

"It would be a terrible shame if there were no other people with which to share the Land," Raimi replied carefully. "But the Seal should not let anyone in who is not willing to follow the values of good magic." She paused, wary of contradicting the dragon, but also she had been struck with a unique idea. "That's it! We can tie their desire to come into the Land with a commitment to the values of the Land. No magicians can come, just those people that wish for freedom from magic and careful cultivation of the Land. And the way we tell their commitment: we tie it to a language spell. Only those that are given the language of the Land will be allowed past the Seal."

"*That would be a deep piece of magic indeed,*" Mohan commented. "*You would have to bind it to the Land itself, not to yourself as a source of the power.*"

"Deep magic indeed," Raimi murmured and then carefully waded into the river. "Do you think other people will come to the Land after the dragons have fallen asleep?"

With the river around her knees, Raimi felt a deep conviction that other people would come, but saying it aloud somehow made it real. "The Land must always be a haven for good magic," Raimi promised, and accordingly put herself back into her royal costume, this time in a shimmering fabric that did not soak up the water. She sighed with irritation at the interruption, removed the veil and then continued. "If the Wise Ones are the only ones here, perhaps we will all be given the gift of the same tongue by God, but what of those that come and wish to enter but who are not magicians? Should they not have the same opportunity?"

"*God has not said that He will even allow others beyond the Seal,*" Imzuli pointed out logically.

"Magic is for the service of others," Raimi replied evenly. "If the only humans here are other Wise Ones, what is magic's purpose? No, I know in my bones that God will allow other humans into the Land. It might even be the reason why dragons are going to sleep. I don't think humans could be here and not disturb the dragons if you were awake. You need your space and humans do have a way of spreading far and wide, filling the space they are given. This language spell will be a means of helping us know those that can limit themselves to the laws of the Land."

"*Will the humans disturb the dragons who are sleeping?*" Imzuli countered. "*You say that humans have a habit of spreading everywhere.*"

"The Wise Ones won't allow that," Raimi promised, renewing her transition into her glorious costume. "These mountains along the south…they don't have any dragons in them right now. If humans need resources like ore or timber from the mountains they must utilize these without dragons in them. We will not disturb you."

Then, giving up on making oaths, Raimi plunged into the river, luxuriating in the wonder of the water and strangely being able to breathe in it.

"*Aren't you cold?*" the dragon commented. "*It reminds me of my home in the north. And you do not feel this cold?*"

Raimi could care less about how cold it might be. Her desire to float along the river felt stronger than ever. "No, not at all. You should try swimming," Raimi replied with a teasing note of challenge and then changed the subject. "It is my river affinity. Do dragons have these affinities as well?"

Imzuli did not try to swim but instead kept a close eye on her human friend. "*I do not think we have the affinities as the Wise Ones will. For us, it is a location to which we are tied. I love my mountains in the northeast, the lake, and the tundra. It is too warm here in the south.*"

"Very well, so you don't have affinities precisely as humans, but surely there is some magic that you like, that you can share with me. I know very little. I can conjure, read minds, use my shields and now I like the idea of a language spell, but I have not tried other magic."

"*Can you travel magically?*" Imzuli asked. "*It should not be hard for you.*"

"You mean, like with the orbs that show a place as it truly is? That reminds me, I need to make an orb for Owailion that shows this place." She had been floating on her back, but now rolled over and saw Imzuli perched between the trees on the bank of the island. Carefully Raimi imagined a globe that would capture the charming place.

"*No,*" the dragon replied. "*That is Owailion's way to see where he needs to go. What will be your way to travel? For me, I draw on minds in other lands to go elsewhere on the planet.*"

Imzuli's suggestion fascinated Raimi, but a niggling doubt kept her at bay. She worried about that latent memory of harming others unintentionally. Ripples would follow her actions. Was that a Wise One's instinct? If so she intended to obey it. "I don't think I should try to leave the Land. I only just arrived here. Can we try traveling within the Seal instead?"

Accordingly, she swam to shore and then stood on the sandy bank wondering how to get dry in the autumn chill. Could she use magic to dry herself? Experimentally Raimi closed her eyes, concentrated and then felt a warm puff of air that lifted from the ground. It left her steamy, dry and content.

Imzuli approved her experiment and then added a challenge. "*Close your eyes. Think of a place…any place where you want to be. Picture it in your mind. Do you see it clearly? Now, wish yourself there.*"

Immediately Raimi pictured the river where her first memory resided, where she first met Owailion. She easily remembered the place on the delta, the island where her mansion would one day be built. She loved the beauty there; almost a garden designed by God just for her. She could smell the water at Lolar, the cascades of mist off the waterfall where it plunged into the pristine calm of the valley itself. She needed only to remember the water to return. She pushed against her magic and wished to shift to the delta at Lolar.

And when she opened her eyes, she saw all that she had imagined. The distant splash of waterfalls and the scent of the river's musk greeted her. "I'm here," Raimi called to her dragon escort, clear across the continent.

"*That was easy for you,*" Imzuli replied as she burst into the air right above her human and her winging downdrafts stirred the water. "*Can you travel to someplace where there is no river?*"

Raimi thought of all the traveling she had done so far. Only one spot, the building site at Paleone where Owailion had proposed came to mind. She pictured the open plains and white walls rising, overlooking the ocean and concentrated, but something resisted her. She could not return there.

"*Then perhaps you are limited. You need flowing water to travel someplace?*" Imzuli suggested as she heard Raimi's struggles.

Raimi frowned with discontent. "That means I will have to walk most places, especially out on the plains. And what if I have not been to someplace enough to picture it?"

"*There is a danger in that,*" Imzuli warned. "*What if you send yourself to a place where there are sorcerers, or you go to a place that does not exist? You are not like the dragons, born with the instinct. That is why Owailion makes his orbs; so he can see how things have changed.*"

"Would going to a river in a different time be that dangerous?" Raimi asked. "Or what if I went with Owailion and left the Land?" Her true concern lurked about going to another territory and not being able to return through the Seal, forever cut off from Owailion and her duties here.

"*No, but there are other kinds of danger,*" Imzuli replied. "*You have not had to worry about name magic or demons. Confronting that is far worse than dying.*"

"Name magic?" asked Raimi. She didn't understand half of what the dragon explained, about name magic and how something could be worse than dying. She only knew it distressed the white dragon.

Unaccountably, Imzuli chose to ignore that question. Instead, she changed the subject. "*I think we should go and find your Heart Stone. I cannot believe we have neglected that aspect of your training for so long. Owailion claims that your Heart Stone is probably in this river where you arrived. Can you sense it?*"

Raimi allowed herself to be redirected and she used her magic instincts to begin looking at the bottom of the river, seeking an orb such as the one Owailion had shown her, but that did not mean she had dropped the other topic.

"So explain to me about the dangers of this…this name magic. Owailion didn't tell me about it, though he did introduce about demons."

Imzuli settled herself on the shoreline, furled her wings and seemed content. "*You know dragons do not go by their full name, just part of it? That is because a name holds power over you. If a dragon…no, if any magician of any species is strong enough, and knows your name, he or she can command you to do anything and you will be unable to resist.*"

"Owailion does not know his real name," commented Raimi. "That's probably why he didn't mention this name magic to me."

"*Mohan probably has not taught Owailion fully about name magic either for that reason. Is Raimi your real name then?*"

"As far as I know," the woman replied. "Owailion was surprised that I even remembered it. Yes, I came out of the water right here and introduced myself." Then, without warning her friend she added. "I am not going to find my Heart Stone by looking from the surface. I'm going swimming."

And Raimi put words into action. She had no idea if she was familiar with swimming underwater but gradually she recognized that with magic, nothing was impossible as long as she could imagine it. She dove below the surface, opened her eyes and stared in wonder. Despite the murky flow she had observed from above, she could see with crystal clarity here underwater. The silt in the channel glistened like diamonds in her eyes. She could swim forever here.

Raimi dove deeper, down into the darker water and then stretched out her mind, seeking magic, not of her own making. The Heart Stone would have drifted if left in nature's flow, but was it powerful enough to go upstream? Some instinctive calculating let her sense where magic would have taken a small orb that weighed no more than a river stone. Would it have mired itself in the silt at the bottom? No, the current was strong, despite being placid at the surface. And her instincts still claimed it had moved upstream, not down.

Then an idea occurred to Raimi. Call to it. Without knowing what would happen, Raimi paused in her dive and opened her mouth. Sound traveled differently underwater but it still traveled, she knew. The echo of muted music emerged from her throat. She called and then Raimi let her body drift against the pull of the river and she used a gentle stroke to propel herself along the bottom of the channel. The light from the weak autumn sun above did little to illuminate her way, but magic made up for it all. She floated effortlessly and kept her concentration on the call to find the stone.

Then Raimi thought she saw a flash of a tropical golden fish. Such a fish would be alien here in these cold streams. Curiously, Raimi swam after the flicker of gold. It had to be magical. Perhaps something going demon? Could she catch up with it? She looked about intently for her guide and then she saw something more important.

A blue glow floated just beyond her reach in the silt-filled water, lightening the murk. She reached for it and felt the reassuring cool of an orb. It swirled with blue and white, like the sky with clouds passing by. She had found her Heart Stone. Raimi directed her stroke upward and broke the surface in triumph.

She looked around the new terrain in wonder. Everything had changed. No silvery dragon waited on the shore. The sheltered valley had disappeared as well as the crash of cascades in the distance. Instead, she had entered a forest creek flowing out of a forest and joining the Lara River. She had come so far upriver, hundreds of miles in a matter of minutes. Well, there was a new way to travel magically.

Raimi held the glowing orb, her Heart Stone up into the air. So with it theoretically she could do any magic that led to good. She felt no different having discovered her Heart Stone. Experimentally Raimi placed the orb near her heart the way Owailion did and it disappeared. Now she was protected from temptation to do evil with her magic.

She considered what she wanted to explore next. Before, when she used magic to shift back to her 'birthplace', she had her memory to draw upon. Did she have to remember a place to do this travel?

Experimentally Raimi drew her mind to a place she could only imagine, one she had not yet visited. Her mind flowed even farther upstream, to where the Lara River split in two, coming out of the mountains. Here the water rushed until it met the other equally strong branch and she felt it settle. The temperature of the air and the angle of the sun changed noticeably and Raimi then opened her eyes. Evening gloom had descended here. Thoughtfully Raimi walked the thin shores, wondering why she had again chosen to come to this place. She had established that she could travel from place to place without having to see a place.

But she had to admit also that it reminded her of Owailion and for no discernible reason. And here, she had come on the off chance that Owailion might be here.

Yes, she had come here alone to think about Owailion.

Are you really that in love with him, after only a matter of a few days? Was that even reasonable? Wise Ones, indeed! She had come here to this empty strand of the river to think without the risk of having dragons or handsome distractions prevent her from thinking clearly. She knew that serious thought needed isolation. How was she to comprehend the unfathomable yearning she had toward a virtual stranger? Yet she felt so at peace. Nothing but God crafting this magic could account for her inner feelings.

Raimi yearned to learn more about Owailion. Sometimes she became mesmerized by the dark of his eyes, or the strange, snow-white hair. Had she always enjoyed those features in men she found attractive or was this just him? She loved the shape of his calloused hands, gentle and strong. His mind, always thinking and speculating, kept her concentration about him rather than fearing the new, alarming world she had waded into. Was that by design? If so, whose design? Again, could she blame God?

Some forgotten memory of a higher power brought her to her knees in the soft sand beside the river. As the stars began to break out beyond the misty hilltops, Raimi prayed. She had to have some reason to make this leap beyond just her own desires. The words would not come aloud, but she knew Someone heard them.

And the comfort came to her heart. She knew.

If she felt at peace with her bond with magic and Owailion before, having that confirmation from He who gave these gifts to her, that brought her to tears. She wept in joy and let the drops fall to the earth to blend with the river.

But something magical happened. Through her tears, Raimi saw something strange occur. Where her tears touched the earth, the soil and sand disappeared in whole handfuls. Fascinated and a little alarmed, she wiped her eyes to gain a better view of the phenomena happening right before her. Something niggled at her mind and she used a little magic to add more water to the hole forming before her, which deepened again until she could not physically reach the bottom of the fist-sized pit.

Raimi instead used her mind and explored down into the dark, sensing the river wanted to fill it in but magic not of her creation held it back. Then Raimi's mind reached the bedrock level. She felt something there and magically and lifted it free from the mud. At first, she thought it simply a dirty stone, so she carried it to the water to rinse it free. In the dark, she could not make out its shape, but under the water, her vision cleared. She washed the mud-free and saw a box with a simple lid which she lifted free. She then tipped out the box's contents.

In her hands, she held a charming little bowl. It would barely hold two or three handfuls of water, but she could imagine a lily floating in it and growing, or a pearl swirling about in it only to transform into a fish. The vessel had three short legs to hold it steady on a table, and silver lilies and reeds etched around its base. Obviously, it was magical, for how else had it called to her? But what did it do?

Without answers, Raimi followed an instinct, bent and filled the bowl with water from the bank. In the reflection there she saw the moon, but also, something else. She lowered her head to see more clearly. On the water's surface, Raimi saw Owailion sitting cross-legged on the island at Lolar. She recognized the bend in the river and the stones on the shore, but the image was in the daylight, during summer with the cool trees above his head, casting the river into shadow. He sat with a simple stone in his hands. He examined it, turning it over and over, concentrating on it. Then the stone dissolved into three powders. Fascinated, she watched as he mixed the powders and then pressed them into shape. She saw the whole episode; casting the vessel, etching the decoration and even the burial of the very bowl that now showed her the past. But how had it come to be here, so far away from its original burial place? Or maybe it had come to her here.

When the ground closed up again beneath Owailion's hand, the vision in the bowl faded and only the moonlight remained cast in the still water she held. Raimi found she had been holding her breath, for she let it out, rippling the liquid in the bowl, and with it the remains of the spell. Well, she had her answers. The vessel had been made for her by Owailion and hidden until she found it. She had wanted to see something of Owailion's past and now she had. The bowl's purpose was clear; to show the past. Perhaps it was fitting; she was the Queen of Rivers, always moving on into the future.

She would tell Owailion how she had discovered his little bowl when they met that night. Raimi looked up into the sky and realized she had been gone from Imzuli for hours. She would hold the bowl for a surprise when they reunited.

With little fear of her traveling magically now, Raimi stretched her mind out toward the river bank where she knew instinctively Imzuli waited for her and stepped toward the dragon who excitedly awaited her and watched the stars.

Chapter 12

Malornia

Owailion and Mohan flew directly up the Lara River, covering the empty plains rapidly, with a far different mission. "*We must plan before we go,*" Mohan warned. "*It is a dangerous place and what you propose is no pleasure trip.*"

"I was under the impression that you had never left the Land," Owailion commented.

"*Before you first came, I had not. But while you were waiting for your lady, I did go. I wanted to ask some questions of an exiled dragon there. It was not a pleasant interview. He knew nothing of the Sleep, of your coming, or even God's plans for the Land. He did, however, tell me that those runestones would be very valuable to humans in Malornia.*"

Owailion considered that for a moment. "Someone might believe that the writing might speak of how to break the Seal. If someone can read the stones, they may be able to enter the Land. That is my greatest fear," Owailion muttered gloomily. He did not want to go to Malornia, but he must if he were to find the stones.

Just then, as they were flying up the river, he felt a now-familiar itch. Something directly below him demanded his attention. "Mohan…" he began to tell him, but the dragon must have felt the itch for himself and had already begun to spiral down toward the river that snaked below them.

"*Is it another palace?*"

"I would assume so," Owailion replied, "but I won't know until I sleep and dream about it. I hope the dreams include Raimi again."

After Mohan landed, Owailion slid off and looked around the empty place. "Who would want to live here out in the middle of nowhere?" As far as the eye could see, vast flat plains spread in every direction. In the winter this place would be buried in blizzards and in the summer it would bake in the sun. Not a single tree or small hillock to break up the scenery. Only the river right before them gave any relief from the dead and dying grasslands.

Without knowing what he was doing, Owailion began strolling along the river bank where reeds and lilies grew. The swampy land refused to make way for the trees, and here he walked, heedless of the mud into which he sank. Then without warning Owailion reached down and scooped up two fists full of the reeds, jerking them cleanly out of the marshland.

"*What are you doing?*" Mohan asked.

"Something was starting there. I think these reeds are 'going demon'," replied Owailion and carried his gleanings up onto the bank. "They were listening to us and whispering to each other."

Mohan rocked back in surprise. "*I had not sensed that….until you pointed it out to me. My, you are very good. You heard them whispering?*"

"No, not heard precisely. I just…knew." Owailion walked up past the river bank and up to the grasslands where eventually he would build the palace he had felt. With Mohan watching he conjured a blanket and set the reeds out neatly on the surface, spaced evenly and well away from each other. "They wanted to combine together, teaming up and whisper spells. I sensed the magic and the reeds were perfect to do it. In the winter winds, they would have completed the job, coming together to whisper evil things. And now I know exactly what I shall do with them."

"*Do with them?*" Mohan asked, almost bewildered. "*You are going to make a Talisman with them. And you know someone will need these…these reeds? For what?*" The dragon's curiosity worked to keep Mohan awake quite nicely.

"Hopefully it will have some gift for magic. That bowl showed me the past when the runestones were stolen," Owailion reminded the dragon.

Owailion looked at the assembled reeds and began arranging them, largest to smallest. He didn't dare yet allow them to touch each other yet or they might start to whisper again, but he could see his creation in his mind's eye. He would dry, cut, sand and polish them with lacquer, bind them together and have a set of pipes fit for a Queen. Mohan must have tapped into Owailion's mind, for he saw the final instrument and asked the obvious question.

"*What is it?*"

"They are a set of pipes; a musical instrument. I don't know what magic it will craft, or how she will use it, but the Queen of Rivers must have a set of pipes. These are for her, a second Talisman."

"*How long will it take to create this Talisman*?" Mohan asked, looking at the sun high in the sky and thinking loudly that he might go hunting.

"It took about a day with the bowl. That was simpler in structure but I also had no idea what I was doing. You go and eat. I will call you when I am ready. I won't start this palace until after the pipes are formed."

Mohan agreed to the plan and then departed. Meanwhile, Owailion began physically manipulating the reeds. He dried them with a thought, cleaning out the pulp from within them and conjured a little brush to sweep inside each. He next conjured a fine lacquer to brush over them as he judged size and circumference. He dared even to blow on each reed, listening to the tone and discarding three of them as flawed. Did he even have a musical background? Owailion doubted it, but he understood the dynamics of sound enough to recognize all the notes he would need to make a suitable set of pipes. Next, he conjured a sharp knife to start cutting each reed to the length needed for the notes required.

Overhead the sun passed and then night fell. He didn't remember conjuring a fire, but somehow there was light as he worked obsessively. He could not stop in the middle of this project, for it demanded every bit of his magical attention. Indeed, he doubted that the palaces he had started would continue rising during this time and he would have to consciously reactivate the work there, but he did not care. He had to prevent a demon from forming and he worked feverishly at it. Then he wrapped the pipes together with silver and gold twine he conjured. Finally, he decorated the hefty pack of pipes in silver lilies and gold reeds just like the decoration he had placed on the bowl he had made earlier.

Finally, at dawn, he lay back with the completed instrument at his side and fell asleep, at last, done. Fortunately, the Queen of the Rivers floated through his dreams to distract him. All he lacked now was a place to hide his gift for her.

When he woke, instinctively he reached out to Raimi, seeking her mind somewhere in the Land. His thoughts drifted toward the northeast, up along the Lara River. There he found her thinking of him.

"Good morning," she called to him. "You were asleep and so I didn't want to interrupt you. What were you doing that you are sleeping in until almost noon?"

He smiled at her implied jealousy. "Making a gift for you," he replied, keeping his secret behind his shields.

"I know, I can see them. They're pretty. Another Talisman?"

"What…how?" he sputtered.

"You are sitting right next to the river. I've learned I can see many things in reflections. I also found my Heart Stone and the little bowl you made me. It showed me how you built it as a Talisman and now I've been watching you, both in the river and in the bowl."

Owailion felt a profound sense of pride in her accomplishments in just a little over a day. "You are doing very well," he complimented her. "As for my progress, I found another palace here in the middle of nowhere that I must start. Then, if I don't find a place to hide these pipes, I will be going to Malornia…probably tonight. I don't know if it will be safe for me to contact you, or even what time it will be there if I can."

"Then I will expect you to call when you can... and hide those pipes. I like the bowl and look forward to finding what the pipes can do." Then her voice grew conspiratorial. "And remember, I will be watching you." She laughed boldly, and Owailion could not help but laugh with her.

After he broke off his contact with Raimi, he began the excavation for the palace he had dreamed of, still escorted by the lovely Queen of Rivers. Later that afternoon Mohan returned from his feeding and Owailion was excited to begin his next adventure; traveling to Malornia.

"So you have never really explored other lands?" Owailion asked Mohan as they left the Lara riverbank, departing with yet another palace underway. "You would not know where we should look for a priest then?" asked Owailion.

As they flew northwest, as if they would fly there direct, Mohan taught him what he knew: Malornia to the west, Demion to the east and Marwen to the south. "*All of them are ruled by humans but I am sure that Marwen has driven the dragons away and Demion has no mountains unless you count the Great Chain that they share with the Land's borders. I fear we only have Malornia as an option. I think the humans in Malornia are clustered near the sea.*"

"Why would you use those words, 'I fear we only have Malornia'? Is it so bad then?" queried Owailion.

"*Malornia, the land from where the outlander ships have always sailed. I think of it as the nation of the outlanders. Demion has demons and Marwen shuts us out but Malornia is aggressive. Is there a priest there? Surely, but we must be cautious there. Dragons go there in exile and become slaves to the sorcerers. If you wish me to accompany you we must be careful. It may seem strange to see free dragons about.*"

"Do you want me to go alone?" Owailion asked, assuming Mohan's reluctance. "You can get me to a port and I could sail there."

Mohan muttered in discontent. "*No, there is no need for that. We can fly there instantly and I will let you walk into the first city we come near.*

I should be there to protect you if things go awry but I don't need to go in with you. I can hide outside."

Owailion looked around at the plains they were crossing, grassy and featureless. "Then let's go now," he suggested.

"*It will still be dark on the Malornian coast if we arrive now. This will be good.*"

A bleak disc of sun showed through the overcast sky as they prepared to leave the Land. Owailion felt a sense of foreboding as they prepared to depart the Land. "*And be sure to wear your shields as strongly as you can... without putting yourself into your royal clothes. That would not be wise. There are both demons and evil men here who will be interested in a stranger even if they do not know you for a magician. Strong shields and no other magic if you can avoid it,*" the dragon advised.

Then Mohan banked west as if he would fly to Malornia direct, down swept his wings and transitioned through the Seal.

Pitch black night greeted them and Owailion could only make out the ground as a series of thin white lines moving against the darkness. He peered down, studying it out until he recognized the crests of waves meeting the darkness of the beach beneath them. Without asking his input or advice, Mohan turned south along the beach, following it closely but still aloft so that anyone out at this hour might think he was simply a gull on the wind.

"There," Owailion called. "Just there. Lights from a town. Most people live near the sea. It's a sure means to find food and one less direction to defend in case of an attack."

"*Unless you consider a sea attack,*" added Mohan. "*I will set down here and hide in those trees there... with invisibility, for they do not look to be particularly tall trees. Then you can walk the rest of the way.*"

Owailion squinted into the dark but could only make out the difference between sea and sand because of the surf. He trusted that Mohan knew what he was about and leaned back as the dragon slowed and landed on the beach. Then he slithered down the dragon's back.

"What should I wear and carry with me?" he asked as Mohan stamped his way into a grove of trees on the shoreline's edge, with predictable devastation.

"*How would I know? I've never met a human other than you and Raimi,*" the dragon replied. "*You know more about mankind than I ever will. Good luck and call me when you are ready.*"

Owailion turned reluctantly and began tramping down the beach, wondering how far away the lights had been as he walked. Could he even do magic here? Experimentally he conjured himself a hat to see if that skill functioned here in this foreign land. When the felt hat appeared as he ordered, Owailion sighed with relief. He added a less insulated cloak than the one he was wearing when aloft with Mohan. He hoped that a priest would not think him too destitute to support a wife. Nor did he wish to seem rich enough to rob. With that thought, Owailion conjured himself a sturdy sword in an unmarked sheath and a small purse of gold to pay for anything he might need.

By the time dawn arrived Owailion could make out the sturdy stone walls of a small port town with two jetties and dozens of ships leaving the protection there. The forest pushed right up against the walls and he looked closely for clues on how to approach. No roads left this outpost village on the north side so he could not claim he had come from some outer village. That is if he could speak the language. That question just occurred to him as he hiked up the side of the north jetty and looked over the town.

The walls that surrounded the village were marked with arcane symbols he could not understand. They were not writing but stars and beasts painted on the stone as if in blood. He gulped in fear, tasting the potency of magic here. So how was he to tell the sorcerers from the non-practitioners?

"*Truth spell,*" Mohan sent to him helpfully.

Owailion thanked his mentor for the reminder and began walking up the boardwalk atop the jetty, toward the town. Perhaps he could pretend he had come from another land on a ship that had just docked, although this village seemed very small for foreigners to visit. And the gate, iron-clad and sturdy, spoke more of the fear this town harbored toward attack than its wealth. So he would not come in as a tourist. The fishing boats leaving port provided most of the foot traffic but as he passed a donkey-drawn cart of fish he helped push the heaping load in through the gates and no one looked at him twice as a visitor or someone out of place.

Inside he paused to listen to the chatter and realized that he could understand it even though the words were completely different from what he had been speaking with Mohan. He looked around for a sign above a shop and was delighted that he could read them as well although the characters were strange. Greatly daring, he threw a truth spell over the streets as he walked toward the village green filling up with fishwives selling their wares.

And what he saw made him almost vomit. The roadways flowed with sewage and blood. Demonic lizards and thorny vines clung to the walls and roof of almost every building as they were innocent like house pets and kitchen herbs. And those passing fishwives appeared to be leprous invalids, creeping under the weight of chains bound to their necks. A few soldiers stood in the doorways wearing steel armor that fairly glowed with protection spells. Even the trees planted at the corners of the village green took on the look of twisted spikes with hissing snakes for leaves. What kind of spells had this place undergone?

Owailion let the truth spell fall and breathed better for it. He did not want to suspect all the evil magic required to impose all he had witnessed. Instead, he looked around for a church on the square. If his memory served a church should be visible from a town square. And it was. Owailion saw the tall building with double doors and a bell tower. He did not dare cast a spell on the church as he approached. Better to save that, and his probable reaction, for the priest instead. He walked up the steps and pulled open the door.

Even without the truth spell, he recognized a poor church when he saw it. Only a few benches in the atrium lined the aisle and no one had tended the stubs of candles that poorly lit the hall. Its windows were dirty and plain and the woodwork in need of polish; a very rustic church for an even more rustic town that ignored its religious life. A priest here was more likely to be starving himself than able to help those less fortunate. He would probably be among the poorest of his members.

But he had excellent hearing. The door creaking echoed and brought an old man scurrying into the hall, pulling on a threadbare robe as if he had just been wakened. "Welcome, sir. How can I be of service?" the old priest asked, smiling a nearly toothless grin.

Warily Owailion threw a truth spell over the man and observed what it could share with him. Other than fine teeth and a straighter bearing, this man changed little. So, he was a good man with nothing to hide and no poisonous spells cast over him.

"Sir," Owailion began. "I am looking for a priest to perform a marriage. In a few months we plan to be married but... but not here; across the sea. My lady will not come here, so we must go to her. Are you willing to marry us? I will provide for your transportation and lodging as well as putting money in your coffers to keep your church for a year."

The priest rocked back on his feet at that offer. His amazement passed unchecked across his face. "Across the sea? I cannot leave my flock for so long, sir. How far...?"

"Your flock seems to have left you long ago, sir. It will be at most two days you will be gone. I will bring you there by magic... " and Owailion waited to see how the churchman reacted to magic. Were magic and God opposed here? Or was there an acknowledgment that all gifts came from above, as Owailion had learned since his own arrival in the Land.

The priest did not react visibly but he grew still as if waiting for something more. "What is your name, my son?"

Something strange burned across Owailion's mind and he recognized the hand of fortune had brought him here. He need not fear this man, for he was meant to come. "I am Owailion, King of Creating."

"From the Land?" the priest added with the last rags of his breath.

"Yes. You know me?" Owailion gasped in wonder at his luck.

The priest reached for Owailion, drawing him down to sit on one of the worn benches. "I have been waiting for you all my life. I am...I am your servant. When I was a child I found my way into the church because I have a gift. I was given something to pass on to you. It is a key. You will use it to open the palace that is yours. Each of the Wise Ones will have a door steward that holds a pendant. That pendant will open their palace. Each must Seek them as they would the Talismans. You have sought me, and I have been found. I have your pendant and I am your door steward. You may call me Enok. I have no gift for magic but I am over four hundred years old and have waited for you to come most of my life. I am your servant, my Lord."

Then the truly ancient man pressed into Owailion's hand a small cut gem. It looked like one of the stones he had seen cut on Lake Ameloni, milky and hard as ice but lined with black flecks of jet. And within the stone, he could see a tiny replica of a tall towering palace, exactly as he would eventually craft it. His palace set in ice.

"Your pendant, sire, for when you need it."

Owailion looked up again at the priest as the old man closed Owailion's hand over the gift. "I...I cannot," he answered breathlessly.

"I know right now this is all too new for you and we must not speak of it," Enok whispered as if the very walls would overhear them. "You have far to go but I will be there to support you. My only gift is a long life...and my loyalty. I am your man."

Owailion found he could start breathing again. "Are you safe here? With all the evil magic about, how can you bear it?"

Enok scoffed at that. "Blood magic, we call it. Animals, plants, and sometimes even people are sacrificed to call up the demons that bring this magic. I've lived with it all my life. I am well enough here. The leaders do not bother me for I keep the people at ease and do not make demands on them. The demons do not know me for a magical being and so I am worthless to possess. But I do look forward to coming to the Land and witnessing your work there. It will be wondrous."

Owailion felt overwhelmed and on the verge of tears at the amazing coincidence. "You are the first person I have spoken to in this whole nation. How did I come upon you of all the citizens of Malornia? I have only just arrived."

Enok gave Owailion a strange look. "Why, the same way you came to the Land. God has guided you in all your work. Do you doubt this?"

Owailion shook his head. Of course, he did not doubt, seeing as the magic he had been given had infused every breath he took and every memory he carried, but it still amazed him that it kept happening; God moving the pieces of his life. "I do not doubt. I only feel amazed. I also came to Malornia with another goal that perhaps you can help with. In the Land, there were some runestones. They disappeared. In a land sealed against invasion and inhabited only by dragons, these stones had human writing on them. I have reason to suspect they came here to Malornia."

"And you think I might know of them? No, not here. In this small town, we have little interaction with the powers in the capitol. The King of Malornia is very powerful in blood magic and he will never have enough. No, do not try to find the stones here. One day these stones will be found again perhaps, but for now, while you are so new to the Land, wait until the right time."

"The right time?"

"When the Wise Ones are all at full power," Enok insisted. "You do not know what you will be facing."

Owailion sighed. Of course, he did not know what he faced, but he also had a mandate from God to find out who had taken the stones. Owailion's thoughts ground to a halt. He was told to find who had taken the stones, not retrieve them, not read them. No, he had to learn first and only then act. That he could do and still remain safe. Eventually, maybe in a thousand years, he would know what the stones had to say and why they were lost, but for now, he only had to find the thief.

"So, will you come with me? I really am looking for a priest. I have a fiancé and..."

Enok interrupted, "Of course, but not yet. You said in three months?"

"On Mid-Winter's day. The dragons must approve and are most curious about how a human marriage is to be performed. Shall I come and get you then?"

Enok smiled like he had been given a present. "My greetings to your lady," he almost laughed. "I must tie up my dealings here but I will await your return."

"Raimi will be delighted," Owailion replied and then rose to leave, putting the precious pendant in his pocket. Then stopped by a stricken look that passed over Enok's weathered face.

"Do not speak her name again, I pray," he hissed in alarm. "There are ears everywhere.

Owailion froze in shock. He knew about name magic. He had been foolish, using her name.

Enok shook him into action. "Go now, and do not come here again. Instead just speak to me as you would your dragon friends, from a distance. I will hear."

And with that, the old priest scurried back into his confessional and left Owailion to walk out of the church alone. As he left the dilapidated building, he shook free of the momentary fear. He should be elated. He was not alone now that he knew Enok.

Owailion did not notice the soldiers in the doorways, the demon lizards on the walls or the blind stares of the fishwives as he departed the nameless town. He only knew he had a new friend and a hope for the future.

Chapter 13

Demon on the Mountain

Raimi had to insist, as they traveled up the Don, that Imzuli feed every night. Over the weeks the urge to hibernate had descended on the young dragon like the change of season. Although the Great Chain Mountains now dominated the horizon and Raimi had found two sites for palaces, little could keep Imzuli's concentration. She seemed distracted and too often Raimi had to insist she go do something else so she herself could eat or sleep regularly. A conversation about humans no longer even stimulated the expected excitement.

"What am I going to do with her?" Raimi asked Owailion during one of their nightly meetings. "I feel like I am harassing her even to simply talk to me. What could have happened to make her so…depressed?"

Owailion could not advise her, for he had little of that problem with Mohan. The gold dragon had willingly gone out of his way to help traverse Malornia, looking over the strange land, finding whole pockets of magic, the major ports and reconnoitering the capitol. That the dragon had to do so invisibly and had to feed inside dangerous forests might be enough to keep Mohan more alert.

"Imzuli is young," Owailion suggested. "Perhaps she is not happy about the Sleep. She has so little experience. Shall I ask Mohan to speak to her?"

Raimi, with her independent streak, rejected that idea. "No, I will make do. It's like I'm flying alone. It makes me question if the dragons will even make it to mid-winter. If we let them, they would drift off right now. I'm going to miss them," she added regretfully, feeling her eyes ache with unshed tears at the idea.

"Think on this then, we will be alone together at that point. I will not be stuck here in Malornia much longer. Have hope for that."

Raimi smiled at that suggestion and in response, sent Owailion a magically blown kiss. They would be together soon enough.

At dawn Imzuli came back from feeding and Raimi greeted her with as much cheer as she felt would not be offensive. "I think today we will pass over Zema. I wish to see where those stones were, and then you can take me up to your mountain. It is close by, is it not?"

Imzuli gave a non-committal rumble. "*Yes, it is close by.*"

Rather than comment on that, Raimi climbed aboard and they were off, skimming over the forest and through looming clouds that threatened snow, the first of the season that would reach the valley floor. "Would you rather go higher, out from beneath the clouds?" Raimi asked politely.

"*Here is Zema. Be wary,*" Imzuli warned curtly as she spiraled down into the forest.

Even in the brightest summer sun, the place would have seemed gloomy, Raimi noted. Imzuli set down yards away from the bare spot in the forest as if she dare not use the obvious center of the ring as a landing spot and would rather battle the branches fouling her wings than enter Zema. Raimi thanked the dragon as she slid down. "If you do not want to be here, I will understand. Go to your home, my friend, if that will ease your mind."

"*No,*" Imzuli grumbled. "*I just do not like this place. It brings me bad memories. I will wait here for you.*"

And that was as much as the dragon had spoken in over a week. Raimi patted Imzuli on the flank and then turned to weave her way toward the strange bare patch in the forest. The rain arrived before Raimi managed to push her way through the undergrowth and saw the light of the sky. Her first impression of Zema was the smell; it reeked of dead flesh. The ground within the circle was muddy from near-constant rain without any plant material to absorb it. No trees, grass, ferns or even moss would grow in the space.

Then Raimi looked closer. Something, she thought perhaps the roots of trees, was trying to push up through the mud. Without entering the circle itself, Raimi squatted at the edge and brushed at the stubby growth that had pushed up perhaps a hand-width from the floor of Zema. It wasn't a root. It was made of stone.

"There's something growing here," Raimi announced aloud, knowing Imzuli would hear her. "What do you make of this?"

That did indeed get Imzuli's attention. Raimi felt the dragon's presence in her mind, utilizing her eyes and could hear the muttered snarls as the dragon belatedly tried to weave her mass through the trees so she could see for herself. "*That smell, it is a demon,*" the dragon announced.

"A demon start? I've not found one of those yet."

"*No,*" Imzuli insisted as she finally made it physically to the edge of the clearing. "*That smell is a full-blown demon, coming here from wherever we banish them. I think Zema is a portal to that other place. This is where demons come, bypassing the Seal. And that portal has not been used since…*"

"Since the stones were stolen? And what about these little stones, the ones that are popping up here like weeds? Are they the remains of the old stones or are these new ones, growing here faster than new trees can sprout?"

"*In the summer when Owailion came here to investigate, there was grass and a few other plants in the clearing and no little spikes of stone. These have come up here since then and all the plants have gone. It is the entrance of a demon…and very recently. That smell…*"

Raimi did not hesitate. She pulled her bag from her back and dug inside, pulling out the Talisman bowl. She conjured water into the bowl and then waited for the surface to settle. She had to place her head directly over the reflection to keep the steady rain from marring the image. Staring at her own reflection she concentrated and then made her command. "Show me what has happened here at Zema to make the stones start growing back and the plants to disappear."

Raimi watched as the gloomy clouds of the reflection shifted and she saw the dark deepen as night fell on the image of Zema. The trees dripped with rain and in the circle, a blanket of moss and low grass had struggled to fill in the clearing. No little knobs of stone had poked through the earth. Then, as they watched, a blood-red light began to form in the center of the clearing, floating a few feet above the ground. The glow began to pulse and then with a snap, disappeared, leaving something misshapen in its place.

The creature in the center of the circle stood on the shaggy hind legs of a man-sized goat but the upper half of its body appeared to boast stumpy tentacles of a WARPED squid and the smashed face of something that might have been a pumpkin once but now had been stove in and rotted to form glowing eyes and a sagging mouth. The demon looked toward the sky and then leaped from the center of the circle into the clouds above. The observers were left to see the steady rain had marred any hoof prints left behind in the circle where now not a single plant remained. Finally, the bowl showed that only an instant later sixteen small stones thrust up through the mud like teeth growing through gums.

Disgusted by what she had witnessed, Raimi dumped the water from the bowl, adding it to the mud of the circle they dare not enter.

"A true demon," Raimi whispered in horror.

Imzuli began groaning as if in pain. "*The stones arise when a demon comes through. How many might have come over the ages to have them grow so tall in that time? We did not know. They were... the stones were so much more than we thought.*"

"We do not know that those stones grew every time a new demon entered. Perhaps they stopped demons from entering like a cork stops up a bottle. Do the other dragons know this is a portal or was that a theory of your own?" Raimi asked as she put away the bowl. "Should we share what we have learned?"

Imzuli shook herself in irritation. "*No, I never told my suspicions. None of us gave Zema a thought. We know where the smell comes from now. We must hunt down that demon right now. Then we can share this at the conclave. Climb aboard.*"

"What if a demon took the stones originally?" Raimi suggested. "They apparently can breach the Seal." Meanwhile, she did as Imzuli asked and clambered up onto her customary spot on the dragon's back.

Imzuli launched herself into the sky before she replied. "*No, if this is their portal, they would not wish it damaged. They would want it open. Changes in it would only draw attention. The demons did not take the stones.*"

Raimi trusted the dragon's instincts on this matter, as well as her nose. The dreadful smell of rotten flesh guided Imzuli up into the mountains. They traced it as it leaped from peak to mountain peak, hopping vast distances, but always landing on a different mountain's height, as if it could not fly exclusively. And the stench grew stronger as Imzuli flew after it.

"What should I do when we finally catch up? I don't think I can blow fire like a dragon and I should learn how to do this for myself before the dragons are asleep," Raimi called to her friend as they streaked across the mountain range.

"*Let me manage that,*" Imzuli insisted. "*The demon is mine to burn.*"

Raimi did not argue. The fierce tone made her hold her tongue. She could wait to understand. For weeks Imzuli had been depressed. Now, with a demon to hunt she had shifted to into a driven demon herself. What about this demon would ignite such passion in the gentle dragon? Why would she suddenly insist on doing this for herself when she should have been allowing Raimi to use this as a learning experience?

"Please let me help," suggested Raimi. "Use me as bait. The demon won't stop bouncing about unless you give it a reason to stop. Put me on a mountain peak somewhere and I will call it. That's what a demon wants, isn't it? A body to inhabit? I'll shield myself and then when it comes attacking me, then you can roast it."

This ploy at least got Imzuli to focus on something instead of fixating on chasing the demon all across the Great Chain. She finally stopped and hovered long enough to consider the benefits and then wordlessly transitioned to one particular peak.

"*This is my mountain,*" Imzuli explained as she alighted delicately on the topmost ridge. "*You must use your strongest shields. Do not let him push you over the sides. I will lurk below, invisible. A demon does not die but he cannot escape when he is in my flames. He will agree to leave the Land and go back to where he came from in order to make it stop. Do not let your shields down no matter how hot it becomes or how much he howls.*"

Raimi agreed to this plan if only to have a part in conquering a demon. She slid down the dragon's side, but standing there on the snowy ridge, balanced carefully on a slope worn down by a few dragons alighting was not safe in itself. And something was strange here. Raimi did not mention it, but something about this peak gave her that familiar itch she associated with a site for a Wise One palace. How could a Wise One palace be created here at the top of Imzuli's mountain? It made no sense. But now was not the time to puzzle out that riddle.

Instead, Raimi strengthened her shields and broadened them out until she was using magic so strongly, she put herself into her royal clothing. She wore fine silk in blue and gray with a waterfall of silver down the sides in a river that washed off the ridge. This costume was not fit for the bitter wind passing up the mountainside and she added a warm, richly decorated coat, gloves, and a hat rather than the bothersome veil. Once she was ready, Imzuli launched herself back into the air.

"*I will be right here, below you on the slope, invisible.*" Then Raimi watched as the dragon shimmered into nothing, blending in with the whitened mountainside.

Raimi looked out over the vistas, wondering where to direct her call to the demon. There was no way of knowing where the creature had bounced to, so in her strongest voice, both physical and mental, she drew back and shouted.

"Demon! Come and get me!"

Of course, the first blow came from behind her, nearly bowling her off the ridge, but that was probably for the best, for if she had seen the attack coming, she might have been frightened. When she managed to turn and see all the tentacles thudding against her shields, only inches from her face, and the rotting gourd of a face, the horror hit just as hard.

"What? Don't like what you see?" asked the demon in a surprisingly scintillating voice. Then the misshapen creature changed into something angelic, with gossamer wings and a lovely, golden face. "Perhaps you find this more appealing when I am you."

Then Imzuli's fire erupted. All Raimi could see of the angel was its writhing body, burning and yet not being consumed. The creature shrieked in horrifying pain and morphed back into the goat/squid and then even into a mist under the rain of fire. Within her shields, Raimi too felt some heat and pain, but she gritted her teeth and spoke firmly to the demon.

"You will go back to where you came from and not return."

The enraged demon could only screech at her, piercing her shields only with sound. It thrashed and beat against her defenses, rotating wildly between its three forms, seeking one of them that would allow its escape.

"Go back," Raimi reiterated calmly. "You cannot escape unless you leave this Land."

It might have taken hours or even days, but the demon finally capitulated. It did not say so, but one moment the purple mist swirled into the goat/squid and then with a crack, it disappeared entirely. Imzuli's fire continued blasting against Raimi's shields with withering heat, and the human shouted above the roar of flames. "He's gone I think."

"*Do you smell it still?*" Imzuli asked.

"Your sense of smell is far stronger than mine but, no, I cannot see or smell it any longer."

With that reassurance, Imzuli cut off her fire. Raimi looked around at the ground that glowed and the stones that had now become glass that flowed down the slopes. All down the sides all the snow had long since melted and Raimi felt a surge of energy just sensing the waters that now would go flowing off this mountain and into her rivers.

"*I've ruined my mountain,*" Imzuli groused but came to light on her somewhat shrunken peak.

"You've done beautifully. You fought a full-grown demon and driven him back. We've learned where they enter the Land. You can watch Zema. Keep an eye on it and perhaps even prevent others from coming. It's wonderful."

"*It was a good plan,*" Imzuli agreed. "*I think I will go and feed now. That was the longest I have ever blown fire and we were chasing him for a long time before.*"

"And I will go to my place on the delta to rest as well," Raimi smiled as she patted the dragon on the neck. "Yes, you did well, my friend, and I will have quite a story to share with Owailion tonight."

Chapter 14

Together

Owailion returned to the island on the Lara delta with hope and relief. Mohan brought him, settling on the far shore to enjoy the weak sunlight. Now that mid-winter was approaching, neither one could wait to shift to a new phase of their life. Mohan could not abide hunting in Malornia, not with the demon-possessed prey, nor the slime coated minds of all the people they encountered. For his part, Owailion had learned more than he cared about blood magic and the toxic government in Malornia. They both came away convinced that the runestones had come to Malornia. And together they decided to not return any time soon. Being away from the Land had taken too much out of them.

"Aren't you worried about falling asleep?" Owailion asked the dragon as he wallowed in the beach sand, seeking a comfortable bed. "It's only two days before the conclave but you'll fall asleep if you don't keep going."

"*No,*" the dragon replied carefully. "*I've got enough questions to keep me awake a while longer. For instance, why aren't you worried about coming back a little early? Aren't you concerned that Raimi will know you are here and you'll be tempted to do something you shouldn't?*"

"You just want to watch us," Owailion replied, hoping it was a tease, but deep inside he might have resented the dragon's fascination with human intimacy. Certainly, Owailion felt torn; wanting to be alone with Raimi, but distrusting his ability to resist her charms. And how could you tell a dragon that his presence was both an inhibitor as well as a protective relief? Mohan would simply not understand.

"*I do find you two very interesting. Dragons do not form pairings as you have. Your thoughts are full of Raimi constantly.*"

"As they should be," Owailion replied. "I've come back here because I still do not know what kind of palace to start here. I was hoping to dream of the design or find a place to hide her pipes. It just seems strange that I still cannot do anything magical to prepare her for becoming a Wise One."

"*And if she sees you here and wants to join you?*"

"Then I'll welcome her. We won't give in to temptation at this late date." At least Owailion hoped that was the case.

As if by design, Imzuli, with Raimi on board appeared in the sky above. They began spiraling down toward the island. Owailion swallowed in nervous anticipation as his fiancé slid off the dragon's back and fairly danced over to him. She reached for him and gave him a long, sumptuous kiss that drove all other thoughts from his mind. Finally, with Imzuli's rumbling in appreciation echoing in the background, Owailion came up for air.

"Hello," he whispered shakily.

Raimi almost giggled at him. "I love that I can do that to you. But we have an audience." She looked over at Mohan and Imzuli who both watched the couple intently. So it made her nervous too. Instead, she reached for Owailion's hand and they began walking around the shoreline of the island as if on a stroll. As they moved away, she gave him the huge scroll of the map she had added to. It included her more detailed markings. Owailion noted how Raimi had sensed the itch of three locations for palaces; one at the mouth of the Don River, one at the southern tip of the Great Chain and a final one, much to her worry, at the top of Imzuli's birth mountain.

It had taken some self-control to not tell Imzuli about that; perhaps the dragon's continuing depression encouraged her silence. She had even waited until they were physically together to tell Owailion of this.

"I do not have the mandate to build these palaces," she told him in a tightly shielded thought since the dragons were still intent on observing them as they walked. "You will have to confirm all I have discovered. I must be wrong. A palace cannot possibly occupy Imzuli's mountain."

Owailion agreed with her uneasily. "We will investigate this after...after the conclave." He did not dare share his conviction that the dragons would go to sleep immediately after the gathering and they would be alone from that point on. Was he excited or worried about that prospect?

Abruptly he dropped that difficult topic and instead eagerly gave her something he had withheld from their nightly chats. "I found a priest," he revealed. "And he knew I was coming. You see, each Wise One will also have a door steward, someone who holds the key to getting into our palace." He then brought out the pendant that Enok had given him.

Raimi listened eagerly to his tale and then took the jewel from him to examine it more closely. "Deep magic," she whispered in awe.

"What do you mean, deep magic?" Owailion asked, watching the sunlight on the river catch in her eyes.

"Imzuli taught me about it. She explained that certain spells, God based spells, are deep magic that binds to the earth, not to the magician. God gives these door stewards a long life in order for them to be part of the Wise Ones' world. Like the language spell over us, the Seal, the Sleep and even bringing the Wise Ones into being. Even after the magician is gone, the spell continues because it is bound to the earth itself. Deep magic."

"Is that why I had so much trouble with making seals when Tamaar was trying to teach me? I wasn't tying it to the earth, but to myself?"

"Probably," Raimi confirmed. "Most of it is done by God, but we can invoke it if we put careful parameters on it. That's how I found out I can see anything within the reflection of the rivers. I was going deep, following the water as it seeped into the ground and could see...I could see anything. I've seen the inside of the earth and the whole world from the highest clouds because they are water too. Where water goes, so do I."

"Have you looked for the rune stones?" Owailion asked in excitement at this insight.

Raimi blinked in surprise. "I've not tried." She sat down abruptly on the ground and pulled out the Talisman bowl and filled it with water. Then she verbally commanded the bowl. "Show me where the rune stones are right now."

Owailion squatted down beside her to look at the reflection, but all he felt was a disappointment. The reflection grew dark and they could see nothing. "It's blank," he muttered.

"No," Raimi corrected him. "It shows where the stones are – in a dark, waterless place. It would not be a cave, but maybe a room away from everything that might provide light. It cannot show what cannot be seen. We have learned that much."

"Well," he sighed, "it's something. My mandate is not to find them, but to find the thief. I was corrected in that. I have plenty of other things to do without fighting a war to get the stones back here in the Land."

Raimi agreed with him and then handed back his pendent. "If there is a key, then there must be a door and you haven't built either of us a door. You still haven't felt any inspiration for what to build here, just that this is the place for my palace?" She looked up longingly through the trees to the cascades that plunged down into this wondrous valley.

"No, and that worries me. Why would your home be forgotten? Maybe you don't need a home, except in my arms. Now that we are back together, I can concentrate on that again." Owailion wrapped his arms around her and she felt enveloped in his warmth. "I've missed you," he whispered as he buried his lips into her hair.

"And I you,"

Somewhere on the other side of the river, Imzuli shifted so she could see them cuddling. Wordlessly the two humans began walking again, out of direct observation.

"Do you want to see what's growing at Zema?" Raimi asked and before he could agree, Raimi magically refilled the bowl to provide the reflection. "Every evening I've watched what you have been doing, your trek across the sea, spying on Malornia. I've even gone back to see when you arrived in the Land. It has been..."

"How disturbing, you've been watching me?" Owailion teased, and then shifted toward what he could not discover on his trek to the outland. "I wonder if I can ask your bowl to show us how the rune stones even came to the Land?" he asked. "God would not have actually set up a portal to bring demons to the Land, would He?"

Raimi stopped their walk, refilled the bowl and then waited until the water stilled. Then she closed her eyes in concentration. "Show us how the Zema rune stones came to be in the Land."

The light in the white sky, threatening the first snowstorm this far south now reflected flatly on the water's surface and for a moment Raimi wondered if the bowl would show anything. Then she saw a ripple that had nothing to do with movement in the water. She saw what looked like a cyclone racing across the sky and then it touched down on the golden plains, snaking and weaving eastward wildly. When the view wheeled around to a more parallel angle she could see the approach toward the mountains. She recognized the particular peaks. The forest at the range's base loomed out like a wall standing against the cyclone and when the storm collided with the trees they swayed violently. The shafts of the trees shattered. The tornado dissipated there, bashing against the strong branches and when it faded the stones, markings and all, stood there full-grown, placed by the hand of God. No sorcerer had left them and no demon entered with their arrival. Perhaps they were the corks meant to block the demons from coming. Was the Seal even there at the time? There was simply no way to tell.

Again, Owailion wished the image to pull closer to the stones so maybe he could read them but the surface of the water in the bowl was simply too small to make out the markings and so he pulled away from the dish, satisfied with what he had seen in Raimi's bowl. "They came from God then," he whispered. "I doubt they were set there as a portal, but God set them up to block entry, as well as with a message for humans."

Raimi nodded and then added, "You don't want to see how they disappeared?"

Owailion looked over toward the dragons who were no longer physically in view and then on a private line answered her. "No, I've seen it before and this is a dragon matter. I've learned to not get involved in it. I'm fairly certain Mohan has gone back in time to see for himself. Maybe he will confront the dragon involved; perhaps in private at the conclave, if he learns the identity of the thief before then."

Raimi shuddered. "I cannot imagine such a discussion. The dragons seemed so civilized and even-tempered. It's hard to conceive of a thief among them. Accusing one of them of a crime…it seems alien." Then she shifted the subject toward a more pleasant future. "Tell me about what to expect at the conclave," Raimi suggested aloud. "I asked Imzuli about it and all I got was 'a meeting of dragons'."

Rather than explain with words, Owailion magically shared with her the memory of his one attendance at a conclave. He showed her the island of diamonds, the clouds and having them burned away with Mohan's fire breathing. Owailion displayed for her the overwhelming beauty of the attending dragons, with their hides glittering like jewels. Then for good measure, he pictured something from the dream he had enjoyed – Raimi in her royal garb, white and shimmering with her copper hair and alabaster hands the only bit visible. Finally, he added from his imagination an image of them both standing ankle deep on a shoreline made up of uncut gems. They both wore their royal costumes, facing each other, holding hands as his Priest Enok stood before them, speaking the words of a promise.

Raimi smiled shyly in anticipation. "When?"

"Mohan is calling the conclave for tomorrow. This will be more complicated than just a wedding. Apparently, the dragons have memories they want to share with me. I also expect that Mohan will want to address the issue of who stole the stones. And they will talk about the

Sleep. I think that other than Imzuli and Mohan, all the dragons are barely holding on at this point, ready to go into their mountains and never come out again. Our marriage vows will probably be a minor part of the conclave, at least to the dragons and we are only guests there."

"Do you think the Sleep fall on them quickly? Will they all go off to their mountain and suddenly the skies are clear?" Raimi asked, thinking of Imzuli and how vibrant she was at the beginning, always asking questions and finding something new and beautiful to show to her friend, and then how she faded. Raimi would miss Imzuli terribly. Would the dragons ever wake again? It seemed wrong for them to go to sleep not be seen again.

Owailion sighed with regret. "I do not know, and it's going to be sad no matter what. I've come to love Mohan in the time I've been with him. Every Wise One should have a dragon friend, but it is not to be. God has a purpose for the Sleep and we might never know. I wish… "

"Wish what?" Raimi asked when he petered out and put shields up around his thoughts.

"I wish that your Talisman bowl could show the future as well," Owailion whispered. "Somehow it sounds a little greedy to hope for something no one should know."

Raimi blinked with surprise. "I thought it was a miracle to see the past. It never occurred to me to ask the bowl for the future. How do we know it cannot show us until we try?"

Owailion did not speak aloud his misgivings but neither did he hesitate to at least think about them and let her read his mind. She listened in about his instincts. "The future is too open to so many choices. It was one thing to learn from the past and quite another to manipulate things in the future."

Without listening to his nonverbal protest, Raimi tossed out the water from the previous vision and then refilled it magically. Then she closed her eyes in concentration as the water settled. For his benefit she let Owailion hear the thoughts she used as she carefully directed the image bowl to exactly what she wanted to witness. "Show us our future wedding."

The water went white with fog and they could barely make out individual shapes of dragons perched on the volcano above the lake. The two of them stood hand in hand, just as in Owailion's manufactured vision, looking in each other's eyes but something was missing.

"Where is Enok?" Owailion asked of no one.

But the Talisman bowl took his question as a request for a vision. Their wedding image faded to reveal something new. Raimi recognized the church from Owailion's memories of his visit to Malornia. She saw how Owailion had just left and the door closed behind him. Then a dark-robed figure crept out of the alcove at the back of the chapel. He snuck forward toward the altar and called out for the priest. Enok came out to meet this newcomer but looked startled when he saw who had entered like he recognized this visitor and knew the danger he posed. Raimi had a difficult time holding the image steady as the imposter caught Enok by the collar and dragged him kicking and fighting up to his own altar. The far more powerful enemy threw the old man onto the stone and proceeded to plunge his knife into the heart of the priest. Enok was dead not minutes after Owailion had left him.

The water sloshed and Raimi dropped the bowl.

"No," Owailion gasped. "I only just found him. How...they must have known I was coming and followed me there. They dare not attack me, so instead, they hoped to stop me by killing him."

Raimi cast her mind out, seeking some way to comfort Owailion in this horrid moment. She again thought of how everything she touched must go awry, but this was not her door steward. It had only been her Talisman that showed this evil. She enfolded Owailion in her arms and rocked with him in his grief, holding onto him as his only solace.

Owailion stirred again morosely. "I wanted to see something wonderful. Is there ever going to be something beautiful in our lives?"

Raimi had no words for him. The past that they had just witnessed had been horrid. Could the future be better? She lifted the bowl, filled it with water and then closed her eyes to make her wish. "How will the Land be after the dragons fall asleep?"

Then she opened her eyes to witness the results. Owailion's dark sorrowful eyes turned with her to look avidly, desperately for hope. Despite his misgivings of witnessing the future, he wanted that hope. Again the surface reflected the flat white winter sky. Then the image shifted to the snow of the mountains. The scene followed along the Great Chain, showing the peaks one after the other in a now-familiar succession. It briefly flashed by a few of Owailion's grand palaces located where he had not yet found them. Now completed the palaces stood with luxurious gardens that defied the climate and altitude at which they were set. Then the vision raced around the Elbow where the mountain chain bent southward.

Beside him, Raimi gasped. "That's where Imzuli's peak is…was." They both saw the entire mountain was gone and in its place, a stunning garden had taken root in the crater left behind. Before they could register a building there the image moved farther south. Were there other mountains missing now? Were they gone or crushed or…it moved too fast to be sure of the changes.

Then the scene shifted out over the forest along the Don River, but they witnessed something strange happening. The trees began dying, turning brown and withering as the image flew by at dragon speeds down to the sea. Villages popped up along the river, cutting back the sparse trees that had survived whatever killed the forest. "People are coming inside the Seal?" Owailion observed. "I wondered…"

"Why would the forest die? How will people get inside the Seal?" asked Raimi even as she saw the land around the Don River rippling from earthquakes and other forces. "This is hundreds of years of change," she added as the forest had given in to the influence of the plains and then was lost, and the image shifted west toward the Southern Mountains. Mines and more towns emerged throughout them. A volcano erupted off the coast to the south in a black flash and they missed seeing more. Their next little vision shifted to the Lara River and they both gasped.

The island on the delta where they stood at this very moment, their favorite place, had dissolved into a swampland. The hills surrounding the river were gone, along with the waterfall and the trees. Instead, marshes and mist filled in the place. A palace, presumably Raimi's, stood in the middle of the swamp and they saw it only briefly before it crumbled, becoming marble chunks in the marshlands. Raimi's hand trembled at the sight and the image rippled, and she dropped the bowl into the sand.

Raimi found herself crying uncontrollably and Owailion tried to comfort her when he felt like weeping himself. Neither one of them could stand the thought of their Land changing so much, but seeing it in first person, watching it crumble before their eyes, they felt it as if the blows were physically assaulting them. It was worse than seeing Enok's demise. That at least hopelessly fell in the past.

"It's like a storm hit the Land," Raimi whispered mentally, recalling the former vision the bowl had shown them, of how the stones arrived by a cyclone.

"No, this was slow. We have watched hundreds of years of alterations. Any place can change in a thousand years. God would not destroy all that we have built. I can see the forest dying off and maybe some of the mountains eroding, but not…"

"Imzuli's mountain? Where will she go to sleep?" Raimi asked in her pain. "A palace, that can be rebuilt anytime, but you cannot rebuild a mountain with her inside. She'll be crushed!"

Raimi felt Owailion trying to comfort her, shushing her while the grief and unknown nearly overwhelmed them both. "We'll ask at the conclave. Mohan will have some ideas. We cannot let them go to Sleep if that is what happens when they are not watching. They trust us as stewards. We will share this at the conclave. They will have to…"

Raimi shook her head, rejecting his notion. "Owailion, their instincts are already set. They can hardly stay awake right now. How will we do this on our own?" She barely could get the words out in a whisper. Fearfully she knew this vision was true. She had been born to the Land knowing something she did would go wrong. "We will have to get through this on our own."

Owailion sighed in regret. "Not again. We will never use the bowl to see the future."

"Don't swear that," warned Raimi. "A Wise One must keep their oaths. Someday we may regret everything we have ever done. It is a storm we will have to pass and somehow we will."

"But Mohan's right here. He'll know…How can we not tell?"

"How? Close your mind off," Raimi warned. "How do you think I've been able to keep it secret that Imzuli's mountain is gone? It's been hard, but I had to. We have to. They cannot know…know…how we fail."

"We will not fail," Owailion swore, and he wanted this oath to be binding.

Chapter 15

Midwinter

It was a much-muted pair of humans that arrived at the shore of Lake Ameloni the next day and stood on the diamond shore at dawn awaiting the call to Conclave. The winter settled overhead, frosty and cold but at least the stormy winter did not threaten to make the gathering buried in a blizzard. Raimi reached down to the stones on the shoreline and as Owailion recalled from his dream, she easily cut perfectly faceted gems of the rough stones with just a brush of her hand or by blowing away the stone dust. She picked up a dozen, breathed on them and then let them fall like snowflakes back onto the shore.

The dragons arrived one at a time and made themselves known by taking their place on the island's side with a roar and a mental greeting. Imzuli came and wanted immediately to ask for more examples of kissing, the most energetic thing she found interesting of late. Some things needed to remain private, so Raimi put her off. Neither human had fully processed the visions from the bowl. How did you speak with a dragon about what would happen in the future to Imzuli's mountain? Instead, they put on a brave face and spoke only privately with each other.

"What should we do about the priest? We haven't discussed it," he mentally whispered.

"The dragons will expect something grand," Raimi added, noting Imzuli's love of romance.

"I don't know," Owailion replied in like tones. "Perhaps we have a bonding like the dragons, without a priest but with them as witnesses. It is the only way we can do this. I don't dare return to Malornia and find another priest."

Raimi nodded her agreement and Owailion could hear her thoughts. Sometimes even when they did everything correctly it still did not work as expected. It had been her greatest fear from the beginning. All the things she touched would go wrong.

"No, my love, not this, this will not go wrong," Owailion tried to reassure her, dispelling the gloom, wishing magic could make it true.

Gradually the island filled with dragons and the sense of anticipation spread about the island felt thick enough to lift the malaise the humans felt. For the most part, the dragons looked forward with anticipation and excitement for this next adventure; the Sleep. They speculated loudly about dreaming as humans did and how the Land would change while they were unaware. Meanwhile, Raimi and Owailion kept their thoughts on the subject tightly behind their personal shields and clung to each other for comfort. They knew some of the answers to the dragon questions but did not want to share. The truth would put too much of a damper on the draconic enthusiasm.

As the dragon who had called for this conclave, Mohan took the top of the volcano's peak and opened the meeting formally. Owailion and Raimi remained far below on the shore, looking up into the winter sky to see him but that distance did not keep them from knowing precisely all that was discussed.

"*Thank you all for coming to this conclave. We have many things that must be accomplished at this time. First, we wish to introduce Raimi, the mate of Owailion. She is the second Wise One, the Queen of Rivers.*"

Raimi stepped forward and surged a little in her magic so that she put herself into her royal raiment, silver and a wintery gray that reflected the lake beyond her. In such finery, she fit in perfectly with the dragon magnificence and Owailion smiled in appreciation.

"Thank you for having me," she whispered mentally so the dragons could all hear her, even on the far side of the mountain.

"*Another one? Really, Mohan, is this truly necessary?*" Ruseval grumbled once again in typical fashion. "*Humans breed like rabbits. They'll take over and then when we reawaken, they will be everywhere. One human should be enough.*"

Owailion pulled Raimi back into his arms.

Mohan growled for quiet. "*That is not to be our decision. God has brought her here, but He has assured me that the Wise Ones cannot breed. Their magic is very controlled.*"

This was news to both Owailion and Raimi. No children? After all the other disappointments of the day before, this blow hardly rocked them. It had not been something they had discussed, but if God had declared it so, then who were they to grumble over another limitation. The Land would need their undivided attention apparently. Hopefully, that limitation would be enough to assure Ruseval, if anything could do so.

"*That said,*" Mohan continued, "*They have asked us to witness their union. They call a bonding a marriage. It is only for us to witness and welcome them as a pair. We have no say in their rights to bond. Now, Owailion where is your priest?*"

With a private prayer for his Wise One instincts to guide him, Owailion stepped forward and announced with regret his news. "The priest I approached to perform the marriage has been killed. Therefore, I suggest that we not endanger anyone else on our account. Instead, I request that we have a bonding, just as the dragons do and that the conclave is our witness."

Owailion found himself under the intense gaze of all the dragons, even the ones on the far side who took to the air to watch this event. He felt no fear at this; he had endured it before at his hatching. Instead, he funneled his calm toward Raimi. God was in charge and gave him exactly what they needed to say. Owailion surged magically and put himself into his royal clothing to match Raimi's. Then he turned to face her, holding her hands tightly in his. The words to speak came with inspiration.

"Under the eyes of God, I will love you and cleave to you alone for eternity," he swore, barely making himself heard, but the meaning rang through the skies. Then he pulled out his latest creation; the dream-crafted diamond she had given him months ago before she had even arrived in the Land. He had set it into a ring and now placed it carefully onto her finger.

Raimi's smile caught the light of the diamond as she replied. "And under the eyes of God, I will love you and cleave to you alone for eternity." She replied solemnly, trying and failing to keep the smile out of her water-laced voice.

And knowing they would only be setting the dragons all into a twitter, Owailion leaned down and kissed Raimi long and luxuriously.

The dragons could have watched them for hours as well, but thankfully they had other more important business to accomplish and once they got the hint that this kiss could last forever, the dragons turned to themselves and Owailion and Raimi ignored them.

The next order of business seemed to be the intricacies of the Sleep. The dragons spoke at length about how their eating habits had changed and how they suddenly found hollowing out their mountain homes very interesting.

"*Now it is time to share the Memories,*" Mohan's voice forced its way past the human's shields, deliberately interrupting in order to get his attention. "*Each of us has Memories to give Owailion before we sleep. Will you please join us at the mountain's top?*"

Owailion sighed. He had suspected something like this would be necessary but he had not wanted to mention it to Raimi and now he must leave her. The dragons had no concept of a honeymoon and this certainly would take some time. "I'll be back as soon as they let me. You might want to set up a camp," he advised Raimi, giving her a final kiss and then disappeared up into the presence of the dragons of the conclave.

Once more atop Mohan's neck, Owailion felt a strange sense of remorse. He would never witness this panorama again from this glorious height where it seemed he could see forever. He was already overwhelmed by the vista that spread out before him; the carpet of clouds, gleaming snow, and blindingly bright dragons scattered below him. And that view gave him assurance that the Sleep was immediate. Then Mohan's mind impinged on his, advising him, breaking through his melancholy with a dragon's hope.

"*Owailion, we must now share with you the Memory of the Land for you are God's chosen steward. You will feel the pains of the earth, the flow of the magic and the strength of the Seal in your mind. Each of us holds a piece of the Land's Memories, but it is held also by one who holds it all. Until now that has been me. God has assured me that you are capable to take it instead. You must live with this Memory; keep it alive and sacred. The Land is God's land. He has prepared it and protected it. You are to become its steward and defender. You must live with it as a joy, not a burden. Add to the Memory of the Land and it will grow more powerful. Share it with the other Wise Ones as they come but for now, you must take it and learn from it. Are you ready?*"

How could anyone be ready to absorb the memory of an entire continent? There was nothing to do to prepare except saying you were ready. Owailion assumed God would make him capable of whatever burden this entailed so he nodded his preparation. "Yes," he murmured.

Imzuli, as the youngest, went first, hovering out over the clouds and mist to make eye contact with him. Owailion watched in wonder as he felt his mind invaded by the silver and white dragon. As the youngest of the dragons she held the least but what hit his brain made him gasp. He felt crushed by the weight of mountains, many glaciers' worth of snow and gemstones. She remembered for him the pressure of water springing out of the stones and drawn down into the cracks of the earth, into the Don. She drowned him in the great nameless lake in the northeast and its ice and mists blinded him. He felt the deep chambers and trails through the mountains weave their way through the passages of his mind and his blood filled with ice water runoff. Owailion felt like he had aged a thousand years in the flash of one dragon's silvery eye.

Abruptly Imzuli finished with him and broke off the contact. Owailion groaned at the sudden severing of the connection. His eyes struggled to focus on a simpler panorama than an entire mountain range. The ponderous weight of it all settled like water in the hollow of his skull, dripping slowly. He tried to nod his head toward Imzuli but it hurt too much to move. Instead, he closed his eyes and then gulped as a second dragon took Imzuli's place and a new set of Memories washed over him. How long did this take? It felt like days for just one set of these draconic records to pour into his skull but the sun did not seem to move across the sky. It warmed his back as he now absorbed the gentle wave of wind over prairie grasses, hidden cisterns encrusted with crystals and the frantic cracks of canyons. He lost track of even his name in the picturesque passage of ages. Had he ever been human? Would he be a human again after seeing and sensing this all? Would he survive?

He couldn't even think to ask the question when the third wave hit.

* * *

Raimi walked through the fog on the beach, gathering stones, faceting them and then scattering them again among the raw gems. The day seemed to drag as she listened to the thunder and rumble high above in the cloud cover. The dragons had taken Owailion from her just minutes after they had been married and she resented that even more than being shut out. She felt shielded out of every mind above her on the island and struggled with irritation at it. She knew better than to try to listen in to what was happening. This was for Owailion, not her. He was the pioneer here, but to her surprise, she did not like being alone that much anymore.

To distract herself Raimi walked the entire island, looking for a place to set up a camp as Owailion had suggested. The still lake waters did not call to her nearly as much as a river did, but she still sensed something here that stirred her curiosity. A demon of the lake, or perhaps a ghost lived in the water here and she thought about harnessing its presence. Owailion had once tried to explain the feeling of something 'going demon' and she wasn't sure that was what she felt here but it demanded her attention.

And inspiration struck. Could she instead create a link to the presence inhabiting the lake to frighten diamond hunters away? Eventually, people would come to this island and see all the diamonds and covet them. This lake and its island were sacred to the dragons and therefore she did not want it to be pillaged. She didn't sense anything physical that she could manipulate into a Talisman as Owailion had done, but Raimi carefully experimented with the tenuous contact and persuaded the spirit there to speak with her.

She reached out and caressed the presence with her understanding of water. She sensed a massive dervish of power, throbbing within in the lake, waiting to swallow anything that strayed into the water. She tasted its ambivalent power and its rage at existing, without a purpose or structure, like a ghost stripped of its life but unable to move forward. Could she harness that? Recalling what Imzuli had taught her about linking this deep wishing magic to the Land itself, Raimi reached out to the ghost of the lake and washed it free of devious thoughts by imagining a river passing through the lake, scrubbing away the anger. Then she spoke with the presence and introduced herself.

"I am a Wise One of the Land. You are bound here, but I have a task for you. You must be the protector of this island. No humans may come here without knowing your anger. Shake the island and drive them off. Can you do that for me?" she asked as if she addressed a child.

The ghost's reply felt more like a canine grin and a wagging tail than an actual coherent answer. She sensed an eagerness to help, loyalty and devotion to her simply because of her notice. No one had ever sensed it here, waiting, swirling, tasting the silt and algae but nothing more. Now, since she had noticed, it would do her bidding. No one would walk the shores of the island of Ameloni without a threatening growl from the spirit of the lake. The ghost felt giddy at the opportunity to drive off all comers. Except her. It loved Raimi for asking, for noticing. That spirit would do anything for Raimi.

"Well, don't drive off Owailion or the dragons either. They are safe to let inside. You will be the Guardian of the Lake?" Raimi asked carefully and felt another wiggle of delight from the presence and then it settled back down into the depths of the lake, swirling but with purpose now to await any call to duty.

* * *

Two days later Raimi was frantic with worry for Owailion. In her impatience, she had turned thousands of gemstones into faceted, cut jewels. She paced the shores, watched the weather and worked a little on the parameters of a language spell but she could not concentrate enough to do it justice. She simply yearned for the end of the draconic interference and Owailion's return. The clouds had not lifted from the mountain top and she had not seen a single wing or tail in days. She knew Owailion lived, for she could sense a buzz of life but little else. The loneliness echoed in her head but every time she tried to touch his mind she felt gently but firmly pushed away, like an undertow. She could float and survive outside Owailion's mind but she would never make it past the inexorable tide around him.

She had camped and set a bonfire in front of her in a hopeless attempt to burn through the winter that reflected her mood. She felt a storm coming, blowing away the pervasive fog but not the cloud cover over the dragons to shield their doings on the volcano's peak. Then at dusk, with the gloom of the storm about to break overhead, Raimi looked up from the mesmerizing fire and saw Owailion standing on the other side of the flames; a statue in her eye but a blistering, burning mind across her thoughts. She bolted to her feet and caught him before he fell face-first into the flames.

"Owailion?" she gasped and lowered him down to the ground. His eyes were closed and his skin chill against the back of her hand. She lifted one eyelid and his dark eyes, unresponsive to the blinding of the firelight, stared back at her. Carefully she reached out mentally to hear his thoughts, for he made absolutely no effort to shield his brain. But in doing so she found herself underwater at the bottom of a great well. It was a good thing she could breathe underwater or she would have drowned.

Instead, Raimi pulled her mind free. "What have you done to him?" she asked of the invisible dragons and when they did not reply, she screamed it. "What have you done to him?!"

Finally, Mohan's gentle reply dripped with exhaustion and sincere love. "*We have given all to him. We will now sleep. Farewell.*"

So they were leaving, finally going into hibernation. Raimi realized she was the last witness. It was hard to dredge up the proper emotion to acknowledge what she knew to be true. With the abrupt departure, the artificial clouds overhead lifted and made room for the storm that slammed into the mountainside. It began burying her in the snow like a curtain fell and the act was over. She would grieve for her lost friends later.

Raimi instead clung to the need to tend to Owailion and be sure he recovered. His exhaustion made her bones ache. The very air around him shook with the mental weight of all he must have experienced. Without thinking about it Raimi conjured warm blankets and wrapped Owailion up like a baby. Then she tried to feed him some warm broth. He didn't actually respond to her but she was able to dribble a little in his mouth and he did not choke on it. Next, she redirected the tent she had been using to set over her head and then banked the fire, all while holding him tight as he shivered and moaned in his exhausted sleep.

All through the stormy night she held him, bathed his feverish face with cool water and whispered endearments. She dare not listen to the maelstrom that was his mind. The weather seemed to reflect his trials. Twice the tent almost blew away from over them but she held it firm with conjured river rocks and pure strength of will.

At dawn, the storm finally subsided into an eerie calm and Owailion fell into silent sleep as the winter's bite descended and the clear, bitter cold of a blue sky overhead penetrated the canvas. Raimi peeked out of the tent only once to look up at the snow-covered slope above her, completely bare of dragons. Then she allowed herself to rest as well, curled up against Owailion's exhausted body and they both slept at peace.

Chapter 16

To Name a Thief

Far later a caress woke Raimi. She felt warm and content, unwilling to open her eyes when she sensed Owailion moving a wayward strand of hair from her face. She opened her eyes at that thought and again almost drowned in the black of night in his eyes.

"Some honeymoon," he smiled down at her. The dark circles under his eyes spoke volumes toward his recovery still to come but his intense gaze insisted he was wholly with her now.

"How would we know," she replied. "I've not had a honeymoon yet…though I'm waiting patiently."

They never left the tent that day, nor the next, for neither felt inclined to break the spell of Ameloni Island. Owailion needed to rest and to settle the weight of the world between his ears. The dragons left them alone and empty and while the humans had dozens of questions about what was happening in the Land, nothing urgent enough to interrupt them came to mind. Storms fell on them again, nearly burying the tent but this hardly bothered the lovers. If they were snowed in until spring it didn't disturb them in the least.

As they lay back on the third day in the luxurious bed they had conjured within their tent Raimi finally garnered the nerve to ask what the dragons had done to him and Owailion seemed willing to reply.

"They gave me the Memories of the Land. I didn't know this before but they feel everything the Land feels like it was a living part of them.

Now I feel it too. No wonder they didn't need to have seen a place to be able to travel to it. I've felt it all; the birth of mountains, the slip of an avalanche down a slope, the formation and destruction of demons. I have lived it all. Do you realize that there have been thousands of attempts to break through the Seal over the years and two actually succeeded for a time? Anything that is felt or touched in the Land I sense it, like an itch, ache or burn in my own body."

"Isn't that overwhelming?" she asked as she tried to mask the concern in her voice.

"Frequently, yes...at least at first. Imagine if you had to remember every moment the mechanics of how to walk and concentrate on it or you'd fall over. That's how this feels. It takes time and I'm getting better at it but I still need to concentrate on what I'm sensing or I will be lost under the weight of it all. An entire library of information is hard to carry around in your head. Don't ask me to do too many things at once. I can't find anything in my brain because there's too much through which to sort."

Raimi smiled at the suggestion. "I'll only ask you to love me. Is that too much?"

"Never," he replied playfully and ran his hand down her back, making her think of water flowing. Then he continued. "I can tap into different things now and again; pick and choose whatever floats to the surface. Like right now there are four people on the southwestern border, exploring for a way to get inside, though they aren't sorcerers and have no hope. Do you realize Zema has grown another hand width? The new stones are big enough now for me to see that they don't bear the markings. I'm sure somewhere rattling around in my brain is a Memory of the writing on the original stones and I might be able to read them if I can just locate them in my head."

"But you do have them?" Raimi asked curiously, lifting herself onto her elbow to look into his well-deep eyes. "Are they in our language?"

"It's strange. I can't yet find the actual text in the Memory, just the realization that it is there somewhere. I know that it is an introduction to each of the sixteen Wise Ones; their affinities, weaknesses and some prophecies of what will happen, especially in their training, before they are . . . Seated? I guess that's the word I'd use. We should call them Seeking while a Wise One is still looking for his or her Talismans and learning how to be a magician. We can call them Seated once they've accomplished that goal."

Raimi shuddered and leaned up to look him in the eye. "You said something about prophecies of what will happen...like their future? That's dangerous, isn't it? Seeing the future has not been helpful to us," Raimi declared, reminding him of the awful visions from her Talisman.

"How is any of the Memory helpful? It might as well be Mohan's puzzle rock again. It just is," Owailion commented, and then changed the subject. "Mohan claimed that the thief was almost certainly one of the dragons in the conclave, but if that is so, that might be the one thing withheld from the Memories. Besides, I'm at a loss with what I am supposed to do with a dragon who is also a thief. It's not like I can throw a sleeping dragon into exile as they would."

"I thought you said that it was dragon business. Mohan didn't want to bring a bad reputation to their human interactions."

"It became human business the moment they gave me the Memories and stewardship over the Land. I believe the runestones were sold, and the transaction took place outside the Seal."

Raimi's brow furrowed. "Sold? For what? The dragons have...had no need for money."

Owailion sighed with growing distress in his voice. "Would you sell the stones in exchange for the ability to not give in to the Sleep? If one of the dragons did not want to go into hibernation, they could easily have asked an outlander sorcerer to help them stay awake. It would be easy enough, even with a Heart Stone, to simply pretend to go to sleep and with just two Wise Ones in this great big Land, we would hardly notice if they remained active. But while it would be a makeable bargain, how could a dragon be sure the sorcerer would not betray them?"

Raimi nodded understanding but then added, "Or that there are people who would make such a bargain. The dragons are...were so honest and straightforward, it would never occur to them that anyone would be so false. Do you think you could be able to learn who did it?" She felt chilled at the thought of any of the dragons seeking a deal to avoid a fate they did not like. It seemed so outside their thought process.

Owailion shrugged. "I could probably sift through the Memories until I discovered which one, but again, what would I do with that knowledge? I can't cast them in prison. They're far too powerful. Besides, sleeping is already a type of punishment, an exile."

Raimi thought about it and then remembered something Imzuli had taught her early on. "Name magic. You know all the dragon's names now don't you?"

Owailion nodded uncomfortably. "If I can pronounce them. What does that have to do with the price of the runestones?" he asked guardedly.

"Imzuli told me that if you know someone's true name then you can command that person- dragon or human-to do anything. They might fight it but in the end, even dragons have to obey you. You could wake them to ask if they stole the runestones."

Owailion's expression grew more troubled. "Mohan warned me about this name magic. He implied names held tremendous power. The details are somewhere in the Memories. And I certainly know the names of all the dragons, yet Mohan did not use that knowledge on the others to discover the thief. Perhaps there is a reason. It sounds as if name magic takes away free will. It would be evil…against the Heart Stone. You cannot take another person's free will away without it being an act of evil."

"Not if what you asked of them was not evil in the first place. Ask me…command me to do something. Let's see if it works. Something I would not do without a command but is not evil," she challenged.

Owailion's mind, left open for her to read, muttered at her about this disturbing new form of magic, and he sat up to concentrate. He deliberately explored the Memories and soon recognized that Mohan had not shared much of this with him because of its nature. Name magic was disturbing if misused, impure and evil otherwise. Owailion didn't know his own true name so he was never going to be in danger of being manipulated with name magic, but Raimi, coming to the Land with her name intact, did not bode well for her. Enok had warned him never to use her name again. Since then, they had done nothing to protect her name and had even shared it with all the dragons at the conclave.

"Raimi..." he could think of only one thing he could command her to do that would fit to test the name magic. He conjured a simple wedge of red cabbage. "I know you don't like it but eat this."

She shook her head, warily eyeing the cabbage; not her favorite. "No, you've got to be more forceful and tie my name to it."

He still didn't like it but Owailion tried again with slightly more conviction. "Raimi, eat this cabbage."

Her eyes grew wide and she snatched the slice of vegetable from his hand and began gnawing on it as if she were starving. "Raimi, stop!" he called in alarm.

"Blech!" she gasped. "Oh, that was horrible," Raimi dropped the offending vegetable.

"The cabbage or the name magic?"

"Both," she shook her head and made the awful cabbage disappear. "It feels like you have no choice. I didn't think, oh, goody, cabbage. I didn't think at all. I didn't even feel as if you were commanding me. That's ...that's..."

"Evil, like I said. The Heart Stone didn't block me but it still feels terribly wrong to use it even in a benign sense. Mohan didn't teach me to use name magic for a reason. A Wise One should not use it."

Raimi nodded, now more thoughtfully. "I agree, but what if it is used against us? All the dragons know my name and it would be wrong to strip it from them now even if we could figure out how," she pointed out.

Owailion shifted uncomfortably and looked over at his wife, trying to find a way to ease her fear while dissipating his own. "We must find out who sold those stones. We'll talk to any of the dragons who are awake. They can't all have gone to sleep in an instant. And I'll take the time to think through these Memories and see if I can identify who took the rune stones. If they would sell the stones, they might be willing to use your name. Finally, we need to give you another name, something less dangerous. When other humans come as we foresaw, you'll be safer that way."

"It will be a lie," she pointed out the obvious. "Wise Ones can't lie."

"Hello, you may call me Owailion," he replied simply even though he didn't know what his real name might have been. "It is what you can honestly say."

Raimi sighed and he could hear her trepidation well as resolve. "Very well, if that's the best we can hope for, we should start investigating soon. I have no doubt it will get difficult to find any dragon awake soon."

A week later he had to admit that Raimi was right. Every mind Owailion touched among the dragons was profoundly asleep and he still wasn't comfortable with using name magic to awaken them. He did this exploring work sitting in the center of the foyer of the nearly completed palace at Paleone. He wasn't concentrating on the palace itself. He left that to Raimi who worked on the gardens, despite it being winter. Instead, he was wandering through the Memories, assessing how the complete knowledge of a thousand-year-old dragon could possibly be rolling around in his head and how he could manage to pull one thought, one idea, one act out of all that time. He decided to focus on the one dragon that had expressed dislike of humans in the first place; Ruseval. The green dragon seemed the most likely candidate to want to take the rune stones, but what was his motive?

"You know," Raimi suggested carefully a week after they arrived at Paleone when Owailion came out of his meditation long enough to eat something, "it would be faster if you simply asked them instead of searching the Memories for their plotting. They withheld their theft from the Memories when they knew they would eventually be sharing with you. With name magic, you'll get a reaction to your questions at the least. Make some excuse... oh, visit them and ask each one to hold a future Talisman for you. You're going to have to hide them…including that set of pipes you still won't show me."

Owailion smiled secretively. He had been carrying the pipes for so long he had probably misplaced them at the bottom of his bag, forgotten and neglected, but he still had no inspiration on where to hide them. They were like her palace, still waiting for the spark of an idea that would guide him on how to conceal them. Why would God give him ideas for everything else he needed to do but nothing when it came to Raimi's palace or Talismans? Most puzzling.

"Oh, very well," he relented. "I'll go talk to them. It probably would be nice to be sure they're all settling in now. You'll be safe here alone?"

"You'll come back?" she asked coyly, reminding him of what he would miss if he didn't come back nightly. It was almost like they lived there at Paleone. It was a roof over their heads and had heat, many soft beds to choose from, a kitchen and everything they could desire.

Owailion chuckled with her teasing, rose and gave Raimi a kiss before he disappeared, headed toward a Memory. He elected to start where he left off; with Ruseval. Owailion knew where the green dragon's mountain was, midway down the Great Chain just southwest of Lake Ameloni, up against the southern plains that had been his responsibility. Owailion had not made an orb of the place but the Memories provided the locale and he arrived on the glacier-covered slope in the bitter cold and immediately crafted a bubble of warmth around himself, for he knew this discussion was going to be long and he suspected, tiresome.

"Ruseval, are you awake?" he asked aloud, not bothering to project, just like when he spoke with Mohan.

"*?*" came the distinct impression of some awareness, though the mind behind it sounded terribly sluggish.

"It's Owailion," the human announced, pressing his words into the dragon's mind. "I'm sorry to disturb you but I am asking all the dragons to do something for me…make a deal with me."

Owailion hoped that the word 'deal' would resonate somehow with the dragon, bringing an image of another deal to mind, but Ruseval's sleepy brain remained stony. "*I'd rather make a deal with a demon. At least from them, you can expect to have treachery and can prepare. You humans are all bluster and no faithfulness. Leave me be," he ordered.*

Owailion sighed with regret before he tried the inevitable. "Rusevalnamik, have you made a deal to give the runestones to another?" Owailion had hoped to not use name magic, but now it seemed necessary. He would never get a frank answer from the irascible dragon otherwise.

The grumble echoed right through the mountainside. "*No, I have made no deals. Now go before I roast you.*"

At least the dragon was honest, Owailion noted, and not the least alarmed that his true name had been invoked. Accordingly, the human made a hasty retreat and pulled himself to Mohan's mountain, farther west. In the interest of being equal to all the dragons, Owailion decided to approach Mohan next. Besides, he needed to hear a friendly voice.

And he was very concerned. Was the gift of premonition part of the Wise One magic? If so he still sensed something would go wrong with regard to those rune stones. Owailion did not want his friend and mentor to feel that he had only been able to handle the stewardship for a few days and now was already seeking advice like a green boy, fearful of making a mistake. Already he had violated a trust; using name magic to find answers he could not achieve elsewhere. But he knew that Mohan would want to know and would care. It seemed petty that he was concerned that someone might be misusing Raimi's name, but there were other lurking issues besides a thief. What had become of the stones? Who would destroy Imzuli's mountain? What could devastate the Lara delta? How had humans, non-magical men, made it past the Seal? How did they stop Zema regrowing its lost stones and letting in demons? How could someone kill Enok just after Owailion had discovered him? All these questions lingered as if connected in Owailion's mind and he wanted the answers. Besides, he missed his friend.

"Mohan, are you there?" he whispered, hoping he wasn't intruding. No one liked being awakened in an untimely fashion, even the dragons who had absolutely no experience with it.

An echoing silence sank in Owailion's mind like he had landed in the well of Memories again. "Mohanzelechnekhi?" he called again, this time managing the full name with relative ease. "Can you hear me?"

The reply seemed to come from far away as if the dragon had already fallen into deep dreams of distant places. "*Owailion? Is that you?*"

"It is," the Wise One answered. "There is a serious problem here and...and I need a friend's wisdom. The dragon who took the rune stones...we believe he or she has sold them in a corrupt deal. We have foreseen vast destruction for the Land and the breaking of the Seal. The only magic that could have done this awful thing is... We believe it is name magic. Up till now, Raimi has not hidden her name. It is hers, from birth. Could...would a dragon use name magic against her?"

The distance between them again seemed to stretch and Owailion got the distinct sense that his friend was no longer in the Land. Had he left? If so, how? Owailion's gaping fear nearly swallowed him. Was Mohan dying instead of falling asleep?

"*No, my friend. There is another duty we dragons of the Conclave have been called to do. I am like you, the first. I have left to do as God bids me...on a new planet. The others of the Conclave will eventually follow; those that are humble enough to come. Perhaps not the thief.*"

"And you have no idea of who it is?" Owailion asked desperately, swallowing an effort to wish away the whole terrible situation, go back in time and start Raimi's life in the Land in a bubble of careful protections.

Mohan sighed with regret. "*I have asked and investigated, but have found few answers. In the Memories, can you read the writings? Perhaps they speak of this.*"

"It is too small and dim to read," Owailion replied with regret. "Right now I have no time for such puzzles when I have Raimi's name weighing on my mind. The actual words on the stones aren't worth the worry. I'm more concerned about who would sell them. Anyone willing to cast the stones away would also be capable of selling Raimi's name."

"*And you say you foresee great destruction in the Land, and the Seal was broken?*" Mohan prompted.

"Yes, the Don Forest is... will be gone. Imzuli's mountain is a hollow and the entire delta area of the Lara River is a flattened swamp. It's unrecognizable."

"*And when is this supposed to happen?*" Mohan asked. "*How were you made aware of this destruction?*"

"Do you recall the bowl I made for Raimi? It is a Talisman that shows not only the past but also the future. We looked to the future, asking to see how the Land would change during our stewardship and that's when we saw it. We also witnessed there were colonists and villages all over the Land so we know the Seal is also broken."

Mohan sighed audibly through the connection and Owailion could not tell if it was the exhaustion or grief. "*Then I would confront Imzuli. Her mountain's loss might be her bitter consequence for this foolishness. She is the one who loves humans more than me. She is the youngest, most excited to see the world. Perhaps Imzuli did not want to go to Sleep. She did not know...*" Mohan's tone faded as he fell into deep mourning.

Owailion knew family ties meant very little in the dragon world but surely this was a father worried for his daughter. "I will speak with her and try to see how I can mitigate the situation," Owailion promised. "I hope it is not her, for your sake."

"*For the Land's sake,*" Mohan amended and his mental voice faded away as he broke the connection.

Owailion opened his eyes and stared out at the mountains around him. He did not want to believe Imzuli would sell the stones or give Raimi's name to another magician but he had to confront that possibility. Should he tell Raimi of these suspicions? In a way, he was grateful that Mohan suspected Imzuli. The white dragon would never sell Raimi's name, no matter how many temptations she had entertained. Perhaps the depression Imzuli had felt was due to regret at what she had done. But how would he question Imzuli about this? How could he be gifted to help protect the Land if there was nothing to do to make this better? Nothing.

Owailion waited, hoping some Wise One insight would fall into his mind but nothing came other than to return to Paleone and tell his wife that her best friend might have betrayed them. With that in mind, he felt the tug of his love for Raimi. She was Queen of Rivers. Perhaps she could wash away the past and that was what he wanted right then most of all.

* * *

Raimi watched Owailion go to speak with the dragons and felt a sense of hopelessness. Why did she have the premonition that name magic and the runestones would be their undoing? Was the bowl Talisman supposed to show the future or had she manipulated it? Well, she intended to find out. Deliberately she set aside her landscaping plans and turned to her Talisman bowl. She wanted to see again the moment those rune stones had been stolen. Perhaps the bowl could show what the natural eye could not see.

Raimi sat on the cold marble floor of the kitchen at Paleone, ignoring the lack of a few amenities like chairs for a table. Instead, she sat cross-legged, tucked her skirts in under herself and filled the bowl magically from the water of her memory. She stilled her mind at the same time as the water steadied and then concentrated on what she wanted to see. "Show me the minutes before and after the Zema standing stones disappeared from the Land.

Unexpectedly the image resolved to a warm summer sky overhead and not to the forest at Zema. Instead, the sea swelled, changing Raimi's perspective. More alarming, she saw a ship. It boasted three masts and was manned by a few dozen men, all working hard to bring the vessel into a mooring spot, transitioning from ocean to river. They dropped anchor and waited just outside the Seal and the main flow of the river; the Don River if Raimi's instincts told her properly. How had this changed from the Zema forest? This wasn't the same view of when and where the stones were stolen.

Then the image lifted and a dragon wheeled out of the sky, silver, and white, blinding the men in the bright sunlight. Imzuli alighted delicately on the bowsprit, keeping her wings spread so that she could rise again instantly if the sailors proved dangerous. Raimi felt her hand trembling and she almost dropped the bowl in her shock. Imzuli would not have done this, surely. Give her the benefit of the doubt, advised a little voice in Raimi's head.

Thankfully, in the empty stone kitchen, Raimi could easily hear the men aboard the ship. The captain and a robed man, probably a sorcerer, walked solemnly to the bow to speak with the dragon while the rest of the crew cowered beyond the wheelhouse. "Welcome, Lady Imzuli," the sorcerer called, as if the dragon could not hear his every thought.

"*Stylmach,*" Imzuli addressed the man, "*Were you able to read the stones then?*"

The sorcerer acknowledged the name with a bow and then replied. "Your curiosity does you credit. If the images you shared with me are true, they speak of sixteen guardians of the Land. They will come and protect the Land when...and it says this on the stones...when the dragons leave the Land in Sleep. I have interpreted that to mean the dragons will die."

Imzuli growled and Raimi, just watching this little scenario in the Talisman's surface growled with her.

"*I very much doubt that,*" Imzuli replied imperiously. "*I require the entire translation and then I will agree that you have fulfilled your part of the deal.*"

Without much of a fanfare, the captain held out a rolled-up scroll and unfurled it. Stylmach began to read aloud. Raimi listened to the prophecy, enraptured and yet terrified. All the Wise Ones, their future, and powers laid out for a sorcerer to hear. No wonder the outlanders were so determined to break into the Seal and acquire the magic of the Land. The Wise Ones would be glorious, powerful and the Land would thrive under their gentle hands. They were not to be rulers but stewards and guides.

Finally, when Stylmach ended his recitation he looked up at the dragon. Imzuli stared down at the parchment with an intent eye and it dissolved into ash.

"*Very well, the stones are yours then,*" the dragon announced and a thunderous weight of granite appeared on the mid-deck space, evenly placed so as to not capsize the fragile boat.

"Surely there is more we can do for you, Lady Imzuli?" the sorcerer asked with a barely contained smile, desperate to continue the business dealings with the young dragon.

"*I doubt that, as well,*" the white dragon replied in a cool tone. "*I was only curious. Now the human has arrived and I shall not need your services again.*"

"Oh?" called Stylmach as Imzuli lifted free from the ship's bow. "Perhaps we can meet these new ones? Or I can help you avoid your fate. I only wish to be of help."

Imzuli looked down from higher than the masts now. Her regal glare spoke full well how little she trusted this sorcerer. "*I'm sure the Wise Ones will meet you one day, Stylmach, and you will regret it to your dying day…as humans often do die as well.*"

As if desperate to keep Imzuli's attention he tried once more to bargain with her. "*I can guarantee you a way to not die,*" shouted the sorcerer as he watched his dragon leaving him, flying back through the unseen barrier of the Seal.

But Raimi had been bidden the bowl only to show when the stones had left the Land, not how Imzuli might have answered. Raimi's hands could no longer bear to hold the vessel and she dropped it, spilling water all across the marble floor of Paleone. She could not move, could not think. She wanted only to freeze and make that vision go away. How could her friend betray the Land in such a way?

At that moment Owailion reappeared, standing before her. They looked at each other and in tandem spoke one word.

"Imzuli."

Chapter 17

Night of Dreams

Since they had both come to the same conclusion in different ways and for separate reasons, they felt the need to share, as if this way they could split their grief over what they had learned. They spoke quietly as if someone might overhear them.

"But taking the stones does not necessarily mean she shared your name as well," Owailion qualified. "I cannot imagine Imzuli would ever betray us. Only weeks later she was your escort and not once did she harm you. We need to speak to her."

Raimi's voice froze like ice. "How? She's asleep…hopefully."

Owailion gently comforted his wife. "They are all asleep, preparing to travel to a new world as we did. That is all. Mohan assured me of that."

Raimi sighed with regret dripping from word. "I couldn't bear to confront her about this. She knows my name. Perhaps she was just foolish and young, curious. Maybe that was why she was so gloomy toward the end. Now that I look back at it, when we were approaching Zema was when she grew so aloof. It makes sense now."

"The clearest path is the one behind us," Owailion replied.

"And the one ahead is darkest," his wife added. "If we challenge her actions, won't she defend herself? Can we find some other way to make sure she didn't sell my name? I don't know whether to be sad or angry."

Owailion, in his deepest heart, wanted to wait to speak with Imzuli as well, but he also knew it was foolish to ignore the possibility of betrayal. "I can justify letting all the dragons go to sleep and see if Imzuli had joined them. I'll put a sensor of some kind on her mountain to see if anything has changed there."

"I already did," Raimi admitted miserably.

"I suppose, technically Imzuli has done nothing wrong except in judgment; giving the stones away for an interpretation of them seems a silly motive for endangering the Land. It benefits no one; not the dragons, not the Wise Ones and it remains to be seen how it will influence the outlander sorcerer who purchased them. Very well," he sighed, finally acknowledging that his Wise One instinct held no answers for him. "We will let sleeping dragons lie and see what happens."

Raimi nodded in relief.

And so Owailion reluctantly went back to building palaces as if nothing alarming hovered in the back of his mind. He asked Raimi to continue landscaping the palaces and seeking for her second Talisman even though she knew exactly where it was at the moment; still in Owailion's bag. And together both of them would seek some way to make sense of what Imzuli had done and hope she had not done more. Without actually discussing it, they mutually agreed to never look in the bowl again for fear of what they might see; an image too horrible to contemplate.

Owailion began work on the palace at the mouth of the Don River during the winter and named it Waild, after the draconic word for forest. He then moved on up the river to the palace meant for the base of the Great Chain. This one, animal-themed, he named Fiain after the dragon's word for animals. Occasionally he would even travel to Zema to witness for himself the strange eerie growth of new stones, like fingers stretching out of the ground. He never sensed any of the demons that must have come through the portal. The new stones now stood almost waist-high in the barren circle. Still, he dare not check on the dragons, for he had not reached the mountains quite yet. He justified his delay with reluctance in disturbing them. And each night he returned to Raimi who remained at Paleone finishing the gardens there.

Finally, at the cusp of spring Paleone was completed, the first of the sixteen palaces of the Wise Ones.

"Can you seal it?" Owailion asked his wife after she called him back to inform him of the final details. He transitioned back to Paleone and they stood just outside the fortress walls, peering up into the stormy sky at the blue banner that snapped in the wind. "You have been more successful with seals than I have."

"Deep magic," Raimi confirmed. "She said we had to ground it in the earth itself, not in ourselves. The roots of the earth can take the strain and blows that will descend on it."

Her words, as she set them to action, sent a shiver down Owailion's spine. This palace would indeed take blows and attacks. He might not have the gift of premonition but he knew to his deepest bones that Paleone would be assaulted.

Nothing changed in Owailion's perception as he heard Raimi sigh with completion of that final task. "It is done," she whispered.

Accordingly, Owailion reached out, almost touching the alabaster wall defending the courtyard, but his hand met an invisible resistance. "That is amazing, my love. You have a gift with this deep magic," he murmured, fascinated how her magic had developed, so differently from his and just as powerful.

"I have a gift with dams," she corrected. "And dams can be broken. You know I don't feel that I… All I touch will somehow go awry. Please do not trust that Paleone is safe."

Owailion looked from his wife to the spire again and noted that the banner no longer snaked across the late winter sky, now encased in a bubble of timelessness where even the sea wind could not reach it. "I trust you have done the best that can be done. It is enough."

Unfortunately that night they spent in a tent once again, since even they were sealed out of Paleone. Owailion had not expected to dream, for he had not found a new palace to build, but something stirred his mind and he paid attention. He found himself back again in Malornia, walking toward the church where Enok, his lost door steward had served. This time, instead of feeling merely unsafe, dozens of demons seemed to stalk him, passing through the shadows of the buildings around the square as he passed through the town. The trees and ivy lining the walls of the church teemed with crickets and bats that swelled and spoke in human voices that gave him shivers down his spine. In the dream Owailion was bound to make the doors of the church, hoping for sanctuary. He staggered on the slime of a dozen slug/fish demons coating the stairs. Owailion grasped at the door latch, swatting away the snakes that coiled around the knocker. With relief, he wrenched the door open and slipped inside.

The interior of the humble church felt cool, clean and dark, belying the light that streamed through its dirty windows, but Owailion felt safe from all the evils lurking outside. He let his eyes adjust to the new environment and looked around for Enok even though his sleeping mind knew that the priest was dead and would not be here.

And yet, he was. The old man, wearing his threadbare robes slipped out of the shadows and greeted Owailion like a brother. "I'm glad you have come, King of Creating. It has been difficult to reach you."

"Reach me?" Owailion asked, suspecting a trick.

"Yes," replied the priest. "You know that I have been killed but I have one more message…something you must know. Your Lady's Talisman cannot warn you. She is in danger. The ones who killed me, they had been watching this place and they know." Enok looked around in the shadows of the chamber as if he feared being overheard even in this dream.

"They know what?" Owailion encouraged. "Who are you talking about?"

Enok fixed his great gray eyes on him and then leaned close, with his hand around Owailion's arm like a vice. "Your Lady, the Queen of Rivers…they know her name. Keep her away from the Seal. Please do not trust that she is safe."

Those had been almost the same words she had spoken at the sealing of Paleone. Owailion felt himself jolt awake with shock, but a word came out with his waking.

"How?"

Owailion could not force himself to fall back asleep, no matter how he tried, to find his answers. He lay awake for the remainder of the night, curled up against Raimi who slept on, oblivious to the horror her husband felt covering him, like all the demons that had stalked him to the church in his dream now had come to coat him in a cold slime of dread. Raimi was in danger.

* * *

Raimi also slept restlessly, but on the surface, she barely stirred as she dreamed of water, but not of rivers or streams. Instead, she drifted in the ocean, far from land. This did not distress her, but she could not remain there treading water, trying to see above the crests of the waves. Then she spied something to the south, coming out of the lowering sun. A ship.

Without recourse, Raimi began to swim toward the distant vessel and with magically enhanced strokes she arrived at its gunwales in minutes. She did not ask permission, but latched on and pulled herself aboard. To her surprise she came over the rail in her royal gown, gold and river blue with copper, silver and gold lilies stitched all down the bodice and not a hair out of place under an ornate crown even though she swam all the leagues to arrive on an empty ship.

She looked about the deck and up into the canvas sails, set to full and no one to tend them. The rigging creaked in the wind and the ship must have been making good time. Yet the wheel spun free, shifting with the current. With little understanding beyond her instincts, Raimi reached out and grasped the wayward wheel.

"Thank you for coming, Raimi."

She whirled around and saw a simple man whose appearance tickled at a memory, perhaps from her forgotten past. He was short and somewhat rugged and simple, with dark eyes and an arrogant jutting jaw. Where had he come from? She would have noticed him approaching on this bare deck.

"Who are you, sir?" she asked, feeling little fear, for this was just a dream.

"You may call me Stylmach," the man replied and then approached, putting his hand on the wheel opposite hers. Then he began to turn the wheel, heading east of the sun. "I have called you here to talk to me, Raimi. Tell me about yourself."

Something in Raimi's dream-self began writhing in alarm. This was wrong. She felt no fear of the stranger or the ship so far from land. No, her dread came from the realization that she wanted…no, needed to speak with this stranger. She could not place from where this urgency sprang but it bubbled up like water struck from stone with alarming thoroughness; a river began. She could not resist.

"I know so little sir, but I…I am a pioneer of the Land. I do not know much else, for I came to the Land with amnesia."

"Really? You speak the truth, I see. Very well, tell me about the Land instead," Stylmach insisted and then added, "Raimi, tell me all you know."

She felt her spine stiffen in alarm. She opened her mouth to scream herself awake, calling for Owailion but she felt her breath stolen and Stylmach's gloved hand reached toward her and carefully, caressingly curled around her throat, stealing her voice.

"Raimi, you will not call for help. You will not perform any magic against me. Raimi, you will be mine and when you waken, you will forget everything that has transpired here in your dreams. I will be your master and you will do all that I command. Raimi, you will do this, won't you."

Frozen so she could not even pull away from his leathery grasp, she managed a single dry swallow before she whispered a single, fateful reply.

"Yes."

* * *

Owailion made breakfast over a campfire, conjuring only the barest needs; eggs and a frying pan. He stared at the flames as if intent on his efforts but the fire hypnotized him and he almost burnt breakfast before Raimi stirred and he could stop. He barely looked at her for fear he would remember Enok's words every time she moved across his vision. She seemed distracted too so he did not disturb her and did not comment on her slow waking. He wanted only her peace and nurtured it.

"Tamaar," Raimi opened, as she took the plate Owailion passed to her. "I suppose I need to start work there."

Now Owailion looked at Raimi more closely. The dark circles under her eyes and the lackluster voice worried him. She doubted herself too much, he knew, but now she seemed almost lethargic or was that Enok's warning making him suspicious of every expression that passed across her sweet face. Was she tired or sick? Could a Wise One even get sick?

Owailion shook off his worries and replied to her implied question. "Yes, and I want to give Tamaar something. I have a Talisman in need of a hiding place and this would be a perfect time. I made this horn a few weeks ago from a mountain goat blending with a tree and it needs a home. I'll give it to Tamaar and get her to let you in at the same time."

He pulled a twisted signal horn Talisman out of his pack and handed it over to Raimi. She slowly smiled at its polished beauty. No, he thought, she's just tired.

"It looks like mother-of-pearl," she commented in appreciation. "For whoever is the King or Queen of the Sea?"

"Probably the sea." Owailion was grateful for the distraction and so encouraged it. "Tamaar is a sea dragon so it makes sense. She is also Imzuli's mother. Maybe she'll have some insight into what we should do."

"Good," Raimi added, sounding more resolute. "I also want to ask her about how she seals off her territory. She is better at it if she can bring it down and back up again. It might be important to understand that."

After breakfast and a quick shift via one of Owailion's memory orbs, they stood at the Invader's Cliff and Owailion placed his hand against Tamaar's shield around her territory while Raimi held the horn. "Tiamat," he called, invoking the sea dragon's true name. "We need to speak with you. Are you awake? Please hear us."

"She was the only dragon to seal off her territory," Raimi commented as they waited for a response. "I wonder why."

"Yes," Owailion confirmed. "You should also talk to her about her truth spell. She's the expert on your deep, long-lasting spells. She might even be able to help with the language spell."

Raimi nodded, but Owailion could sense her latent doubt in her ability. Rather than dwell on that, he renewed his call to the dragon. "Tiamat, wake up. We need to speak with you."

"*Go away,*" they heard in triple tone as each of Tamaar's heads snarled at them. "*We have a right to sleep.*"

"Yes, but you have to wake up to let us in. We need to put the finishing touches on that palace and I want to ask you to hold onto a Talisman for me," Owailion insisted.

Tamaar sounded peeved. "*Just you and Raimi? No dragons or other sorcerers?*"

Owailion smiled over at his wife as he replied, "No, we're alone. Rai…my Lady will be staying to work on the gardens, but that should only take a few weeks and she won't disturb you. Can we come in?"

They heard a long-suffering trio of sighs but they also sensed the seal around Tamaar lowered and they could pass through. As soon as they crossed the unseen barrier they felt it rise again behind them like a trap. Owailion shifted them to the nearly completed palace on the southern coast and showed his wife around the grand mansion for a few minutes. Finally, he sat down on one of its many terraces along the cliff to look out to sea. From there he began an awkward conversation with the sea dragon while Raimi began to plan the extensive gardens that would be involved in a cliff-side mansion.

"Tamaar, you have not truly gone to sleep yet, have you?" Owailion began, giving voice to his curiosity about the process.

"*We have responsibilities that are not easy to set aside,*" the dragon groused. "*It is difficult to stay on guard, even one head at a time. The shield around Tamaar is important and we do not know if it weakens after we drift off. One head must always remain awake. It is like going into deep, unexplored waters.*"

"I can understand that," Owailion replied. "Why don't you let me maintain the shield? I can do that for you and then perhaps you will sleep better."

He only got a non-committed grumble.

"Well, consider it an open invitation. Also, I need you to know that eventually there will come a Wise One who will need access to this territory and will not be able to wake you. She is the Queen of the Sea. You must not block her out. If you do, there will be incomplete protection over the Land as a whole," he warned.

"*Is that a threat, human?*" Tamaar replied in the most fearsome tone he had ever heard from any dragon, even Ruseval.

"No," he replied carefully. "This Wise One will be a compliment to your power. She will..." He waited for a moment, feeling the inspiration that accompanied that Wise One statement, "She will have your name. She also will be named Tiamat and that will be how she will find you." He tried to reassure the dragon even as he wondered where that qualification had come from.

"Well, anyway, it would be nice if you would let her in and trust her when she comes. To that end, I have something for you to give to her. You know all the Wise Ones are going to seek these Talismans. To find and approach you will be a formidable task. She must come to Seek you out for this Talisman. If she does so, will you let her in and acknowledge her right to live in the palace?"

Owailion held the horn out into the air. He had no idea where the sea dragon actually was physically but handing an arm-length horn to her would be impossible anyway. By sheer size, Tamaar would have a difficult time holding it. He waited patiently for the dragon to respond, taking it from him magically. He could hear Tamaar's reluctance, dripping with annoyance and was tinged by fear of the unknown. Then, with an almost audible huff, the horn disappeared from his grasp.

Owailion dusted off his hands as if that duty was done and he moved on to another. "Finally, I have one more piece of business, and I don't know how to make this..."

"*Humans are silly, you know,*" Tamaar interrupted. "*They are so worried about the feelings of others that they aren't worried about the truth when it needs to be said.*"

Owailion cleared his throat and then as admonished, blurted out his uncomfortable message. "Imzuli stole the runestones and gave them to an outlander sorcerer," he said quickly, mentally, unwilling to bring the words out into the open where they seemed more real to him.

For a long while, dead silence echoed from Tamaar's cavern. He could imagine the wheels turning behind the rigid shields of the three-headed dragon as she thought through this accusation. Finally, the dragon lowered her shields enough to speak to him again.

"*Show us,*" she ordered flatly.

Owailion obliged reluctantly, pressing the images he had seen in Raimi's bowl into the minds of the dragon. Tamaar absorbed it and added it to whatever she had contemplated privately behind her shield. Only then did Tamaar comment.

"*That hatchling has too much of her father in her. Curiosity does not become her. What will you do to address this?*"

Owailion rocked back in surprise. He had thought – no, hoped and prayed - that the dragons would take Imzuli's consequences under their purview. "Me....I...I had not thought to do anything. She's a dragon, not a human. There is nothing I can do to discipline her and no harm was really done unless the sorcerer who bought them can use them for mischief. We were more concerned that she ...if she is willing to sell the stones, what more might she try to sell?"

Tamaar's grumble grated on his mind. "*Sell? We do not understand this word 'sell'.*"

Owailion explained carefully. "Humans sell one thing for something they want more; their labor for food, something they have made for something they cannot make for themselves. In this case, Imzuli sold the stones for a translation of what was written on them. We fear she might not want to go into the Sleep and was willing to sell… to sell Raimi's name to a sorcerer that could prevent her from falling asleep."

After a long thought, Tamaar asked another question. "*Have you asked her about this?*"

"We have little evidence of such wrongdoing. Would not her Heart Stone prevent her? I have no wish to accuse anyone, especially with so little evidence. You know her far better than I do. How will she react to such an insinuation?"

Tamaar did not reply immediately and Owailion could not even sense her shields activated. Perhaps she had fallen back asleep. But when she did break her silence, Tamaar's mental voices spoke in an eerie tandem.

"*You are the stewards of the Land now. When you address this, do not inform us. We will sleep now.*"

With that dismissal, Tamaar shut Owailion out of her mind.

* * *

Raimi sat on the sheer cliff just outside the walls of the opal palace, looking down into the turquoise waters of a narrow bay and thought deeply about what she needed to do here. The gardens meant little and actually required only a small sliver of her attention. Instead, she hoped to explore the shields that she would craft around each palace. After studying Tamaar's shield that sank into the seafloor just feet beyond the cliff on which she sat, Raimi felt she could make a better, more substantial shield than the one she had attempted at Paleone.

She also wondered how she could craft these shields so that the true owner of each home would be able to get inside. It seemed a problem more troubling than the seals themselves. She meditated on the problem, basking in the warm jungle air despite the wintery sun outside Tamaar's seal. In her hands she held the Talisman bowl, empty of water and let her mind pass through the earth, like the water that ate away mountains and always sought its way free to the oceans. She became the rivers and streams, cleaned by the movement and focused only on the needs of the future. And despite the bowl was empty she began to see a vision.

Alarmingly it displayed not the past, but some unknown future and Raimi longed to open her eyes so the vision would stop. But she was no longer in charge of the deep magic. Instead, she knew God guided her mind now. "*If you seal the palaces, I will provide a door steward to open them. Each Wise One must Seek until they find. Find the one who will open the seal for them,*" chanted the comforting voice in her mind.

Raimi gasped as a panorama of figures flashed through her mind: gentlewomen, mighty men, an eagle, a ghost, a fairy, and even a phoenix passed through her mind like flashes on the water, with barely any time to register behind her eyes. *"These I will make the door stewards like Owailion's Enok. They hold the keys to break the seals. The Wise ones must Seek,"* the voice reiterated and then faded.

With a wrench, Raimi came to herself and felt how the sun had shifted to the far side of the bay as she had concentrated on her deep spell, but now she knew. If she set the seals, the stewards would come as God prepared them. Each would be tied to a Wise One as a loyal companion, devoted to their one queen or king, an immortal and steady friend, meant to serve. Were they even real? Raimi did not know, but she had answers enough. As she knew waters would always flow and eventually meet the sea, so she would have faith that this too would come to fruition.

Yet having successfully created another deep magic spell, Raimi felt little accomplishment. Perhaps she still carried the fears that her magic would cause bad long term effects on those she loved. Perhaps her lingering sense of melancholy stemmed from Owailion's departure. Since she was staying within Tamaar's shield to work on the palace gardens her husband was not free to come to visit her every night and so for the first time since her arrival in the Land Raimi was essentially alone for extended spaces of time. Either way, she had plenty to occupy her time during the days. This palace did not require the stone pathways and strong walls that Paleone did but instead, it dripped with hanging gardens suitable to the tropical seashore it occupied, and this kept Raimi's mind active during the daytime.

However, at night she dreamed with alarming vividness. Owailion had warned her that dreams for a Wise One were important, especially if you remembered them. Owailion often wakened with a perfect design for a palace dripping out of his mind and had shared these stunning images with her so she appreciated why he understood exactly how to build each grand mansion. Raimi's dreams, up until now, came hazily, as if through deep water and the imagery all seemed symbolic.

Now alone in the Tamaar palace Raimi slept in one of the glorious, open rooms with a balcony that looked out over the deep turquoise bay and that water somehow made it into her dreams. A three-mast ship had drawn close into the narrow harbor and dropped anchor just beyond the Seal. In her mind's eye, it was the same vessel from Imzuli's bargain but without a soul aboard. Instead, Raimi just heard a voice in her head.

"Raimi, are you there?" She seemed to recognize the male voice, and it brought discomfort, unlike God's voice. Who was it? Stylmach? She remembered the slight accent and it concerned her dream self but she had to listen anyway.

"Yes," she replied in her dream.

"Will you speak with me?" asked Stylmach seductively. "Please, Raimi, tell me about yourself."

This time she automatically told him all she knew; Queen of Rivers, Wise One magician, married to Owailion, friends with Mohan and Imzuli. At the mention of the white dragon, the sorcerer hummed knowingly but didn't interrupt. Then when she mentioned her Talismans the dream interrogator grew interested enough to ask more probing questions.

"Raimi, tell me more about this bowl. It is magic?"

"It shows the past," Raimi explained, dreaming a familiar sense of alarm. Why was she giving her short life story to this dream character? She deliberately tried not to share what specific things she had seen in the bowl.

And the sorcerer sensed her reluctance, so instead, he switched topics. "That's a lovely mansion you have there. We have seen others coming up across the Land. Is it yours?"

"No," she answered flatly, hoping Stylmach would not go further.

"Where is yours? I assume you are a great enough enchantress to warrant such an elaborate palace as this."

Was he playing to her supposed vanity? Was she so sensitive that she felt shame that Owailion still had not built her a home? No, she wasn't tempted to fall for that ploy but she also was not willing to reveal where hers would eventually be built.

"Mine is coming," Raimi answered since in the dream she didn't feel like she could be rude enough to not say something.

"Ah," the outlander commented knowingly, insinuating that she was further down the list because of perceived weakness on her part. Then he began to feed on her more pernicious instinct. "Everything you touch will go wrong somehow. Look how your guide and friend Imzuli ended up being the thief of the rune stones. Why is Owailion unable to build your palace? He cannot even find someplace to conceal the pipes so you can play hide-and-seek for them. It seems so silly."

Then the sorcerer drew her back away from that distressing line of self-doubt and plunged her into more alarming areas. "Raimi, tell me of the Heart Stone," he commanded.

The order was irresistible. Raimi could not stop herself and part of her realized her deepest fears had come true. That sane portion of her mind still asleep screamed out in alarm, trying to resist, but she was not strong enough to fight the compulsion. There had been a reason to fear this nightmare man but she simply had to tell him about Heart Stones. Could she manipulate that request?

"Heart Stones are a Wise One's conscience," she began, striving to give only the most innocuous details. "It prevents us from using our magic for evil." She hoped it was so, or Stylmach's name magic could force her to do something she would regret for an eternity.

"Ah, and do you have one?" Again Stylmach insinuated that she might be unworthy of such a blessing. Or was he hoping to get more details, such as how to obtain one for himself; plucking them off a riverbank like a skipping stone.

"Yes." She would resist the impulse as much as possible and gave no freely offered information. She would not point out that to be a magician in the Land one must have a Heart Stone or the Seal would block them out. What would happen if an outlander sorcerer acquired one? What if this Stylmach commanded her to give her stone to him? Would he be able to cross the Seal?

"Raimi, tell me how you found your Heart Stone." Again the command washed over her insistently. Without recourse she told him about finding it at the bottom of the river, implying that it was not born with her into this world. She hoped that led the sorcerer astray enough to not ask that she give it to him.

Abruptly the nightmare began to grow too foggy in her mind. Could the sorcerer not maintain the link to her? Raimi squirmed frantically, detesting the connection. A nightmare of demons would be preferable. She was going to betray the Land and all the people she loved.

"It is time for me to go," Stylmach announced eerily. "Raimi, your shields will remain down to me and Raimi, you will forget this conversation completely." With that, the dream faded away but he parted with the final chilling promise. "We will speak again tomorrow night."

Chapter 18

Nightmares

Raimi awoke at dawn feeling unrested. Why must humans have to sleep? As a magician, she should at least have the ability to stay awake like the dragons, she thought groggily. Raimi arose, stretching as she moved onto the balcony and looked out at the brilliant ocean that spilled out from under the cliff. No ships came near the Land – no one to trade with – but she wondered if outlanders would come to try to break through the Seal and she could see them coming as Tamaar claimed. How would a human see them coming?

Well, Raimi thought, she could experiment with some more deep magic. She had already created a language spell and the guardian for Lake Ameloni, as well as the spell that bound the palace shields to the door stewards. She might not be able to see evidence of these spells, but it was worth a try to do another one. Was there a similar spell she could utilize to keep sorcerers away from the Land?

Raimi looked out over the water and drew on the deep magic, grounding it in the roots of the Land. Then she wished that every ship that ... no, she could not capsize ships just because they carried a sorcerer. Perhaps something more benign. Thinking for a moment she instead bound the spell so that every magician traveling over water became seasick, no matter the size of the boat or how strong the remedy they might concoct. Yes, that she could wish into being. Raimi felt restless with the powerful need to do something, anything to defend the Land from the evil she sensed creeping in on her.

Then, to rid herself of these premonitions, Raimi worked hard the day around gardening the palace at Tamaar; roses, wisteria, and exotic plants she could not recall the name of but she imagined they smelled wonderful. These gardens might not be seen or appreciated by anyone for a thousand years but they needed to complement Owailion's work and be self-maintaining until the palaces became occupied, so here again, she crafted deep magic. Besides, in this case, Raimi felt reasonably sure she wasn't going to harm anyone by involving herself or her magic.

Abruptly another thought brought a shiver to Raimi's spine. She knew settlers would come breaking the Seal, building villages all up and down the rivers. She had witnessed it in the Talisman bowl. Perhaps the other distressing events like Imzuli's mountain or the devastation on the Lara Delta were natural and not caused by outlanders. Yet someone had destroyed her home on the delta. Raimi wished passionately that she could unsee that destruction. Perhaps it took place over millennia? Mountains fell and land rose in that kind of time frame. Maybe the Wise Ones could prevent some of the things they had seen and so many beautiful places did not have to be destroyed. But the coming of settlers always had seemed inevitable and somewhat welcome.

Depression followed Raimi's work that day and so at dusk, Raimi went swimming in the bay to wash away her dark mood. She hoped to relax with the realization that she had only a few more days to work on the gardens and then she could go and follow Owailion. The water in the deep harbor she hoped might be just the thing to ease her tension.

However, Raimi was wrong. Instead, she felt as if she would drown, which was silly since her gift with rivers and swimming applied to any body of water. The dark of the deep bay made her feel as if something toothy might come up and nibble on her toes and so after only a few hasty minutes in the water she waded back out and went to bed early.

Unfortunately, the dreams descended again. A ship sailed into her sleep, but she did not remember it from her nightmare before. Oddly enough in this vision, the vessel came across a snowfield, coming up the Lara River to a branching, as if following her retreat, invading her mind. The ship remained unmanned and adrift. She vaguely recalled Stylmach and while familiar, she could not recall where she had heard his accusatory tone.

"You are a naughty little witch, Raimi. You cast a spell on me. I've never been seasick and now suddenly I am? How is that? Answer me, Raimi."

The compulsion on her rocked her head on its neck with the force. Seasick? Had she made him ill? How could she not remember this powerful magic? Was this from her former life? Raimi gulped, and then carefully replied to the mysterious sorcerer, "I did not put a spell on you." It wasn't a lie technically. She had put a spell on all sorcerers, not him specifically.

"Well, it was powerful. What is the cure?" the outlander demanded in a sour tone.

Raimi didn't feel the compulsion tied to that question to force her to answer, so she didn't. "What do you want of me that you are invading my dreams?"

"I want you to help me become a Wise One," Stylmach replied frankly. "And if you don't, I will make you destroy every stone in your Land."

Raimi thought she would shake with fear at that prospect but something of the Wise One slipped into her sleeping mind and she felt a streak of defiance come to the surface. "Rivers might flow upstream once in a while but that's what it will take, you know," she boldly replied.

"Raimi, tell me what it takes to become a Wise One of the Land."

The magical imperative made the snow darken in her nightmare and she could not gather the will to fight it, except in her tone. "You don't. Anyone who manipulates others is unworthy of being a Wise

One. God chooses us, wipes our memory, gives us a Heart Stone and brings us to the Land. He alone selects us. You must ask Him."

This bold reply did not deaden her tormentor's fixation on the subject. "Raimi, will being in possession of a Heart Stone turn me into a Wise One?" Stylmach snarled.

Raimi kicked at the black snow as she fought how this flow was going to pull her away from the Land and all she loved. "I don't know. I do know you cannot be a Wise One because of your manipulation."

Another query burned into her mind. "Raimi, what are some of the limits to your magic with the Heart Stone?"

She was beginning to hate the sound of her own name. If she ever escaped this Stylmach she would change her name without a thought, after she ripped this single-minded sorcerer to shreds. "Yes, many that you will find bothersome. For instance, I cannot lie. I cannot kill unless it is in defense of the Land, others or myself. Also, I may not do anything that is not honorable and good in the eyes of God, such as using name magic to makes slaves of us. I am obligated to protect the Land from demons and sorcerers like you and my life is dedicated to that. And…and I cannot have children."

"Interesting…you cannot lie?" Stylmach sounded doubtful.

"No, not even when you are not forcing me to answer your worthless questions. Now let me go," she ordered, to no effect.

"I am not done with you." Then he stated the words she feared the most. "Give me the Heart Stone, Raimi."

The Queen of Rivers trembled with icy fear and in her mind, she wailed for Owailion's help, but in a nightmare her call failed, blocked by Stylmach's command. Owailion could not help her. And she did not want her husband near to see this shameful act. What if the sorcerer commanded her to attack the man she loved as well? What if Stylmach began manipulating Owailion too?

Raimi tried to delay the inevitable. "How can I give it to you? You're not real. You're only a nightmare." Indeed she hoped that a nightmare was all she faced, but at the moment she was only lying to herself and she knew it.

"Hold the Heart Stone out to the ship, Raimi."

The command slammed into her like rocks at the bottom of a waterfall, crushing and icy. She gasped, striving for a path free of the pounding power of that order and could not come up with a way to avoid doing as she was told. Like her hand performed the actions of a puppet, she reached into her soul and pulled free the little blue orb. In her nightmare, she closed her eyes and held it out over the snowfield toward the boat.

"You will forget that we have had this conversation. You will not speak to anyone about this. You will not do any spells against me, ever Raimi."

Then an invisible hand reached out and snatched the globe from her hand. Raimi remained aware enough to see how the slow pulsing orb abruptly sped up its beat to match the pace of its new owner's heart. Then the nightmare faded and Raimi woke up gasping in the dark.

"Raimi, what's wrong?" she heard Owailion's welcome voice in her mind and she lay back against the pillows in relief.

"Nightmare," she explained to her husband. She could tell he was somewhere in a tent up in the mountains, just rising for the morning while she still had a few hours of starlight, being farther west.

"Tell me about your nightmare," he suggested gently since he couldn't be there with her.

"That's just it; I can't remember anything of it. I just feel….empty." She sighed, wondering what was going on with her. For nights now she had such awful dreams that unaccountably eluded her and she just could not imagine enduring more. "I think I have a good enough grasp of the gardens here that I can complete what I must from a distance. Can I come to join you?"

"I would love your company. I'm up here on the western edge of the Great Chain. Oh, and just be warned. I've finally found a place for your second Talisman."

Raimi smiled through her exhaustion. "I'll tell Tamaar that I'm leaving and then join you."

* * *

Owailion stared in wonder at the change he saw in Raimi after only a few days away from him. The light had fled from the river in her eyes. She looked haggard and the dark circles under her eyes from lack of sleep did not explain it all. Indeed, a Wise One could grow ill? If so, then that was it, but what had caused this change? Raimi might claim that she was not sleeping well, but the lurking prophecy of Enok haunted him.

Well, he would do what he could to help her recover. Owailion conjured a huge luxurious bed in the tent he used while up in the mountains and insisted that she rest there that day. Now here with him again Raimi finally slept peacefully. While she napped, Owailion privately, for he suspected she would not appreciate his investigations, utilized her Talisman bowl to go back and look at her activities during her time in Tamaar. He saw her working on the gardens, the deep spells, occasionally swimming and then going to bed every night. Nothing else seemed to happen. With no disturbing dreams, Raimi awoke after a few hours and then came to find him at his worksite.

"So you finally hid the pipes," she began as she looked over the stunning scenery of a great pit set in the pass between two huge mountains as Owailion guided a white foundation stone into the hole.

Owailion nodded and she could see the secret smile on his lips. "I realized that I would not get any more inspired ideas until I faced my fears. And when I did, I found a place for your pipes. I knew then that the thing you and I want least to do is confront Imzuli. The minute I thought about that, I knew the pipes belonged with her."

Raimi looked better for her nap, Owailion noted but her look of puzzlement slowed him pointing that out. She finally asked, "You went and spoke with her? And you also hid the pipes with Imzuli? Now you are telling me where they are? Isn't that defeating the purpose of hiding the Talismans?"

"No, the purpose isn't to hide them," he countered. "The idea is to challenge you, force you to pass some kind of magical task. You and I are both reluctant to talk to Imzuli. I passed my part of the trial when I went to give her the pipes and saw that she was indeed asleep. I know she did not make the deal with that sorcerer to stay awake. Now it's your turn to speak with her about the stones...and ask for the pipes. That is your trial."

Raimi swallowed with worry. "That's going to be another nightmare. You know that I worry about everything I involve myself in ends up for the worse, and this could very easily go sideways."

"You'll do fine," Owailion assured her. "You have not made anything worse being here in the Land. You've only made things better."

Owailion saw the doubt still in her haunted eyes and added. "You've made me better. And look at all the deep spells you have developed. Here, I'll give you her true name so you can wake her." He then conjured a little piece of paper and a stylus and wrote out Imzuli's true name that he had received from the Memories.

Raimi looked at the little slip he held out to her with trepidation but took it. Then she kissed Owailion passionately, to show her thankfulness for his support even though there was little he could actually do to help her. If she wanted to eventually face her character flaws and challenge her personal demons then she must deal with confrontation sometime. He overheard her chanting that mantra that as she latched magically onto a tiny brook that ran off a glacier at the base of Imzuli's mountain and transferred herself there with a magical thought.

Chapter 19

Winning the Pipes

Raimi realized as she looked up at the mountain that loomed above her, that she had never actually been to any of the mountains without a dragon escort. She felt like an invader. However, she recalled the gaping hole that she had seen in the Talisman bowl with this mountain gone and instead a Wise One's palace with stunning gardens had grown here. That was another thing about which she needed to speak with Imzuli. How did you tell someone their home was going to disappear? That issue could be another nightmare all in itself.

Raimi looked down at the little strip of paper Owailion had given her and then took a steadying breath. "Tethimzuliel? Wake up," she commanded.

At first, the response wasn't even in words. Something in Raimi's mind sensed the dragon rolling over deep within the mountain, ignoring the call, or only disturbed by it. "Tethimzuliel, it's me, Raimi. I need to talk to you. Can I come in and see your cave?"

"*Raimi?*" Imzuli's voice, heavy with sleep and confusion took concentration to hear. "*You woke me. How long has it been?*"

"Only a few months, my friend. May I come in?" Raimi replied. Standing out on the mountainside did not seem like a good place to speak, not with ice and avalanches hanging above her in the early spring and the sudden feeling that listening ears would always haunt her and want to hear a name.

In reply Imzuli reached out and abruptly pulled Raimi to her, bringing her into the cavern within the mountain. The human gasped at the sudden change of setting. The cave, lit by orbs like Owailion often used, seemed made of Imzuli's glittering hide; brightly polished silver. The smooth walls, completely free of stalactites or even rubble, felt like the inside of some chromed egg, and easily double the size of Imzuli herself who lounged in the middle like a queen on a throne, looking down at Raimi with her glittering silver eyes still adjusting to the light she had conjured.

"*I might not be a proper judge of human appearance,*" Imzuli commented, "*but you don't look well. Are you sick?*"

Raimi tried not to laugh. "That's exactly what Owailion said to me. No, I'm just having nightmares. Do you dream while you sleep?" she asked, suddenly curious now that the subject came up.

"*I do not think so. I do not understand the concept; a story or a vision while I sleep? No, I do not think I have dreamed, but then I have not been asleep for very long.*"

Awkwardly Raimi stalled. "You have a beautiful home here. I still do not have one, but I am with Owailion so that is good. That is one of the things that brought me here to speak with you and I do not know how to say this without hurting you, my friend. Owailion has found one of the Wise One's palaces is supposed to be built...built where your mountain is located."

Imzuli blinked in surprise but said nothing. In typical dragon fashion, the shields over her mind slammed into place so she could do her thinking in private, but there was nothing to say. "*He knows this?*" the dragon eventually asked.

To help her friend understand Raimi gathered a slower, shorter version of the bowl vision and then shared it so that the dragon could see the images that passed over the Great Chain. Imzuli would recognize the mountains she knew so well by shape and size and then when the missing mountain came into view Raimi brought the visuals down directly into the valley that had been formed. They both saw the details of waterfalls feeding a tropical paradise where before a glorious mountain had once sat. Flowers of hundreds of species littered the twisting walkways that filled the valley. The palace at the bottom of the dell appeared to be a series of columns with low roof lines carved in marble rather than high walled and enclosed like all the other palaces had been before, but it was unmistakable: a Wise One's palace.

"I'm sorry," was the only thing Raimi could think of saying.

"*Do you know how this change will happen?*" the dragon asked tonelessly.

Raimi shook her head, but then remembered that dragons rarely could interpret body language. "As long as the mountain is there, we would not even think of building it here, no matter what God says about it. Owailion has two finished palaces, but he has eight others under construction, several not started and three he has yet to even find. He has plenty to think about and we will not disturb you about it…except. We just wanted to ask if you could move somewhere else to sleep; Jonjonel, for example. We have foreseen many terrible changes in the Land that we cannot account for. We would hate for you to be harmed by something unexpected. Will you move so if…when something makes your mountain disappear, that you don't disappear with it. That would be a worse tragedy."

Imzuli did not answer for the longest time. She was thinking deeply, again behind her shields, with her silvery eyes closed in concentration. Raimi had no idea what kind of bond and devotion a dragon might hold with their home mountain, but it had to be strong. The only thing a human might have to compare might be family. Could a dragon even survive moving to another mountain? Dragons were not like her, always moving on, living in a tent and even immigrating to another land. For Raimi, it would be easy to leave her home, but she knew enough to recognize that for a dragon, even one as young and open-minded as Imzuli, it would never be an easy decision.

Instinctively Raimi reached out and caressed Imzuli on the arm as if a touch would cure the problem. The dragon's eyes flashed open and she looked down at her friend. "*I will have to think about this…if I can stay awake long enough to give it my whole concentration. But this news is not the reason why you have come to talk to me."*

Raimi looked down in trepidation. "No, there are other things... in addition to the pipes that I know you have for me. The trial for me to win the pipes is bringing such difficult things into the light. Imzuli, we know you sold the runestones to an outlander sorcerer. We just could not understand why."

Imzuli grumbled audibly and scooted back so she could lay down with her head at Raimi's level, her silver eyes glittering in the magical lights. Could a dragon's face express shame? Imzuli's silver eyes welled up like mercury and caught flashes from the lights above. The usually blinding white of her hide dulled to almost gray and the tip of her tail began to twitch slightly. It took time but eventually, the dragon explained.

"*That was the most foolish thing I've done in my life,*" Imzuli admitted. "*Have you ever done something you knew was wrong even as you did it, just because you were curious? I have always been fascinated with the idea of humans like Mohan is. I learned about the concept of writing from looking at those stones. I used to study them every time I went near Zema.*"

The dragon sighed gustily and the scent of her sulfurous breath blew around Raimi's skirts. "*You see, I have known humans were coming all my life. I was hatched about the same time the prophecy of the Sleep was given. Mohan made sure I understood that humans were coming to take the stewardship over the Land. I knew my time awake would be limited, so I wanted to experience as much as I could in the short time I was given. I went outside the Seal and visited other lands as soon as I was old enough to fly there. I saw much of how humans live. I saw bargaining and trade. I saw what writing could do and music and dance and I wanted ... I wanted to be a little like a human. Is that foolishness, yes? I have learned more in just six months being your friend than I did in ninety years of exploring other lands. But I made that bargain because I wanted to see how trading worked and the meaning of the words on the stones. I knew they were not mine to give. And then when Owailion discovered the stones were gone and it was too late to return the stones ... and I was too embarrassed to admit my mistake."*

Raimi looked with compassion at the gleaming dragon and realized she could forgive Imzuli's foolishness without a thought. "I'm only six months old, remember. I've done foolish things as well. We all do things we regret. I came to the Land with a feeling that I damage anything in which I get involved. At first, I was unwilling to marry Owailion because I was afraid I would mess that up too, somehow hurting him. There's an old saying; 'I'm only human', and it means we all make mistakes. But it also applies to you, Imzuli. You're only human."

The dragon chuckled, which came out as a soothing rumble that made the whole cavern echo and the lights tremble in the air. "*I would like to be a human, but I am evil to wish for it and I cannot do evil.*"

"Is that why you were so eager to hunt that demon that came from Zema?" Raimi asked now that all had been resolved. The dragon dropped her jaw again and rumbled in the positive. "*I should have revealed the truth earlier. I knew all about Zema except there was no proof. I had hoped that the writing on the stones would explain how to stop the demons from coming. But I was wrong. You know what the stones say, don't you?*"

"Yes, and nothing was lost that we cannot learn for ourselves."

"*That is good, for I withheld what I had learned from the Memories that I gave to Owailion. I am ashamed of that as well. Will you forgive me?*"

Raimi did not hesitate. She reached out and gave an enthusiastic, very human hug to the dragon's snout, about the only thing she could wrap her arms around. "Forgiven." Then she doggedly went on to the next subject she needed to broach. "For a time we were concerned that if you were willing to take something that did not belong to you to sell it, you might take something else to sell as well. My name."

That brought Imzuli's head up quickly in alarm. "*That sorcerer did offer me a chance to not go to sleep in exchange for something but he did not suggest your name. That would have been truly evil and I might have roasted him just for suggesting it. I did not have anything else to sell and it would have been so wrong I would have lost my soul. No, going to sleep is the right path for me. I will have other adventures someday."*

"I am glad of that," Raimi replied, feeling much better for her friend. "Please think about moving to Jonjonel. I'm worried for you."

"*I will think about it.*" Then the dragon blinked her silver eyes meaningfully, drawing out the next question with a human inflection. "*But is this really what you came to speak with me about?*"

"Oh yes, the pipes."

Imzuli did not demand anything of her friend in exchange for the pipes. She had placed them inside one of the glowing globes that hovered above their heads near the ceiling of the cavern. The dragon brought the light down with a magical nudge and placed it into Raimi's outstretched hands where it popped like a soap bubble and the human caught them.

"They're beautiful," Raimi whispered, turning the glossy set of reeds over to see the decoration, gold and silver inlay all across the set.

"*What do they do? Owailion said they were not his to explain,*" Imzuli's enthusiastic curiosity had returned.

"Owailion did not know…well, generally reeds make music but since these are a Talisman they will also have another purpose, a magical ability like my bowl can show me the past. Should I try to play them?"

"*Yes please,*" Imzuli almost giggled and then added with belated caution. "*Will they do something harmful? Can you even play a song?*"

Raimi knew instinctively that she could play because this was her Talisman; meant to invoke magic for her just as the bowl could. Yet she feared its effect. The bowl, while amazing in its capabilities, also brought sorrow in profound ways. Carefully Raimi closed her eyes to concentrate and abandon herself to the impulses that would come with the reeds. She didn't actively participate in what she was about to do. This was an automatic reflex. The song flowed easily. A sweet, mournful and yet charming tune emerged from the pipes and she felt its magic caress her mind and body like a refreshing shower under a waterfall. It washed something away from her heart and she felt new. It was as if the sun appeared in the middle of the night.

"Oh," she gasped and stopped playing in sudden terror.

"*Raimi? What are you doing here?*" Imzuli asked in a bewildered tone. Could she not remember the conversation that she had just been having?

"Imzuli, something terrible has happened. I was...I was playing the pipes. I remember."

"*I don't remember giving them to you. Did I fall asleep and you wakened me?*"

The dragon had forgotten and Raimi had just remembered.

Raimi began to weep. She was cursed, as she had suspected. It would all go wrong as she had feared. "Imzuli, this is horrible. I gave my Heart Stone to an outlander sorcerer!" she almost shrieked. Something in Raimi broke open like a dam burst and she snatched at her bag, seeking her Heart Stone or her bowl, anything that might help.

"Raimi?" Owailion's mind voice broke into her concentration. "You're frantic. What's wrong?"

Owailion had sensed her abrupt panic through their love link clear across the continent and Raimi couldn't seem to think straight enough to give him a logical answer. She had none to give. Owailion's mind washed through hers toward Imzuli. The dragon expressed confusion but without reflecting Raimi's panic.

Thankfully he didn't wait; Owailion shifted directly into the dragon's lair, with or without her permission and saw Raimi sitting at the dragon's feet, weeping and hysterical, struggling to get the bowl out of her bag with the pipes tossed aside. He looked up at Imzuli to see if she was the source of his wife's fear, but the dragon looked dumbfounded.

"What happened?" he asked of either of them even as he knelt right in front of Raimi and took her bag from her. With much calmer hands he found her bowl inside and held it, not letting Raimi touch it. He magically filled it with conjured water and then whispered, "Show me what has just happened to make Raimi so frightened."

He could sense both his wife and the dragon looking over his shoulder to see the reflection in the vessel. They all three watched in the bowl as Raimi pressed the pipes to her lips, played a tune and he saw her reaction. The dragon had forgotten the previous hour of conversation and Raimi had abruptly remembered giving away her Heart Stone? How could this happen? Owailion dropped the bowl and took Raimi by the shoulders to try and calm her.

"When did you give your Heart Stone to an outlander?" he asked fearfully, though he remained as calm as possible just because he knew it would do little good to add his fear to hers.

"In the nightmares. The pipes…" she almost babbled, trying to get half phrases out to make herself understood. "He told me to forget. The pipes…they make you remember."

"*Or forget,*" Imzuli provided helpfully. "*I don't remember her arriving here. Can the bowl show us what happened in a nightmare?*"

"Let us hope so," Owailion replied to Imzuli's suggestion. He picked up the bowl, refilled it and then carefully worded his request. "Show me the nightmares Raimi has been having."

The bowl obediently tapped into one of the visuals of what actually had gone on behind Raimi's eyes while she slept. Now they all could understand why she would have not remembered her dreams. She had been ordered to forget them. With name magic.

"*That's the…I know that outlander,*" Imzuli commented even as she looked down into the bowl and saw the ship that had invaded Raimi's dreams. Could there be any doubt that there would be two identical ships with powerful sorcerer's aboard? Imzuli lowered her head, awash in embarrassment that she had any dealings with the man and her anger grew. "*He goes by the name Stylmach. That is the ship that he uses to move around the Land but he speaks the language of Malornia…to the west.*"

"How…how did he get my name?" Raimi shuddered even as the dream vision faded and she began to try to get herself back under control. "You said you did not sell my name."

Imzuli looked confused again. "*How did you know... when did I tell you that?*"

"Just now," Raimi tried to explain. "I came here to ask you about it and to beg you to move to Jonjonel. Do you not remember any of that conversation?"

"*No, I have forgotten. Can that bowl show me what memories have been taken from me?*"

"Let's try. I need to see everything that has gone on here," Owailion commented. He picked up the bowl, filled it a third time and then ordered, "Show us everything that has gone on here in this cavern since Raimi arrived."

Raimi had not forgotten what happened during the interaction she had held with Imzuli so while Owailion and the dragon reviewed the conversation and the winning of the pipes, so she methodically thought through all the things she might have revealed to this Stylmach.

"Since I gave him my Heart Stone, he probably knows I'm a Wise One," she admitted aloud after their review. "I probably told him about all that entails; the Seal, the Sleep and all my powers. I might have told him why we wanted the stones and that there will be more Wise Ones and our affinities. Oh, this is awful. My curse has ruined us all."

"You do not have a curse," Owailion interrupted her grim list. "But we do have a problem and need to plan."

Raimi sighed and tried to regroup her thoughts. "If he was a real person, not a dream, then Stylmach can be made to forget my name, can't he? I hope that is why I have been given a Talisman of forgetfulness."

"*It seems like our best hope. You must get back your Heart Stone, or he may make you do something worse,*" warned Imzuli.

"We will make Stylmach suffer for this as well. I hope Wise Ones are allowed to kill him for his presumption," Owailion promised.

Raimi nodded agreement. "I refuse to be the means of bringing destruction on the Land. I will not let this curse affect all I love."

And so, the three of them began plotting.

Chapter 20

Remembered and Forgotten

Raimi had to sleep. She could not fight it. The magician might have demanded it but this time she did not resist sleep, knowing she would have a dream she did not want to have. However, this time Owailion hovered in the background of her mind and they would try to turn a necessity into an advantage. Raimi remained in Imzuli's cavern, probably the safest place in the Land for her right now, and her husband and the dragon watched over her.

"You tricked me, witch!" was Stylmach's first comment as the dream ship drifted close to her. This time the setting was again on a river, but now the stream ran right through the silver cavern's walls and out again on the far side. The ship somehow managed to fit inside even though this defied logic. "The Heart Stone does not work," Stylmach accused. "It only burns me. It did nothing for my powers. I cannot even hold it."

"Powers?" Raimi tried not to express the private pleasure of having her tormenter suffer. "I never claimed it would give magical powers. I told you it was a Wise One's conscience. It is a judge and a focus, nothing more. It cannot make you a Wise One. God made me a Wise One, not some Heart Stone."

"You…it…," Stylmach's voice spit with fury. "You lied. You said it would block me from doing name magic or any of the magic you term evil."

Raimi had not considered this and it almost surprised her. How could the Heart Stone inhibit her from lying and yet allow this magician to do such vile manipulation? Then her Wise One instincts kicked in. "The stone is a judge only. It sees you, judges you for the pathetic excuse for humanity that you are and allows you to reach that potential, capable of evil magic. That is all."

Stylmach sputtered again before he managed to spit out something in response. "Evil magic? Well, I've got news for you, witch. You're the one who is going to be doing evil magic. Raimi, I am going to have you destroy the Land. You are going to pick apart your beloved nation piece by piece. You're going to give it all to me and nothing you can do will stop me. Raimi, come to me."

She felt the tug, pulling her against the wall of the cavern. "How? This is a dream," she insisted, for her conscious mind could not pass through solid matter if she were still asleep.

"Step into the river, toward the ship. I will do the rest. Come to me, Raimi."

Raimi opened her physical eyes. Owailion's spell of wakefulness had worked. She could pretend to be asleep but Stylmach would not know that she was perfectly capable and aware. But she still must be obedient to the command the sorcerer had given. She reached down, picked up her carefully loaded pack with the pipes in it, leaving the bowl with Owailion and took the required steps forward into the impossible river. She saw the barely contained fear in Owailion's eyes as Stylmach's magic grasped her and pulled her forcefully to his ship.

Her first impressions were she was awake and violently ill. Her seasickness spell had worked a little too well. The rolling of the deck under her feet startled her into opening her eyes and then losing her last meal onto the rough boards.

"It isn't very nice, is it?" Stylmach's actual physical voice sounded even harsher than she expected as she dropped to the deck retching and all she could see of her enemy was his elegantly booted feet. He let her suffer on her hands and knees until she was empty and then shoved a bucket of dank water at her and she made use of it by scooping a few mouthfuls to at least rinse out the taste. Only then did she struggle to her feet to face him.

Stylmach looked like an ordinary man; brown hair, hazel eyes and a magician's robe over a seaman's clothing. The ship now appeared manned, but with most of the crew giving them a wide berth. Raimi looked about her and saw no sign of shore. She shivered with fear at what limits might restrict her here. Did she possess her magic this far away from the Land and without her Heart Stone? Fortunately, she still felt Owailion's presence in the back of her brain gentling her fear, helping her remain positive.

"Where have you brought me?" she demanded, glaring at the sorcerer.

"Raimi, you will not use magic against me. You will not contact anyone who remains in the Land. And Raimi, you will do exactly what I tell you to do." Stylmach immediately reset his restrictions, and then he added to her question, "You are far from the sources of your power. If you are truly a Wise One you should not be able to tap into your powers. They are meant strictly for the Land. The stones Imzuli brought me claim as much."

"And you're using name magic on me," she noted bitterly. "How did an outlander like you find my name?" It was something that concerned them greatly when the three of them planned this confrontation. If they had to strip her name from every soul on the planet it was going to be more difficult than just dealing with Stylmach.

The sorcerer chuckled. "That was easy. I took the stones from your pet dragon and then I shared them with my master who was following a certain priest. While there, your Owailion visited the priest and spoke your name. I followed him back as my master dealt with the priest and found you with him. You don't remember, but we have now had several conversations. You have shared a great deal with me about how Heart Stones and Wise One magic are used."

Raimi felt a sense of relief; no one in the Land had betrayed her. She could feel Owailion's fury lurking across their link. He would understand at least now why Enok had died.

Stylmach went on. "Imzuli made a deal with me before. Perhaps she will trade with me again. I would rather have a pet dragon than a pet magician...although you are quite lovely," Stylmach added and Raimi felt like retching again. The sorcerer drew close to her, bringing his hand along her jawline and she was tempted to bite him, but she didn't want a physical restriction as well as a magical one placed on her so she just swallowed. She easily sensed Owailion resisting the temptation to come and wipe the smirk off the sorcerer's face with an avalanche, but not yet; not while her name remained in Stylmach's grasp. "Yes, quite lovely."

"What do you want of me?" she reiterated, hoping to speed up this distressing conversation. She felt Owailion struggling to not intervene.

"Isn't that obvious?" replied Stylmach and then looked out at the spring sky as if he had grown suspicious of someone listening in on them. "Come with me Raimi," and he drew his hand down her arm, sending her shivers of revulsion. Then he grasped her hand. He led her to the hatch and down into the ship's hold. Toward the back of the ship, he had a stateroom with fine furniture, a huge bed set with silk coverings and even thick glass windows so that he could see the ocean beyond the ship. It probably had been the captain's cabin but Stylmach had commandeered it for his own purposes.

Stylmach ordered her to sit in a finely carved chair with velvet cushions and he poured blood-red wine for them both. When she did not take the glass he offered, he drank anyway without forcing her to partake. It would probably just come back up on her anyway. The seasickness had not abated. Instead, she glared at him until he set the goblet back down and then sat in a second chair.

"I want power. I could get it from demons but then they control me, which is worse than not having what I want. You have power but it still eludes me how you tap into it. Do I have to make it inside the Seal to use the Heart Stone? Raimi, answer me."

"No," she replied flatly. "Being inside the Seal will change nothing for you."

"Can you do magic outside the Seal? Far away from your ley lines?" he continued as if her magic were a game of twenty questions.

She felt Owailion's curiosity. He had not heard of ley lines either, even in the Memories. Imzuli also confirmed that she too had not heard of them. So Raimi asked the obvious question, "Ley lines?" Asking also provided a desperate attempt to avoid revealing that she could do magic anywhere, no matter how far from the Land she might be.

Stylmach huffed impatiently at her ignorance of this type of magic. "The veins where magic flows. Surely you can sense them. The reason I can do magic at all here at sea is that I have a map of the ley lines that are under the ocean's bed. That is more than most sorcerers can claim." He seemed inordinately proud of this fact, assuming it made him more powerful than his fellows.

Raimi remained tight-lipped about her thoughts on his ley lines but Stylmach was expecting a reply.

"I don't sense the ley lines, but then, I am very new to magic." Perhaps that would misguide him enough to forget his question about her ability to do magic out here at sea. "You want my power so you can show your fellows that I am your magical puppet? What good is that?"

"My fellows?" Stylmach shook his head in wonder. "No, you must be new at magic to not understand. I cannot even safely pull your strings without others hearing your name and taking over. I simply crave a power no others can control. All sorcerers compete. If they saw me manipulating you, they would come after me in other ways and I detest looking over my shoulder. No, my mentor suspects I found you but no one else must know. That is why I want beyond the Seal. If I am the most powerful magician in the Land, no one can challenge me, not even my mentor. So I ask, can you bring down the Seal and then put it up again? Answer me truthfully, Raimi."

She felt the slamming jerk of the compulsion and she snarled back at him. "I told you, a Wise One cannot lie. You don't have to force me to be honest. And I don't know about the Seal. It is something the dragons built, so it is based on their magic, not a human's. If the Seal comes down it is likely to stay down."

Stylmach did not look happy about this news. He growled under his breath, stood, poured another glass of wine, threw it back in one long gulp and then walked to the back of the cabin to look out the windows, as he feared a spying ship trailing them.

To distract his plotting Raimi began her own questioning. "What is the Seal to you?" she asked, exploring his goals and interests. "If you are strong enough to get inside, you obviously are powerful enough to not worry about outsiders attacking, even if there is no Seal?" she asked.

Raimi could not interpret the look he gave her; pity, amusement, disgust? She couldn't tell, but he returned to his chair in front of her. "You really don't understand power, do you? If no one knows you have it, it's worth nothing. If I break the Seal and rule the Land, I will have to defend it and I don't want to deal with that. The people and resources within the Seal are mine to control and the sorcerers outside need to look in jealously, seeing but never touching. I want what you have Raimi; complete control with no competition. I would wager, other than dragons, there are very few magicians on the other side of the Seal."

Raimi sat there for a bit, staring at him, wondering how to react. Then she burst out laughing at his ignorance. "You are a fool!" she mocked him. "You think there are riches, or crowds ready to worship you and magic dropping from the trees like fruit? It is the other way around. I don't have a single thing of value except for love on the other side of that Seal. I have been sleeping on the ground or in someone else's home since the day I arrived. Almost everything I own is in my pack," she explained. Her mention of the bag only encouraged him to do the one thing she wanted him to try.

Stylmach's eyes turned toward the pack on her back. "Give your bag to me, Raimi," he ordered. She didn't fight too much, just a token snarl before she slipped her satchel off her shoulder and handed it over to him. He looked inside and then poured the contents onto the table unceremoniously. She had packed it carefully with everything she wanted him to find, hiding the things not for Stylmach's eyes. Out for display, a simple tin plate and cup, a wooden spoon, a wool blanket, and a warm jacket. She even had a belt knife and a spare skirt, but little else of value except for the exquisite set of reed pipes that just happened to land on top of the other items.

"Raimi, you didn't tell me. Are you a musician?" He picked up the pipes and examined them thoroughly. "There is a spell on them, I can tell."

Her heart fell. Their plan would not work unless she was able to play for him.

"They are lovely," he commented as if he wanted a set for himself. "Raimi, tell me how you got them?"

That was a question she actually wanted to answer. At least Stylmach wasn't going to shatter them before she got a chance to explain. "My husband gave them to me. He made them."

"Your husband? Oh yes, Owailion. You did manage to get married then. Tell me about your husband, Raimi."

This compulsion she fought with all her might, spitting the words out between her teeth as if she was going to scratch his eyes out for asking. "He is the first Wise One. He is the King of Creating. He builds the palaces and he makes things…all kinds of things like pipes and bowls and tools."

"Is Owailion his real name?" Stylmach asked casually.

"No, and before you ask, I don't know his given name. He doesn't either. He wasn't born in the Land, but was brought here as an adult, with no memories of his former life."

"So why do you know what your name is if you also came with no other memories as he did?" Stylmach asked.

Raimi shrugged. "Bad luck? Everything I try to do goes awry. I am cursed that way."

Stylmach seemed to grow irritated and admitted, "I suppose I am cursed that way as well. It is always bad to be under the control of those who came before." Then his eyes drifted as if he were drawn once again to the pipes he was fingering. He obviously felt attracted to power and sensed the intensity of it. Owailion's spell also subtly enforced this from afar. "How were these pipes made, Raimi?"

She sighed with false exhaustion as if she were now resigned and not fighting him anymore. Indeed Raimi did not fight to answer this for it fed Stylmach's desires. "Owailion heard the reeds were 'going demon' and stopped them by putting them into this form, channeling the magic into something else. That is one of a Wise One's duties; prevent demon formation."

"Really? I always thought demons came from the Other side. Perhaps that is where you send them when you are done battling them if they manage to go all the way into being demons. So what do these pipes do?"

"They made me a musician," she commented since there was no compulsion. She didn't have to tell him all they did. "I don't remember being musical, but it came naturally when I first played them."

"And would it do the same thing for me?" Stylmach asked speculatively.

"I really do not know," Raimi admitted. Privately she hoped it did make Stylmach musical enough to wipe his memory. At least she had managed to reveal only one of the pipe's capabilities and Stylmach had not yet insisted that she continue. "Please, play them," she wished though the magic wish was powerless to affect him. The mandate to not cast any spell on him still held strong.

But curiosity was stronger still. Stylmach put the reeds to his lips and blew through them experimentally. When nothing magical happened, other than a simple pure tone gliding through the air, he set his hands over more stops and then began to play. The sorcerer's song reflected his roots; evil and unctuous. It felt like something might come creeping up behind them unseen and attack. Raimi fought the spell of the music by chanting a silent spell over herself.

"Raimi, you will not hear the song. Raimi, you will not forget. Stylmach will forget my name but I will not forget the plan. The river has passed and will never be the same again. It is in the past. It is all new. Raimi will not forget the plan."

"Good girl, Raimi," Owailion whispered into her mind and she could hear the tension in his voice.

Stylmach played the entire song before he showed any sign of a change. He blinked, looked over at her and then brought the pipes down in abrupt fear. Raimi stood up and realized with a start that she had changed into her royal clothing, but with some added details. She now wore a breastplate of bronze, inlaid with gold, emeralds, and sapphires over the silk gown that had turned a coppery green, almost aflame. In her hand, she held a fishing spear with a wicked bronze hook at its tip. Her hair, loose under her crown dripped with water as if she had just come ashore.

"Who…?" the sorcerer stammered.

Before Stylmach could say anything more she spoke for him. "I am the Queen of Rivers and I have come to strip my name from you." She had not forgotten! It had worked. She had to remind herself constantly but she remembered the plan.

"And I am her husband, the King of Creating," Owailion announced as he appeared in the cabin, wearing his royal costume under etched steel armor. "You will surrender your mind to her."

Stylmach might have forgotten the one trump card he held, her name, but that did not mean he was powerless. He threw a bolt of pure power at Owailion who deflected it with a thought and the glass windows shattered. The fine furniture exploded into bits.

"You will not," Stylmach snapped, and held up the pipes that he still had not relinquished, threatening to smash them. He brought a hammer into being, ready to strike.

Just then the weight of a white and silver dragon landing on the prow pushed them all around, making the seasickness critical. It would not do to vomit all over her regalia so Raimi reiterated; "You will give me the pipes or we will crush your ship. There is a dragon on deck and she will have no qualms about setting you afire along with the entire crew. You will give me the pipes and allow me to remove your entire memory or you will die."

Anger rippled through the ship but Stylmach's most powerful shield could not withstand the Wise Ones' attack. His mind fell open to them and revealed that he barely recalled his goal; to get into the Land without shattering the Seal.

"You are from the Land?" Stylmach asked desperately. He finally guessed at least where these two glorious magicians had come from. He felt certain he should know who he was battling.

"We are the Wise Ones, guardians of the Land and you have taken things that do not belong to you. The runestones, a Heart Stone and a name," Owailion announced, his dark eyes glittering like obsidian.

"The runestones…I got them from a dragon…in fair trade," Stylmach protested but above on the deck a dragon's roar nearly deafened them all.

"I thought the dragons were all dead by now."

"You thought wrong. Now do you have the stones or not?" Raimi repeated and brought the hooked spear forward to prod him, easily piercing the magical shield Stylmach held around himself.

"No, I exchanged them…in Malornia," he protested, backing up against the broken bed. But as he spoke, Raimi saw the flicker of a forked tongue escape from behind his teeth. The tongue of a liar?

With only her instinct, Raimi wished to see everything, including Stylmach as he truly was. Accordingly, the sorcerer's appearance changed as much as hers had, if not more. His forked tongue was joined by vomit down his front and the weight of hundreds of chains so heavy he crumpled under them. In his hand, he held a vile of poison that smoked evilly and in the other a bloody sword. His face sunk in and huge gaping holes marred his graying cheeks.

Stylmach didn't witness the profound change in his appearance but another stab with Raimi's spear made him recognize he might need to speak the truth to her, so he clarified. "I…well didn't give the stones. I sold them to Malornia."

"To whom?" Owailion asked fiercely.

"To the king, in exchange for a dragon's name."

Another name; this time a dragon's name? Would it ever end? Both Owailion and Raimi almost groaned with dread. In a silent warning, she sent to Owailion, "I still cannot cast a spell on him unless it is on all of us. Can you bind him somehow so he cannot use a name again?" Raimi asked in her head. Owailion would hear her despite her inability to fully project to him.

Owailion nodded and then stepped past his wife, bringing a glittering platinum sword up under the chin of the withered magician. "You have two choices here. You give me your true name and I will wipe your memory of all names and magic, or I simply kill you. Choose?"

They could both hear his distrust of this bargain. Stylmach feared Owailion's sword held the power to kill him right through his shield but he also distrusted what they would do to him after these Wise Ones stripped him of all magic. They would hold his name and then could torture him as he had tortured Raimi.

"You keep forgetting, a Wise One cannot lie to you," Raimi reminded him. "If he says he will take only your magic and memories, he will do nothing more to you, but he will kill you if you don't surrender to our demands."

Stylmach managed to nod without getting himself cut on Owailion's sharp blade and then began speaking. "The dragon name I was given was Tiamat. I had not found the time to test it out for one must be close to use it." For some reason, Stylmach could not fathom that got a terrible roar from the dragon on the deck who could witness everything that happened below decks. "And... and my name is ... Gnalish."

Raimi looked for the flick of a snake tongue and saw none. She nodded her approval and then Owailion spoke. "Gnalish, you will now forget everything of magic you have ever known. You do not know the name of any dragon or Wise One. Your magic is gone Gnalish. And you have been a sailor on this ship for some time. Go home."

"Oh, and Gnalish, give me my Heart Stone," Raimi ordered imperiously as she felt his last tentacles of power over her fall away. She held out her hand as if Gnalish had it to give her, but he had completely forgotten where it was. All the name magic she could invoke would not change that. Instead, she concentrated on the puzzle and felt the little orb's presence in a chest tucked under the bed and retrieved it with a thought. With that Owailion took Raimi by the hand, signaled Imzuli of their departure and they instantly returned to the Land.

Chapter 21

Erosion

"What are we going to do?" Raimi asked Owailion frankly as soon as they returned to the Land. He had brought them to the waterfall just below the animal palace he had almost finished. He looked over at Imzuli who settled on the shore wearily.

"First, we make a nesting spot for you," he ordered. "Imzuli, we thank you for your help in dealing with Stylmach, but it is time that you went back to sleep. Will you consider moving to Jonjonel? It is unoccupied and we know you won't be disturbed there."

"It seems I must," the dragon sighed gustily. "Can we plate it in silver?"

Owailion chuckled and began doing just that from a distance. "It should be ready for you when you arrive," he promised. With a final farewell, the two Wise Ones watched Imzuli lift away from the ground and disappear.

"I'm going to miss her," Raimi whispered wistfully.

"And you…" Owailion interrupted her before Raimi grew too distressed, "you need to stay away from the ocean. Until we know that the Stylmach's mentor does not know you, he must never see you. I will go to Malornia and seek him out. You stay here."

Raimi almost argued that his restriction was a useless precaution but Owailion's expression stopped her cold. She dare not let herself fall into another trap. "Perhaps," she speculated, "that is why you have no inspiration to build my home on the delta; too close to the sea. Very well, I will stay here and work in the gardens. Please see if you can deal with the king that bought the stones and knows Tamaar's name. I fear that they will be misused."

Owailion agreed heartily and then with a kiss, he disappeared from her arms.

And Raimi remained behind in the gardens of Fiain, working quietly within the walls but her mind ranged elsewhere. Daily she began picking away at the mysteries that remained; why the forests had died, why her delta had become a swamp, how Imzuli's mountain could possibly become a valley with a Wise One's palace sunk into it. She had no answers for such questions and it distressed her. If Stylmach's mentor also knew her name, could he also perform the magic to destroy those things in the Land? Working on gardens did not distract her enough from the uncomfortable changes they had foreseen and still could not fathom. The bowl's disturbing premonitions lingered.

Thankfully Owailion returned to her every night and shared his progress or she would have gone mad with worry. "The demons have completely left Enok's village," he reported. "It's as if their work was done and they have moved on."

"What will you do now?" she asked, although she really feared to know.

"I'm moving south along the coast, headed toward their capital city," Owailion explained. "I'm hoping that Stylmach's mentor is attached to the crown and I can confront both he and the king at the same time. However, since the Memories have no references for Malornia, I must spy out my path as I go."

Raimi did not suggest he join a ship's crew rather than trekking by land. Her seasickness spell afflicted anyone who possessed magic, even a Wise One. Having him gone was tedious for both of them and Raimi had to pick up the slack in addressing demons and continued working on gardens while Owailion traversed Malornia. For weeks they endured this routine into the summer.

Then, on midsummer's night, after celebrating Owailion's 'birthday', Raimi woke from sleep terrorized. She sat up in the dark of one of Lara's newly completed bedrooms, panting at a dream she could not remember.

Owailion roused and stretched out an arm to her. "What is it?"

"A dream…and I cannot remember it." She shuddered and almost could not get the words out. "Do you think…?"

"We wiped Stylmach's mind and I have not been able to find his master," replied Owailion as he pulled his sweetheart into his arms and rocked her, hoping to comfort her while he hid his own fears. "In the morning we will look in the bowl and see what you saw."

Raimi would not be comforted. Instead, she revealed something more. "I have put warning spells on Imzuli's mountain and the delta. I want to know if any magic is used near them, just in case," she advised him. She had continued experimenting with deep spells that left no trace until triggered and so forgot to tell him until this dream reminded her. Deep spells were like deep water, unnoticed until someone drowned. "No alarm went off."

Owailion approved her precautions by kissing the top of her head and settling a dreamless sleep spell over Raimi's mind.

The next morning, testing out the newly finished kitchen at Lara, Raimi wandered in to discuss what had happened in the night. She carried with her the bowl and pipes, knowing they would be needed. She thought deeply of the impressions of her dream out in the open so Owailion would know what she feared. For her, dreams had rarely been enlightening. She brought forward the bowl and whispered her request. "Show me my dream last night."

In the bowl's reflection, they both watched as Raimi walked through the deep Don Forest. She drew her hands along the bark, seeking the sickness that would one day make this forest die-off; one of the lesser damages they had witnessed in the bowl's prophesies for the Land. She found no sign of fading here, for the trees stood so thickly that she found it hard to find a path.

"Why am I here?" dream Raimi asked of no one.

The trees seemed to whisper something to her and she could not understand the language they spoke. "I cannot understand you," she replied.

Then her perspective turned. She was still in the Don Forest but instead of near the sea she found the Great Chain looming before her. This time the mountains whispered to her and while the words seemed clearer, she could not understand the language of stone any more than the language of the trees.

Then a third time her location changed and she stood knee-deep in the river, where the forest surrounded her and she looked down, hearing the words oozing from the mountains and trees still. The river added to the melodious song. Raimi looked down in the flow and saw there a reflection of mountains, not the forest around her. Puzzled, she asked again, "What are you saying?"

To her surprise, a glowing Heart Stone came rolling down through the clear water. It had come down from the mountains, through this forest and now was headed out to sea, she thought. Raimi reached for it, but unaccountably, it rolled away from her. Usually, the river would bring her anything she asked for, but this Heart Stone had a mind of its own. It scurried away too quickly for her to keep up though it remained always in sight. She followed it downstream until the trees began to thin and she could taste salt water from the ocean in the flow. The trees began to give way to seagrasses and the Heart Stone stopped rolling away from her. Raimi plucked it out of the water and looked up into the open sky.

"You will meet here. The next Wise One's name will be Gilead," whispered the forest, the river, and the mountains. In a surprise, Raimi gasped as she finally understood the words. With that, she awakened.

Both Owailion and Raimi blinked, as if they had been under a spell and then looked down into the bowl. There, as if it had been waiting the whole time, a new Heart Stone rested in the shallow dish. Amazed, Raimi picked it up and noted how it did not beat to her heart's pace.

"Gilead, the next Wise One?" She grinned as she said it. This might be closest to having a child they would ever get and it felt much the same. They both laughed at their alarm in an innocent dream and kissed in congratulations. At last, they knew something positive that was bound to happen in the future. They had no clues as to when or how, but Raimi now understood that the new Wise One would come at the Don River Delta.

"Maybe we should work on the palace at Don," suggested Owailion eagerly. "It's probably livable now and we can keep an eye open for him…or her. It is just strange that you have the Heart Stone now to give him."

"Or her," Raimi qualified. "I wonder which affinity he or she might have. Forest, mountain, sea; they all showed up in the dream."

"There's a definite mountain palace, one for the sea and the one on the Don might be a forest palace." Owailion reminded her. "Let's go and see how the architecture is coming together. It's not too close to the sea where an outlander might see you."

They traveled instantly to the delta of the Don River using one of Owailion's orbs and looked around, hoping for an arriving Wise One, but there was nothing. It was several miles to the open ocean so they did not fear that some Malornian sorcerer might spy Raimi there. Besides the palace, there had been under construction for some time and she could remain inside, out of sight. The building still lacked the more appreciated things like a hearth they could put wood into or running water. This did not stop them from camping inside the kitchen. Raimi looked into the architecture to see signs of what the affinity here would be and some hope to indicate it belonged to a King or Queen of the Forest, but she saw nothing definitive.

"Should we ask about the future, to see who is coming as the next Wise One," she wondered as she pulled out the bowl. Seeing something good in it had restored her faith in the Talisman.

Owailion wanted to stop her. The future, while available to be seen, always seemed cursed when they looked at it. He felt the Talisman should be exclusively for the past where it had always been more helpful. However, it was not his to command, so he nodded and then stepped away to see if he could speed up the placement of hearthstones so they could have a fire.

Raimi looked into the water of her bowl, whispered the words she wanted, "Show me the future occupant of this castle."

But the bowl remained lifeless, showing only the ceiling of the kitchen. That was curious. Raimi's doubts washed back in. Maybe she was being too pushy, demanding too much from her magic instead of letting it come naturally. A little voice in her mind whispered again that the things she touched always went awry. She would get into trouble; trying to do too much and not being patient with God's time.

Raimi shivered and contented herself to go find a bed for them in the half-finished palace.

* * *

Nightmares again plagued her and this time Raimi could not escape them.

"Good girl, you've come. You now have a perfectly legitimate reason to stay down here near the sea. Now, remember, you will not react to any of these communications, Raimi. You are worried that your curse might hurt Owailion, so you will not tell him, Raimi. Now, let's see how subtle you can be. Raimi, I want you to kill the Don Forest but do not destroy it all at once. Make it a slow death that Owailion will not notice."

This soft, insinuating voice did not ask questions, did not engage in conversation and did a far better job of binding her within the name magic that Stylmach. She could not conceive of any way to mitigate the commands. She had already been forced to turn off the alarms she had set on the delta and Imzuli's mountain. A slow death for the forest; how was she supposed to manage that? She knew copper was how you killed a tree's roots. Drive a copper nail into a stump and the trunk would slowly decay and never spring back up. So could she accomplish the same thing by bringing copper into the soil, slowly poisoning a forest?

The streams of Raimi's mind knew the paths in which the Don's headwaters could flow where it might pick up copper in the mountains and start upping the mineral levels in the Don River. Subtly she shifted the paths of a few creeks far up in the eastern arm of the Great Chain, washing them overexposed copper ore and she pushed a spring up through one especially copper-rich area so that the water table would do the rest. Shifting the water around would be enough to over time destroy the Don Forest and no one, not even a Wise One would know unless they suspected her deceit and looked into her mind.

"That's good, Raimi. Now, erase this dream from the bowl's visions. You will sleep well Raimi and when you wake you will forget this whole conversation." The voice whispered subtly, insinuating itself into her dreams as it had for weeks now. Sending Owailion to Malornia had been a waste when the enemy was already with the gates of her mind. She would forget the specifics but something inside remembered the manipulation. She knew that this was worse than before, but that knowledge never followed her into the waking world.

* * *

Raimi thanked Owailion for finishing a hearth and the pump system for the Don palace quickly, as they intended to stay here until the new Wise One arrived. Owailion's work at finding the Malornian Master had borne no fruit and it was too dangerous to go out looking for more. They could set up housekeeping here as well as anywhere else. Raimi carefully encouraged this settling in. Perhaps he would notice what Raimi would not, could not let him see; how depressed she felt. She smiled brightly. She kissed him often and the gardens expanded wonderfully in the growing summer weather.

But keeping Owailion away from home only worsened Raimi's fear for other reasons. She disliked coming so close to the ocean. There might be another ship out there, initiating name magic manipulation on her again. She knew something was wrong despite the lost memories, so rather than give in to that fear, she took action. One morning Raimi called on the mind of a seagull that lived on the delta and asked it to head toward the open ocean, seeking any interactions with mankind beyond the Seal. The bird flew away into the bright sun and she went back to work on the gardens again.

At dusk, the gull returned to her and she spoke with it. The bright-eyed bird did not see anything unusual, at least on the human level but there had been strange changes out to sea just beyond the Seal. A new island, shaped like a pointing finger now stood out among the waves. It had only a few trees upon it and the birds were just now investigating it for a rookery, so it had not been there the season before. While Owailion investigated the still growing stones at Zema Raimi sent her mind out on the delta as far as she dared without leaving the Seal and tried to see what the bird had described but the fog hid it from view. Was it an outpost for the magician that stalked and used her, free from the seasickness that kept others at bay? Could she ask Owailion about the finger island?

"No," replied the voice that night when he rummaged through her mind and heard her plotting. "You are trying to discover who I am and how I am using your exquisite magic. Raimi, you will do nothing that will reveal me to you. You are under my control and it will remain that way eternally."

And to emphasize the point, the gull she had used as a spy dropped into her lap dead in the middle of her nightmare. This one she would remember.

However, she wasn't allowed the dignity of crying over her lost freedom or integrity because that would be a sign that something was wrong and Owailion would notice. She was beginning to dread going to sleep. Could she perhaps survive without it?

"Then I would only invade your thoughts waking as well. As punishment for your rebellion with the gull, I want you to destroy a mountain. You know which one I want. I know the dragon has moved on thanks to your manipulation. However, I know the dragon will be hard put to forgive you. I want you to crush Imzuli's mountain, Raimi."

Raimi tried to fight it, pointing out that Owailion would know something had happened. You could not change the face of the Land without him being aware. The Memories provided every detail of the Land and he would feel it in his bones.

"And yet you will not leave behind a trace in your magic," droned the voice. "You will tear the memory of that mountain from his mind and Raimi, I will watch to be sure you do it perfectly. Raimi, do as I say."

"Why that mountain?" she begged as she woke in the dark. She had to delay the inevitable. The subtle sorcerer, her Tormenter did not reply, leaving behind his mandate and no other recourse. The mandate forced her out of bed well before dawn so she could plan.

After breakfast the next day Raimi checked to be sure Owailion was well occupied at his latest project, a palace just south of the Fallon Forest, for she also must answer to the compulsion to avoid detection. She then began working on how to destroy a mountain so no one would notice.

She considered what she knew about Imzuli's mountain; its location, rivers, and creeks that cut down its sides and the glaciers that fed them. Her creeks could erode stone but that took time, which was not on her side. Inside the mountain, with that great hollow chamber reinforced magically with a coating of silver, titanium or steel, she could eliminate that and weaken the structure, but mountains like that did not just simply collapse. If it were a volcano that might be another matter but the whole north/south stretch of the Great Chain was formed from uplift due to earthquake faults, not volcanoes. And an earthquake would only leave a mountain of debris that would be impossible to explain. She didn't know a great deal about the mountains, but she knew that much. Briefly, she felt grateful that the King or Queen of Mountains had not emerged yet or Raimi would certainly be caught.

With a twist of her mind, she gathered all the lining Imzuli had done to her cave and turned the cavern into simple stone. She thought briefly about taking all the metal and forging herself a sword to kill herself rather than being forced to inflict pain on the Land. It would not be a guarantee. Could a sword ever kill her? Besides, her Tormenter would hear her, stop her before the blade fell, and then punish her. Supposedly a Wise One could not die, or so she had been led to believe. So instead she made Imzuli's silver casing disappear back into the magic of the world.

Next Raimi examined the way water, her forte might undermine the roots of the mountain from underneath. Natural aquifers within the rock, the sources of springs and slow corrosion were at her disposal so she began lifting the water through the cracks and crevasses that it could always find. She did enough erosion in a day to compare with a century of time if it were to happen naturally. But still, the mighty mountain stood firm and unchanged in appearance. She stopped her efforts when Owailion returned for the evening and hoped the progress she had made would satisfy the Tormenter.

"Very disappointing, Raimi," Tormentor's words invaded her sleep that night. "You were supposed to bring down the mountain. As a consequence…"

"You gave me a mandate that this should be as subtle as possible and that Owailion must not know I'm behind it. I've started working on grinding down the mountain but it's going to be obvious soon," she interrupted the Tormentor.

"As obvious as stripping you of all your friends and loved ones so that you will turn to me?" The unseen sorcerer laughed in a toxic way. "Raimi, you've got to try harder."

"And when Owailion traces this destruction to me, what will my consequences be then?" she snapped at him. "I will never be free of your demands, will I? What do you want of me?"

The pause lingered in the dream's air like the flakes of snow that floated on the bitter air. "I want you, Raimi. I want the Land and all the magic in it. But most of all, I want you, Raimi, Queen of Rivers."

That reply so stunned her that she grasped fruitlessly for something to say. No one else on the planet had even met her. She wasn't, at least in her opinion, a great beauty or particularly intelligent. She had too bold of a personality, recklessly brazen and had few talents that were not directly magical. Why would anyone want her?

"You are the hardest on yourself, Raimi. You sell yourself short at every turn. So I know you can make a better effort on the mountain," the voice chided.

"I will do whatever you want," Raimi began begging. "I will leave the Land and go with you willingly if that will stop this destruction. I swear I will not fight you if you will stop forcing me to do harm to the Land and the people that I love." In her dream, the oath even put her into her royal regalia as she spoke with the disembodied magician.

"Ah, if only it was that easy. My hope is that you will come to me eventually without having to swear it. You see, Raimi, you will have nothing left to protect and so I will not need to worry that you will slip away, back to your friends. All the dragons will be gone and all the Wise Ones will fade away. The Land will be ours together along with all its power."

Raimi shuddered when not even a curse could come from her mouth. She felt broken. She would crush Imzuli's mountain because she had no choice, but hopefully a Wise One idea of how to deal with the binding in which she found herself entangled would come if she gave it time. Since the sorcerer seemed to be done with her, Raimi forced herself awake and slipped out of bed, seeking a quiet place to cry. Her eyes just seemed to dry up whenever Owailion was near and her words washed away in a flood when she wished to share her burden.

In the dark of the kitchen, she stirred the fire and then conjured a chair and table at which to sit. At times like this, alone and dream free, she could grieve and plan. To that end, she kept her pack with her constantly so if the sorcerer demanded she leave, she would not have to surrender all she possessed. From it she pulled out her clothes and dressed and then brought out her bowl and pipes, wondering if they could somehow help her. The two Talismans tickled at her mind, hinting at possibilities. Right now, the conflicting compulsions to destroy the mountain and to not allow Owailion to be aware of it competed. Could she make him forget the existence of the mountain with her pipes? Perhaps, yes, but how would she hide the gaping hole? She could just make the peak disappear but the magic would be obvious. Only earthquakes, volcanoes, and simple erosion would not bring obvious questions.

The bowl nudged at her mind. It showed the past…the river of the past. Time flowed like the waters. Could she make waters rush by faster than normal? Of course, so it stood to reason she could speed up time by the same means. If she sped up the erosion of a mountain, how many years would it take to grind it down to a valley? She would not touch the mountains around it. That is what she must try.

In the quiet dark of night, in the bare kitchen, Raimi concentrated on what she had to do. She conjured a copy of Owailion's map and reminded herself to alter it once she completed the work, then she circled the proper mountain on the map and began her wishing. In that area, only the passage of time would increase by a factor of millions. Storms and wind, rain and icy fractures would erode away the mountain. Millennia would pass in an hour. In her mind's eye, she saw the weathering and looked into the bowl to judge when to stop. This work meant creeks that normally fell around the mountain now flowed steeply into the valley she had formed. A lake would soon fill up the dell, making it impossible for Owailion to build a palace there in the future. That would not do; she could fix it by blowing out another path out of the valley and down toward a river that would eventually flow into the huge nameless lake in the northeast. She had created a new river as well as destroyed a mountain.

Then Raimi stopped the river of time she had crafted. The mountain she had destroyed and the path of a new river it caused now had been cut into the map she had conjured. With a flick of thought, she used her copy to replace the one Owailion kept. He must not be aware of her treachery. Her husband would never trust her again as it was if he ever found out how she was betraying the Land. She mourned the loss of that trust most of all.

Mournfully Raimi picked up her pipes and like a puppet, stilted and awkward, walked back to the bedroom they were utilizing. Rather than wake him, she simply sat on the edge of the bed, concentrated on the very specific thing she wanted him to forget, even to the point of ripping it from the dragon-gifted Memories and then played his recollection of Imzuli's home away. The white dragon had always lived in Jonjonel and now she slept there peacefully. Maybe in a thousand years when the dragons awoke again, Raimi would admit what she was doing.

"Dragons will be extinct in a thousand years. They will be long forgotten," the sorcerer slipped into her mind, deepening her sadness.

Raimi turned away from her husband's sleeping figure, feeling unfaithful. "I have done what you asked. Now I will ask something of you. Will you leave the Land be, leave Owailion alone and the dragons and all of it, if I come to you, ...without name magic?"

"Now, Raimi, why would I want that? It is so much more delicious to watch you eroding your life away, eating your own heart."

Before she did something that would warrant a new punishment, Raimi set aside the pipes and put a spell on herself to encourage dreamless sleep. She knew now her curse was true; everything she touched would be destroyed. So she slept on anyway, dreaming of murder and suicide.

Chapter 22

Ultimatum

Owailion knew something was wrong despite everything. Raimi's eyes hid a dark mood and jumpy fears plagued her. He had not shared with her Enok's warning dream but now in late summer Owailion rarely left her side as they worked on various palaces. Raimi sometimes made excuses to go swimming in the river after working on gardens all day. Owailion watched her through a memory globe but learned little. He so earnestly yearned to speak with her, to beg her to somehow explain her anxiety. Could she again be ensnared in name magic? This odd behavior seemed to echo how Imzuli had acted just weeks before the Sleep when she stopped talking as well.

Finally one day Owailion suggested a picnic, just to get her to respond to him.

"Yes," Raimi agreed. "Let's go out to the beach where that finger rock is."

Owailion felt a stab of alarm. He had seen that island that rose above the mist and was visible just offshore, but it was not part of the Memories. That it was so near the sea did not worry him half as much as that she suggested it at all. She should have feared going there.

When they arrived, Raimi initially just stared at the finger rock, saying nothing. She pursed her lips, folding her arms across herself, and let the river waters meet the sea before her. This place seemed to symbolize her conflict. In her mind, Owailion heard how she felt like a river being swallowed and overwhelmed by the ocean.

Owailion kept his thoughts to himself. It was a rotten day for a picnic on the beach, but it was her 'birthday' and agreeing to go to such an unwelcoming place had been enough to tell her that he was concerned. The sand blew in their eyes and the wind grew chilly, but Owailion knew instinctively she needed to tell him something that she could hopefully reveal here. He sat alone on the blanket that they brought, just watching her. Rather than speculating, Owailion trusted his instincts and watched her staring.

"Raimi, please talk to me," he suggested finally. There was no name magic behind Owailion's request, simply love. She didn't even turn back to look at him. In her mind, he heard how she felt mesmerized by his dark eyes or the mysteriously white hair on a young face. He had power over her without magic.

When she finally did think of something to say, she said it mentally, not aloud, as if they might have been overheard. "You know I always felt that everything I touch is going to go wrong? I still feel that way."

"Yes," he replied. "But it is not so."

He could not resist. Owailion approached her and whispered her name, and slipped into her mind, close so even the wind could not overhear them. "Raimi, are you being controlled again by someone?"

Raimi could not get her mouth to move or even mental words, but she did manage to look at him seriously. Owailion's protective bubble warmed all around them, keeping her hopefully safe, but she still could not make a sound.

"Is he out on that rock there?" Owailion felt a pit of dread drop in his stomach, but he continued the careful questioning knowing that even positive and negative moves might be too difficult for her to make if name magic manipulated her. She blinked out to sea and then down at the ground. So Owailion interpreted that her Tormentor was everywhere.

"Is he inside the Seal?"

She shook her hair out of the nonexistent wind. She didn't think the sorcerer had made it that far but it would not take much for the Tormentor to command her to drop the Seal and then he could walk right in.

"Has he commanded you to harm something already?"

In reply, she turned inland, toward the mountains. "The dragons?" Owailion speculated. "No, not yet. The Land? Me?" Owailion ran his comforting hands on her arms and down her back to keep her from crumbling. He knew and understood even if he had not struck on precisely the damages she had done.

"I forgive you, my love," he whispered into her ear. "This is not you or your curse. This is evil that the Wise Ones must face. Now, do you think he is Stylmach's mentor?" Owailion asked, continuing the line of questioning.

She looked out to the sea again and tried to smile as if she knew she was being watched. Owailion kissed her to help the charade. "Is he contacting you through dreams?" She sighed with exhaustion so he knew it was more than just dreams.

"Does he ask you questions?" Raimi frowned so he would understand the difference. She had been entirely unable to engage this Tormenter in revealing himself with a conversation.

"Can he reach you if we move inland again?" Raimi blinked a positive; there was no escaping this one. "Does he know about the next Wise One coming here?"

This time Raimi's eyes grew wide with alarm. She didn't know how much the Tormenter knew about why they had come to the mouth of the Don River. Had it been a true dream, or an artificial excuse just to get her near the sea again? She didn't seem to know.

"Very well, we need to protect him as well as you," Owailion decided for them, knowing she was at her wit's end when it came to outwitting this sorcerer. "I think you need to go be with Imzuli. Don't wake her. Just camp in her mountain and…and that is….Jonjonel? Has something changed there?"

Raimi's eyes grew so wide he could see his own reflection in her stormy green eyes. "I'll figure it out. Leave the pipes with me and I'll remember. Go to Imzuli, put a shield around the mountain and do not come out until I tell you it is safe. Can you do that?"

Raimi's brow furrowed in worry. She couldn't be sure one way or the other. What if the Tormenter commanded her to come to him?

"I'll use name magic to enforce it. Let's see which command you have to obey. Raimi, do not come out of Imzuli's cavern until you hear from me."

In response she reached out and finally touched him back, kissing him soundly, deeply and then, as she did as he suggested she pressed her pipes and the new-comer's Heart Stone into his hands.

"I love you," she managed at least to speak.

Owailion's mind followed, monitored her magic as she reached for the creek at the base of Jonjonel and faded from his arms.

* * *

Getting away from the sea felt like a relief, Raimi realized, even though her Tormentor had no problem reaching her much farther inland. Obedient to Owailion's name magic she stretched out her thoughts toward the cavern Owailion had crafted for Imzuli and found a bit of water that leaked into it for a pulling point. She entered the dark of the cavern and didn't even bother lighting her way in the profound darkness. She could hear the dragon's gentle breathing, half rumble, half sigh warm in her mind. Raimi conjured herself a human-sized pillow, lay down and with a final experiment told herself, with firm name magic, "Raimi, sleep without dreams."

But dreams were not all the Tormentor possessed.

* * *

When he had first begun to understand magic, Owailion had thought how amazing it all was, and that there would be little trouble being a steward of the Land. No one would invade, they would never want for anything and the specter of sadness and fear would never raise its head. What a fool had he been to think that way? With great power, there always came a need to use it. He could not imagine what Raimi was going through but he feared he would sacrifice everything, even the Land itself if there was a way to save her.

The problem was, he didn't know how to go about it. A new Wise One was coming and that might help, as long as there was time to train him. Owailion knew the new-comer's name and Raimi had left him the pipes as well as the extra Heart Stone as another clue of how she was being manipulated. Obviously, she didn't trust herself with these items and she had been compelled to make Owailion forget something. Now she wanted him to remember all she had been forced to erase? Owailion felt he must investigate that before he decided how to deal with this Tormentor. He dared not go Seeking the next Wise One for his help, or it would alert the sorcerer to a new and vulnerable Wise One. Best to first confront this sorcerer who had Raimi as his puppet. And to do that he needed to know what had passed between his wife and the Tormenter. With that decided Owailion gathered up his blanket and, as if he were only following Raimi home he went back to the cold hearth in the palace at Don.

Owailion sat at the table and then pulled out the pipes with trepidation. Could he specifically instruct it to give him the memory that had been taken from him? Well, it was worth a try. He set the reeds to his lips and blew. He concentrated on producing music and found that a song that reflected his mood came forward, effortlessly. He deftly played a call to arms and if he did not think about it, Owailion began to remember what had been taken from him; an entire mountain. Under the song's spell Owailion abruptly recalled how Raimi had asked Imzuli to move and the dragon had done so. Then, over the ensuing weeks and months, under the command of her Tormenter, Raimi had washed the dragon's mountain away, from his memories as well as all their maps. Also stunning him, Owailion recognized that Raimi had killed the forest. And worst of all she had hidden these things from him.

But Owailion wasn't hurt by it. He was terrified. Owailion knew Raimi's weakness; her belief in the curse that anything she touched would be destroyed. And all these spells performed under name magic would only help reinforce that belief. He wished briefly that he had taken her Talisman bowl as well so he could go back and listen to her thoughts as she dealt with this invasion of her magic. There had to be some way to sever the link between Raimi and the Tormenter. Could Owailion find the sorcerer and snap his neck before he asked Raimi to do something that truly hurt others? He must do something soon or the sorcerer would expose the Land to pure evil at Raimi's hand. She had not killed anyone yet and had done everything she could to avoid causing harm but it was only a matter of time.

Owailion reached across the continent to Jonjonel, to where he knew Imzuli hibernated and felt his wife also there, peacefully sleeping and hopefully without invading dreams. Now, how could he protect her?

* * *

"Tethimzuliel? Wake up," the voice ordered.

Imzuli growled at the interruption. Wasn't she supposed to be allowed to sleep? But this voice was insistent. Unfamiliar and she wondered if it was Owailion, the only other human male she knew… other than that Gnalish whom she felt inclined to roast at this point. This Voice seemed to be neither and had invoked her name. Imzuli sat up and almost struck her head on the ceiling of the cavern and then she remembered. She had moved to Jonjonel.

"Tethimzuliel, you must obey me. Raimi is in that cavern with you. Bring her to me, Tethimzuliel."

Name magic! The dragon knew it instantly. A magician was trying to manipulate her. She dare not move. If Raimi was there in the cavern with her she might accidentally step on her friend before she found her. Imzuli sparked a single light in the cavern and found her human friend curled up sleeping right under her wing.

"*Where shall I bring her to you?*" the dragon called, delaying the imperative, though it hurt to resist. Dragons could often manipulate name magic if given enough ways to delay and qualify the order.

An image of a ship…again that damnable ship, in a harbor was pressed into the dragon's mind. Imzuli knew the place; Raimi's favorite location on the mouth of the Lara River where her palace would one day be built. The dragon sighed, feeling the compulsion and no way out.

"*Owailion!*" Imzuli called, but the voice blocked her.

"Ah, ah, no calling to anyone else Tethimzuliel," the magician qualified. "Just pick her up and bring her here."

Imzuli reluctantly stretched out a delicate claw and scooped up her friend, pillow and all. Raimi did not stir at the movement, as if she was in a spell. Well, given the situation, it was probably a truth. The white dragon shifted to the top of Jonjonel, balancing on the volcanic peak carefully before she spread her wings and then transitioned, this time to the delta.

The river snaked past the low delta islands and out to sea defying the tide. Against that flow, Imzuli saw the ship struggling, but unable to come closer for the Seal. She flew through the invisible barrier and landed on the deck, squeezing between two masts. Thankfully the canvas was furled or she would never have fit.

She gently set her friend on the deck and felt the release of at least that order. She still could not call one of the other dragons for help or to Owailion to tell him what was happening. Instead, Imzuli looked around the ship and finally saw a man coming forward, wearing a black leather suit, polished to a dragon shine and over it a silver cloak with gold markings running down his back. Imzuli began to feel a growl rising like a volcano in her gut and stepped over Raimi as if she would defend her physically.

"Do not bother, Tethimzuliel," the magician spoke proudly. "Thank you for your services. You can go back to sleep now Tethimzuliel."

The dragon had little chance to catch herself before she collapsed on the deck, asleep with her muzzle snapping the railing on the starboard side, almost dragging in the water, her hindquarters flopping overboard on the port side and her tail acting as a sudden second rudder. The spread wings hid Raimi from view and the magician sighed. What a bother exact wording had become.

And moving a dragon would wear him out. Well, he could not do his next work with a dragon nearly capsizing the ship. The sorcerer pushed up his sleeves and then made a lifting motion. The massive body moved with his hands. He carefully wove the dragon out of the vital structures of the ship and then spun her away, back through the Seal and onto the shore. Imzuli did not move a muscle as she landed with a thud on the sandy beach.

The Tormentor turned back to Raimi who slept on, oblivious to her changed location. He had to agree with his apprentice, Stylmach, that this magician was lovely. Her stunning hair and pale skin particularly appealed to him and almost he could forgive her for destroying all the hard work he had put into his protégé. Almost. If perhaps he could do the same to her, make her a puppet, obedient and barely magical she would make a fine wife. The Tormenter lifted a lock of her coppery hair, luxuriating in its scent. Then he gave himself a shake. Time to get to work. She needed disciplined.

"Raimi, wake up," he ordered harshly. He then quickly reset all his controls before she could even fully obey the first directive. "Raimi, you will use no magic on me or this ship until I tell you. Raimi, you will not contact anyone in the Land."

She woke bewildered and a little sick. "Yes, your seasickness spell still is working," he warned as her ice-green eyes focused on him and he saw the rage there. She would crush him the instant he slipped up.

It did not take long. Somewhere deep within Raimi began plotting her acts of rebellion. What could she still do? Instinctively she reached toward the Lara River and began damming it up like her magic was blocked behind a more than physical shield. Just beyond the Seal the water that spread across the beach just yards from the ship started to soak away, drawn back by her magic. She could justify it since she wasn't attacking her Tormentor or the ship; she was simply damming a river. But she dare not think of this act or he would know.

Meanwhile, the sorcerer continued picking at her aching soul with his words. "Oh dear," he began, "you should not have tried to get away with it. Somehow you brought Owailion into our little relationship. You abandoned him and hid instead. Did the white dragon forgive you for what you did to her mountain? How about the fact that you have given me her name as well?"

Raimi cringed for she did not even remember that betrayal. Miserably she looked around the ship's deck, struggled up from her bed and peered north toward home. She recognized the lovely cliffs and green coastline where the Lara River cut out of the high plains. She squinted and could see Imzuli's bulk, shining brighter and whiter than the sand on which she lay.

"Yes, you gave me her name when I asked," the Tormenter reminded her.

"I thought you did not want a dragon as much as you wanted me," Raimi snapped, keeping her eye on the Land, her friend, her hopes.

"I have you…and now I have a dragon too. I wanted the dragon as an object lesson. You see, there is a myth that dragons cannot die. Indeed, they seem to be deathless but there are a few rare things that can kill a magnificent creature like that; her name being one of them."

That got Raimi to turn to face him. "No, please," she whispered in fear.

"You have two choices. I kill your dragon or you lower the Seal. Which shall it be?" The flickering in this sorcerer's alien eyes spoke of pleasure at the manipulation. "I could always ask her to make the same choice instead. Would Tethimzuliel choose Raimi over the Seal? Shall I wake her to ask?"

Raimi was powerless. She wept even as her mind struggled to grasp the choice. Without waiting for the dilemma to even sink in the sorcerer did as promised. "Tethimzuliel, wake up. Tethimzuliel, you can do no magic. You cannot fly or call out to anyone."

Imzuli, just a few yards up on the shore lifted her head with alarm and oriented herself with much the same look as her human friend if that was possible. They made eye contact across the water and then Imzuli roared in her frustration. She hopped gracelessly and tried to blow fire in a futile attempt to escape the name magic bonds. None of her more draconic skills remained to her and she was pinned to the shore, handicapped and furious.

"Tethimzuliel," the insufferable sorcerer began explaining the ultimatum. "I have given Raimi a choice: bring down the Seal on the Land or kill you. It is a simple choice in my mind, but then, you are not my friend. Dragons and humans have been enemies for ages. I do not see how two different species of magicians can possibly share the same territory. Is that why the dragons were put to sleep?"

"They are our friends," Raimi insisted, for she knew Imzuli could not reply. "Only a monster would ask me to make such a choice."

"A monster, am I?" Her Tormentor lifted an eyebrow and smirked. "Very well, I will make the choice for you." He then turned away imperiously from Raimi who could only look on with horror. Then in a voice loud enough to carry over the water he called.

"Tethimzuliel, die."

Chapter 23

Lost One

Raimi almost stopped breathing just as Imzuli did. Without so much as a growl, the silver dragon collapsed in a heap and did not twitch. "NO!" Raimi shrieked in pure emotion. She could not attack her Tormentor nor perform magic against him but she had to do something.

Without thinking, Raimi dove over the side of the ship. She might not be able to use magic against him, but she could swim. And the Tormenter let her go. He basked in what he had done, enjoying this despicable experience. He had killed an immortal dragon. Raimi, for her part, let her tears flow and add to the ocean. In moments she staggered out of the surf, reached Imzuli and threw herself on her friend's neck. Rage and grief mingled to dam up Raimi's mind for a moment.

Desperately the Queen of Rivers sought for some recourse and felt the waterway beyond her that had already provided it. She had known something was going to snap and now she understood why. She filled every fountain up the river miles upstream, beyond the delta and now she knew what had caused that terrible future Talisman vision. She herself was destroying the most beautiful place she had known. In the bowl, she had seen the whole area turned into a swamp and the protective hillsides gone. Well, her Tormenter wanted her to eliminate mountains; this would do it. Raimi justified it because she would only be burying Imzuli, not directing magic against her Tormenter or the ship. And if they happened to get caught in the aftermath, so be it.

Meanwhile, as the pressure built behind Raimi's invisible dam the Tormenter watched her suffer as she powerlessly commanded her friend to live again. Then he added his commentary. "You could have avoided this if you had decided to break the Seal instead," he called from the safety of the ship. "Why must you always make it such an ordeal of using the magic you have? I would be the King of the Land and you would be my Queen. All the people would worship us."

Raimi did not raise her head from her grief to look back at him but she did reply if only to keep him talking so that there would be more pressure behind the dam when she shattered it. "You're a fool," she said grimly, letting her contempt show, hoping to egg him into attacking her rather than just simply using her as a puppet. "You don't understand the Land. There are no people here to worship you; just me, Owailion and a few dragons asleep for millennia. You will gain nothing if you come here to rule."

"People will come," he reminded her, making it sound like a threat.

Had the Tormentor seen the bowl's prediction of the future in her mind? Had he been listening to her every thought for months? Raimi hoped not or he would suspect what she was plotting right then.

Instead, the Tormentor continued to blather on unaware of her mental rebellion as she turned away from him to look up toward where her home would have been but now never would be built.

"The ley lines that flow in your land must be tremendous for you to have such power. I've seen you move mountains, kill forests and change the world, Raimi. And you will do it again for me Raimi; you and me together."

"You do not know what you are asking," warned Raimi. "You cannot ask me to keep one mandate when there is a second mandate on me that you will not be able to break. I have been sworn to protect the Land from such as you. I cannot do both."

The Tormenter laughed at her cruelly. "I have seen you do both. You made a whole mountain disappear and not even your pathetic husband knew what you were doing. I don't know how he figured out I held your strings, but he's only the King of Buildings. He has abandoned you. Raimi, you are far greater than he is. You deserve better. I can give you all he cannot. He is nothing. He hasn't given you children, nor built you a palace like all the others. Even now he is sputtering around on another river, waiting for nothing. He has not even come to your rescue here. I pity you for being tied to such a man all your life."

Owailion, she thought, tuning out the blathering of the sorcerer. I cannot even say goodbye to you. Then an idea, a Wise One-inspired insight came to her. Yes, I can send a gift. I can give you the bowl. You can see what I am about to do. It is not leaving you a message. I am sending you a gift of the past. It is not magic directed at the Tormenter. I can do that little bit of magic and you might understand my actions. I had no choice.

With a flick of thought, Raimi gave her beloved Owailion her final Talisman. He had it all now; the extra Heart Stone, the Pipes of Forgetting and the Bowl of the Past. Now maybe he would forgive her.

The sorcerer must have sensed her inattentiveness, for he used name magic to bring her back to focus on him. "Raimi, listen to me," he ordered. "You will do this with me. You will be mine. Raimi, break the Seal and let me in."

Belatedly she realized she might have waited just a bit too long. She could sense the water pressure had built to the point she could almost not contain it. She also knew she had to remove her Heart Stone to perform his command. The Tormentor understood nothing of the restrictions of the Heart Stone; she could not obey him and still protect the Land. However, without the judge of the stone, she could kill the monster, she hoped. She was prepared.

Resolved, Raimi reached into her chest and slowly removed her Heart Stone. It glowed in the bright sun and then she wearily turned and set the Heart Stone inside Imzuli's body, right beside the dragon's own and then rose to her feet. In grief, Raimi recalled all she had learned as she studied how the Seal was built. She knew the deep magic well at its roots. She felt how it entwined with Owailion's Memories. She would perform one last sweeping spell.

To help the Tormentor understand that she was about to obey him she lifted her arms high above her head. Across the water, she saw him smile in anticipation and he had brought the ship in closer to the Seal, expecting it would be only a matter of seconds before he could come ashore. Then with a wish, Raimi broke the dam that held the Lara River at bay and brought the Seal down all at once.

Raimi's river of magic flowed on.

* * *

Owailion stood on the misty shore of the Don River, peering out to sea, wondering if he was actually seeing what was there. That single island, just beyond the Seal seemed like a sentinel floating above the fog and he dare not investigate or the sorcerer would know he was being watched. Thankfully Raimi was far away, asleep in a cavern and this sorcerer remained unaware he now had two Wise Ones to fight, one of which he could not name.

Owailion's other great worry was that somewhere here soon a new Wise One would appear. He could feel it in his bones and the newcomer would need to be protected and trained. In his heart, Owailion knew just as he had known when Raimi would first arrive. That first arrival event, coming to the Land, made you vulnerable. He dreaded the thought of fighting a sorcerer at the same moment time as he had to be welcoming a new Wise One. Owailion's mind ran through all the steps: throw a shield over him, and maybe move him inland, prevent him from speaking until after the battle was over and hope for the best, Owailion decided.

Patience was never his best trait, Owailion realized as he brought the blanket back into being and sat down. He had been impatient for Raimi's arrival too. Then it had been loneliness that drove his restlessness but now impending battle made him almost frantic with impatience. He wanted to use the pipes to wipe the sorcerer's mind and be done.

The sun was just setting over the sea when Owailion felt a gentle brush of magic and Raimi's bowl abruptly appeared on the blanket before him. In alarm, he reached for it. Why was she sending him this? He launched his mind to seek hers to find out the purpose of giving him the bowl. Owailion's magic strained to the far side of the continent to find her at Jonjonel when he realized she was not there and a stab of panic lanced through him. He stood up with the bowl in his hands and was about to go seeking her presence elsewhere when the earth shook and he almost fell over, staggering in the thunderous snapping of something. The wrench of pain across his mind tore free from his soul.

Owailion felt the Seal falling.

He gasped, for, with its fall, he could see the bay in front of him filled with ships of all sizes and shapes plying their way back and forth. Most looked to be on a run moving goods either south to Marwen or west toward Malornia but one ship stood at anchor right beside the finger island Raimi had pointed out to him, waiting for this event. Owailion could now see through the Seal. He assumed the Land was open to them as well. His eyes followed the shoreline and noted how a road had been cut along the edge where the Seal would have blocked wagons and horse traffic. Indeed one wagon already on the road stopped and turned off the beaten path toward Owailion.

Owailion felt himself split three ways and could not react to all he abruptly knew he needed to face; a ship with a sorcerer aboard, someone just walking across where the Seal that had burst only moments before and most alarming, Raimi's severing from him.

Unfortunately, the decision was made for him. A wave of pure power launched at Owailion from the ship and he staggered back under the weight of it against his shields. In return, he mounted a stronger invisible bubble of protection around himself and then straightened up. With a flick of thought, Owailion snapped the anchor chain of the ship and bashed the hull against the finger island to which it had latched itself. The vessel began immediately breaking up but the magical attacks continued. The blasts split and this time fell upon the poor travelers who drove their cart across the beach toward Owailion.

Desperately Owailion flung a haphazard shield around the wagon as well and began running toward the travelers. He didn't dare use more blatant magic around someone who was most likely just passing by, but each magical blow at the wagon sent up explosions of sand and grasses that surely alarmed them. Indeed the wagon pulled up and the passengers inside hopped down, trying to hide from the near misses. Owailion threw a wave of power at the finger island and noted that the ship had sunk by now and so the sorcerer must be on the island, protected behind a shield. He would have to destroy the island to distract the sorcerer.

Owailion ducked behind the wagon to face the newcomers, a huge man, his lovely wife and two young boys who cowered behind their cart in terror. "Welcome to the Land," Owailion said between tightly clenched teeth, trying not to shout over the explosions. Owailion could only hope they spoke his language. He did not want the sorcerer to overhear this exchange so he added a bubble of silence over the wagon.

"You can call me Owailion. I've been waiting for you, I think. Your name wouldn't happen to be Gilead, would it?"

The father of the family looked at him like he was being ridiculous, but another blast from the island made them all crouch again. "Yes, but how did you know?" the man replied under his breath. So the newest Wise One had not come to the Land in a miraculous arrival nor without his memory. Instead, he came from a neighboring land with a family in tow. Owailion did not have time to consider the ramifications of that.

Owailion pulled out the new Heart Stone. "I am a magician here in the Land and now so are you. Here, hold this," and Owailion shoved the Heart Stone at the man's huge hands and then continued. "We're under attack from that island. I want you to wish that island ground down and eroded. Direct all your thoughts toward the base of that rock. I will deal with the sorcerer. We must take him out together."

The entire little family gaped at Owailion's hurried explanation. Then another attack beat like a bell against the shield. Gilead was so tall, even on his knees he had to crouch to hide behind his wagon, but that decided him. He did as he was told. The newest Wise One squinted out at the island just offshore and wished the stone would disintegrate. A cry of alarm echoed over the water and Owailion saw a robed man who had been invisible reappear on the top of the crumbling island. He fell like a wounded bird with a splash into the water. For his part, Owailion snapped the sorcerer's neck before he hit the water. Abruptly all the attacks ended with that death and Owailion stood up, joined by the very rattled family.

"Thank you for your help," Owailion began, although his thoughts were skipping far away already, seeking Raimi.

"I....I...what did I do?" Gilead asked as he too rose and dusted off his knees.

Owailion felt a frantic pounding on his heart and wished he could teach this man what had happened but more urgently he needed to find Raimi. He could taste something wrong in the very air around him like she had blocked him completely out of her thoughts. Owailion struggled to concentrate on what he was facing right at the moment. He looked over at Gilead.

"You are magic like I told you. Now, there is much I need to do to explain all of this but there is someone else who needs me more. I will be back as soon as possible. Why don't you and your family go over those dunes there and find some shelter? I will return as soon as I can."

And then without seeing if they would comply, Owailion disappeared, leaving more questions in his wake than anyone could hope to ask.

* * *

The snapping of the Seal thundered across the water and caused earthquakes all across the Land but locally it also masked the roar of approaching water in Raimi's ears. The damned up river now washed away the hillsides and flew off the plateau in a blinding storm, full of the debris eroded away from swamped hills and valleys. Hundreds of trees snapped under the muddy wave. No wonder Owailion lacked the inspiration to build a palace here. It would have been destroyed in her final act. A rock and mud wall of pure fury knocked Raimi down, burying her with Imzuli's corpse and washed a tsunami at the ship.

But the sorcerer was prepared, Raimi realized. The ship crumbled beneath him but her Tormentor escaped unharmed, for she could still sense him from her tomb in the mud, although she was barely conscious and could not breathe or see in the thick mud she had washed over herself. She felt him walking through the debris toward her coming past the fallen Seal. He would command her to stay alive and she did not want to do that…not again. She had fought him to a draw but he still possessed her name. He had commanded her to kill her best friend and she had wounded the Land terribly at his command. Next, she would be forced to fight Owailion. She would not endure it more. But the Tormentor had taught her one thing he had not intended; a way out.

"Raimi," she whispered to herself, thankful that she was already buried next to Imzuli, "die."

Chapter 24

Eulogy

Owailion felt her die. That was how he could find her. He spun through his mind, trying to locate the murky link that abruptly fell away. Raimi's demise hit him like a punch in the gut, blocking him with the wave of magic that had built up and then broke free like a tsunami. Owailion gasped and retched, seeking for the breath he had lost. He staggered toward Raimi mid-transition to a place he failed to recognize.

Owailion arrived on a flooded beach against a bay fouled with debris from an inundation. Behind him, farther up the beach, he did not recognize a thing, even from in the Memories. Snapped trees and a dirty new river cut sharp, slow paths through the mud, oozing like a snake and forming swamps farther inland. Which river was this? He could not think. A large mud-covered bulge marred the uniform flatness of the floodplain. He started to run to the shape but he wasn't thinking straight. He had to find Raimi and she wasn't here.

A blast of light threw him back into one of the streams and Owailion blacked out briefly but frenzied terror drove him back into awareness and he struggled back to his feet to face this new assault. Where was Raimi? "Raimi!" he called into the echoing silence of an absent mind as an unknown sorcerer waded out of the sluggish surf toward him.

"She's mine, Owailion," the Tormenter taunted.

For one perplexing moment, Owailion could not understand how any human could be so evil to not even understand the grief he had caused. Owailion wanted to become a dragon; massive and fire-breathing to roast this enemy into oblivion. Perhaps one day he would manage it, but the fire he could handle. Giving in to his temper, Owailion drew on the Memories and launched a fireball at the sorcerer. Owailion lifted his enemy up into the sky, shooting him straight up, beyond the clouds, beyond the air. Pure rage held the flame in existence even after the oxygen to feed it burned away. When Owailion sensed the magician's shield finally pop and the fire pushed through, he dropped the monster and let him plummet to earth.

Before the sorcerer's cinders landed Owailion waded toward the mound on the shore and using magic he swept away the waist-deep mud. He found the dragon's hide almost unrecognizable and he lifted the whole mass free and seawater out of the ocean to wash her clean. It was Imzuli.

"Tethimzuliel?" he called, hoping the dragon was just asleep again, but he felt the same empty hollow without even a flicker of acknowledgment. "Where is Raimi?" he asked the corpse in his insane desperation.

Still no answer. Finally, covered in mud and barely able to move, some glimmer of logic managed to drip into Owailion's mind. You have magic. Use it. He stopped struggling and began scanning the mud-field with a magical eye, seeking for something specific.

He found Raimi's body face down completely buried in the shallow surf where the tide slowly washed her clean. How could she have drowned, he wondered? She's the Queen of Rivers. She cannot drown. Owailion's mind rattled through half-formed thoughts with no effort to make sense of what might have happened. Instead, he sat in the water and cradled Raimi's pale graceful body until night fell overhead. He wept and railed for hours, alone, oh so alone.

Dawn came before Owailion thought of something more to do. The tide threatened to take them both out to sea and he might have welcomed that except he didn't know how to die with her. So instead he resolutely carried Raimi up the shore and approximately where her palace might have been, he buried her on a newly formed island. He also placed Imzuli's body next to her and then wondered what to do next. He attempted some kind of ceremony as the sun rose but he could think of only one thing to say. "Under the eyes of God, I will always love you and cleave to you alone for eternity."

For once the oath, swearing again their wedding vows, did not change his appearance. He still stood up to his knees in mud, unrecognizable with it drying all over him.

The rest of the day he sat in chilled misery, unwilling to leave the swamp or clean himself up, manage a fire or food; nothing. Perhaps he would become one with the marsh as well. But eventually, he remembered the Talismans he carried with him and pulled them into existence. He simply stared at them with a kind of fear. He wanted to forget his grief and the pipes would help but he didn't want to risk forgetting Raimi. The two were bound together in his mind. He wanted to forget that she was gone and the pipes could not help there. The pipes could never make him forget his love.

Next, he speculated about using the bowl. The idea occurred to him finally that she had given him the bowl to see the past as almost her last act. This Talisman, he feared as well. He did not want to see Raimi's struggle. Would the actuality be worse than what his imagination had dredged up? But if he was going to live forever, he might need to do more than sit in the mud for a few thousand years. Owailion thought carefully about his request of the bowl, filled it with water that wasn't murky with the continued silting of the Lara River and then whispered, "Show me how Raimi came to be here and died."

The vision began at Imzuli's cavern in Jonjonel and fortunately, he was able to hear the mental commands of the Tormenter or he would have assumed the worst of the white dragon. Instead, Owailion watched as Imzuli tried to protect her friend and then when the ultimatum came, he knew exactly why Raimi had decided the way she had. She had set aside her Heart Stone in case it prevented her from dying. She would not be the means of bringing more destruction to her loved ones or the Land. She would never choose; the impossible choice.

Indeed Raimi's curse had followed her to the Land and what she touched had been ruined...even his heart, Owailion thought bitterly. Thankfully her last thoughts had been of him and she had sent him the Talisman so he would know how much she loved him. It was her parting gift to him. She had not wanted to leave him but her duty had demanded it. She had pioneered forward without him.

Owailion sat through another night, drying mud all over him, and thought about all he had seen and known, that if he had been presented with the same dilemma he would have done the exact same thing. So that was why God had not provided him with his name at his 'hatching'. Owailion probably would have taken the easy way out of his eternal life if this was to be his fate; alone forever. He could not be angry at Raimi. She had been wise and that he did not want to forget.

So finally after three days mourning and feeling numb, he acted at last. Owailion buried the bowl and pipes right beside Raimi's body. Then, remembering his duty, he washed himself up a bit in the fresher water upstream and then returned to Gilead and his family on the far side of the continent.

Epilogue

"Mohan? Mohanzelechnekhi? Can you hear me?" Owailion waited for the requisite time to allow his friend to respond. If anything the dragon felt farther away than ever. Human fear of the gold dragon's reaction to all Owailion's failures made each moment seem that much more torturous. He dreaded this conversation but he had to do it.

"*Owailion?*" the golden dragon sounded a little bewildered but answered clearly.

"Yes, it is me. I have some… some bad news. Imzuli is dead… and so is Raimi." He said it in a rush, trying to get it out before he broke down yet again. Owailion expected Mohan's shields to slam up so that he could think and grieve privately, but to his surprise that was not the case.

"*I wondered why she had come so early,*" Mohan commented. "*She isn't making much sense right now and I cannot get her to talk about what happened just yet.*"

"Wait, Imzuli is with you?"

"*Of course,*" Mohan sounded earnest and perfectly sane as he said this. "*She was going to be the next one to come anyway, but not for another hundred years or so. We will all eventually leave the Land and come here… wherever here is. We are sleeping through the trip, but I have not arrived just yet so I do not know. And, having no body she's going to have to make do with me for companionship for a while.*"

"The dragons…. are leaving the Land, not sleeping here?"

"Oh, there will be dragons in the Land sleeping for a long while more. As I said, only once every century will leave but usually, they will come with their bodies. Since you have given a few of them a Talisman as a responsibility, those will be the last to leave. Perhaps by the time all the Wise Ones are in place, we will have all taken our leave of you. I still do not know the full purpose of the Sleep but we all must move on."

Owailion had little energy for this new wondrous news. "I…I…I was just so afraid to tell you that your daughter had been killed in defense of Raimi. Tell her thank you for me."

"I will, and I am sorry about Raimi. Perhaps it was unwise to not warn you of name magic earlier. But it will be all good with time."

Human anger came far too easily to Owailion now with his grief and he struggled to control his tone. "Good with time?" he queried, trying to keep the cynicism out of his voice.

"*Yes, I told you that Wise Ones cannot truly die, didn't I?*" asked Mohan. "*If not, I am sorry that not everything had been taught that should have been.*"

Owailion strained to hold his raw emotions in check. "Explain to me how the Wise Ones cannot die when I have just buried her body."

Mohan, on the other hand, grew gentler with his grieving friend. "*A Wise One's spirit is no different than a dragon's. We are both bound to the Land and that duty holds till the end of time. Her spirit cannot leave the Land and eventually after your duties are fulfilled, you will find a way to bring her back. It is a promise.*"

"After my duties are fulfilled?" Owailion almost snapped, biting his tongue.

"After the Land is Sealed again and you have done all you have been sworn to do…including building her palace. You are the leader of the Wise Ones and you must oversee the Age of Man. Then the Land will be protected by your magic and you may then find her spirit again and join her with a body and be with her again. But you must be patient. That is your weakness, Owailion. Patience. Your time will come. The path is clear and when it is not clear, it will be straight."

Owailion heard those words, the echo of God's promise back after he had first hatched. He dare not be angry in his grief anymore. He might fall from grace and become unworthy of being a Wise One. He would not find Raimi again if he fell into his grief. Slowly Owailion forced himself to be civil. "Thank you, my friend. I will try to remember that. Farewell."

And as he felt the last connection to his friend fade, he sighed. How many ties would be severed from his heart? Owailion looked out across the barren peaks and then up into the sky above the mountain as if someone other than God could hear him. "I will find you, my love, one day, for you are my Talisman."

Dear reader,

We hope you enjoyed reading *Talismans*. Please take a moment to leave a review, even if it's a short one. Your opinion is important to us.

Discover more books by Lisa Lowell at https://www.nextchapter.pub/authors/lisa-lowell

Want to know when one of our books is free or discounted? Join the newsletter at http://eepurl.com/bqqB3H

Best regards,
Lisa Lowell and the Next Chapter Team

The story continues in:

Ley Lines by Lisa Lowell

To read the first chapter for free, please head to:
https://www.nextchapter.pub/books/ley-lines

About the Author

Lisa Lowell was born in 1967 into a large family full of hands-on artists, in southern Oregon. In an effort to avoid conflict, her art of choice was always writing, something both grandmothers taught her. She started with poetry at six on her grandmother's ancient manual typewriter. By her teens she moved on to pen and paper and produced gloomy, angst-ridden fantasy during adolescence. Her mother claims that Lisa shut the door and never came out until she left for university. During this time she felt compelled to draw illustrations throughout the margins that helped supplement her neglect of adjectives and consistent story lines.

A much appreciated English teacher, Mrs. Segetti, collected these moody musings and sent them in to scholarship foundations. Lisa got a scholarship for that rather poor writing, escaped Oregon and went to university. While she loved her family, her only requirement in a school was anywhere too far away to come home on weekends. She got as far as Idaho, Utah and then even Washington D.C. before she truly launched. She traveled to Sweden (Göteborg, Lund and Sundsvall) for a year and a half during college where she also reconnected with her heritage.

During college Lisa also fell in love and then had her heart broken. Suddenly she had something to write about. Every story written since harbors a romance and a tangled journey; a saga as it were, where the tale comes back to the start. She started to tap into Scandinavian myth and overcame fears of writing conflict. All her earlier failed starts and fascinating characters now molded into an actual story. Completing her degrees in Secondary Education and Masters in English as a Second Language at Western Oregon University, Lisa continued to travel and read favorite authors; Lloyd Alexander, David Brin, Patricia McKillip and Anne McCaffrey. She graduated with a teaching degree 1993.

Then, when she came back to Oregon, like a fairy tale, she met Pat Lowell. They met on Sunday, played racquet ball on Monday night and were engaged by the end of the date. The sense of peace in meeting someone with the same goals and values made it right. Four months later they were married. Lisa began reworking childhood manuscripts into credible stories, and this was when Sea Queen began. When children did not arrive as expected, the Lowells adopted three children, Travis, Scott and Kiana. At that point, Lisa chose to ease off writing actively for a time to focus on her family. However, she kept all the ideas and honed her skill while teaching Middle School English. Storytelling remained her true talent and made her a skillful teacher. In 2011 she was named VFW Oregon Teacher of the Year.

In 2012 a friend asked for manuscripts so he could learn how to get a book onto Amazon in e-book form. As she had several half finished works she could contribute, Lisa gave him one and when she saw how easy that seemed, the idea of publishing snuck up on her again. Her children were moving on, and she felt she could again begin to write. She reworked the first book in the Wise Ones series, Sea Queen, and began sharing it with beta readers. However, her friends wanted to hear the back-stories of some of the other characters so she started writing those into full manuscripts and realized that a series was born.

Publishing became more important when Pat had a terrible accident and developed Parkinsons. Lisa had to stay closer to home to help him and he encouraged her writing. She continued to teach English in middle school (someone has to) and blogs on a Facebook page at https://www.facebook.com/vikingauthor/ . At present she is developing a Word Press for her future work and tinkering with her next novels, Markpath, a set of sci-fi novels. She loves to write but also experiments with drawing, dances while she writes, sings when the radio is on and reads a great deal of poorly written essays by thirteen year olds. She still lives in Oregon, near waterfalls and Powells, the best bookstore on earth. She is still in love with her husband Pat and still loves writing tangled journeys.

The Wise Ones

Book 1 - Talismans
Book 2 - Ley Lines

Talismans
ISBN: 978-4-86751-572-3

Published by
Next Chapter
1-60-20 Minami-Otsuka
170-0005 Toshima-Ku, Tokyo
+818035793528
5th July 2021

Lightning Source UK Ltd.
Milton Keynes UK
UKHW010629230721
387648UK00001B/201

9 784867 515723